Edward Peacock

Ralf Skirlaugh - The Lincolnshire Squire

Vol. I

Edward Peacock

Ralf Skirlaugh - The Lincolnshire Squire
Vol. I

ISBN/EAN: 9783337047528

Printed in Europe, USA, Canada, Australia, Japan

Cover: Foto ©Andreas Hilbeck / pixelio.de

More available books at **www.hansebooks.com**

RALF SKIRLAUGH

THE LINCOLNSHIRE SQUIRE.

A Novel.

BY

EDWARD PEACOCK, F.S.A.

IN THREE VOLUMES.

VOL. I.

LONDON:

CHAPMAN AND HALL, 193, PICCADILLY.

1870.

LONDON:
BRADBURY, EVANS, AND CO., PRINTERS, WHITEFRIARS.

RALF SKIRLAUGH.

CHAPTER I.

" . . . . . Such tales as old men tell,
When age has frosted and when toil has numb'd them,
When all the bright and glowing things of life
Have melted into nothing : and there stands
Naught but the rigid frame-work of the past,
A map of life, but not the life we lived."
The Squire's Testament.

It was late in the evening of an early autumn day in the year 175—, that William Skirlaugh, the nephew and partner of Mr. Robert Skirlaugh, a well-known London solicitor, descended from the high perch-like stool which he had occupied almost without intermission since the time of breakfast—an early hour 120 years ago—and proceeded to make things safe for the night. The first duty was to arrange the various papers he had used, many of which strewed the floor around, and to fold up neatly, first in white and then in brown paper, the ponderous deed of eight skins of parchment, the examination of which had occupied his time

during the greater part of the day. These carefully
locked up in his own desk, the next thing was to light
a small dip-candle that stood in an oval brass stick on
the upper ledge of the office desk, the bowl of which
formed a convenient receptacle for ends of sealing-
wax, buttons, pins, and wafers. The light in the
larger candlestick, a fabric of tin, which stood immediately adjoining the writing ledge, was at once put
out, and a search commenced through all the six low
rooms of which the offices consisted to ascertain that
the windows were shut and made secure by the numerous fastenings; for Symon Bedale and Roger Home,
the two clerks on whom this office nominally devolved,
had left their work at six o'clock, and had they been
still on their stools, no man who knew them would
ever have dreamt of trusting anything that required
care or forethought to two young men, who were, indeed,
steady enough as times went, if you gave them a docu-
ment to copy or a message to carry, but who had no
more prudence or thought for the morrow, when left
to themselves, than the choice assortment of 'prentices
with whom they frequented the galleries of the second-
rate theatres, and played at single-stick, football, and
bowls when the toil of the day was over.

After the fulfilment of these minor duties, the great
work of the closed day was to be undertaken. This
Mr. Skirlaugh could trust to no one but himself or his
nephew; and the latter person, although a great
favourite with his uncle, had only been advanced to
this high post of confidence a few months before—at

the time when he was taken into partnership. The work was, indeed, a serious one. It consisted of locking, barring, bolting, and applying a dozen other elaborate contrivances, which we cannot without equivocation call locks, bars, or bolts, to the huge strongbox in which the most important papers of the office were contained. This was an occupation that required much time and a good memory, for if but one screw were touched out of its proper order, or a single spring unloosed ere its time was come, the effect of the whole arrangement came to nothing, or worse than nothing ; not only on these occasions did the box remain unfastened, but bolts and bars shot out of unforeseen places and hindered the lid's being even shut ; nor could these misplaced securities be returned to their proper sheaths until some one who knew the whole secret of the machinery had set matters right again. Notwithstanding that the nephew had been most carefully drilled by his uncle in the intricacies of this complex mechanism, and had more than once been required to rehearse the ceremony of locking and unlocking in that relative's presence, it occasionally happened that, like an ill-said incantation, his labours had produced no further result than a severe trap of the fingers. At these times his fate had been similar to that of the unhappy Caliph of Bagdad, who, when turned into a stork, forgot the formula by aid of which he was to re-assume his human figure ; for when such an unfortunate oversight happened, there was no resource left for the blunderer, but to wait patiently

until his uncle came to look after him; for so tena-
cious and so fearful of loss was that gentleman that
the idea of his nephew leaving the office without
shutting the great chest, even when that office-door
was locked and the key in his pocket, would have very
much displeased him. The younger Skirlaugh, however, had his wits about him. He determined not so
entirely to trust to his memory as to dispense with
external aid. He therefore made a string of verses,
which, while seeming to the ear to struggle after sense
in halting rhyme, contained for the one person for
whose use they were meant, the necessary directions.
By their aid, for they were slowly said over, as each
screw was turned and notch touched, all went well, and
the three keys, a large one and two little ones that
might have hung on a watch-chain, were withdrawn,
the candle extinguished, the office-door shut, and with
a whistle of relief the young man stepped out into the
little narrow court, and breathed what might be called,
when compared with the ill-ventilated room in which
he had spent his day, the free air of heaven.

"Thank God, this drudgery is over for a time, and
one may now think of something else besides pens and
parchment. I wish I'd been a soldier, or even a
grazier, like old Beckwith. He can see clouds and
trees, can feel storm or sunshine when he has a mind.
It is surely quite as becoming for a gentleman to
haggle about the price of steers and sheep as it is to
vend blotted sheepskin and tortuous advice in a room
called an office." So soliloquised the young man as

he passed, weary in body and mind, to what was by
no means a genial home. So most of us dream and
maunder over our present lot. Happily some few keep
this slow dribble of bitter fancies under such check
that their nearest companions hear not the sound
thereof. The greater part of mankind, however, put
no such restraint upon themselves, but give free vent
to the expression of their vain imaginations.

Skirlaugh's sadness was but momentary, a passing
cloud over a cheerful landscape, not a continuous fog
atmosphere; yet our readers might have forgiven him
if his character had possessed a tinge of melancholy.
His life, perhaps, could not be called an unhappy one,
but if, since he had passed from the mystic realm of
infancy, he had met with little of absolute sorrow,
yet there had been scarcely anything to give his
career colour or brightness, to strengthen his hopes,
or stimulate his ambition.

As we shall have much to say about them in the
sequel, it may perhaps be as well to give here at the
outset a few notes on the history of the Skirlaugh
family. To group them all together in one place is to
put before our friends a block of dry reading as hard
and unsavoury as the friar's parched peas. They had
better, however, munch them all for breakfast, rather
than be troubled by finding such hard morsels scattered among more appetising food, when they are
longing for refreshment towards the end of their
journey.

William Skirlaugh, the only member of the family

we have as yet seen, was a young man of about five-
and-twenty years of age, the nephew and almost the
only near relation of a person who stood high in what
it is the fashion among those who do not know the
nature of English institutions to call the lower branch
of the law. The elder Skirlaugh's father had come up
to London in the reign of Charles II. almost portion-
less, a cadet of a cadet of an old feudal family, which
had suffered much both in blood and lands for its
devotion to the monarchy during the great Puritan
revolution. The law seemed the most favourable
means of subsistence ; he therefore entered himself as
a clerk to a solicitor, who was the son of a tenant on
the family estate. By judicious management, and the
advantages of an elegant person and refined manners,
he had succeeded in much increasing the business,
even while in a subordinate position. When, however,
it came to pass in process of time that his master took
him into partnership, and shortly after he became the
husband of his daughter and heiress, Thomas Skirlaugh was enabled to augment the joint funds of the
firm in many ways that had never occurred to the
careful and narrow-minded father-in-law. With increase of business came increase of expense, and as
Thomas and Milescent his wife were not only handsome and clever, but also really accomplished and
agreeable, and as the husband was known to be sprung
of gentle blood, they were, notwithstanding professional impediments, received into society much above
their own rank. The times they lived in were in some

things much more like our own than the intervening generations have been. The old feelings which had bound society together and kept classes apart had been broken up. The restoration of the monarchy had ended, or seemed to have ended, the great struggle for freedom, but it had not refixed life on its old basis. Many of the wealthy men of the day who wished to make a figure in the world knew, in their shortsightedness, no other means of gaining respect or shining in society except that which is the easiest of all—expensive living—and Skirlaugh, with a large professional income, and the consciousness that he had ability and force of character sufficient to make his way in life, was not the man to hold back. He had too much real taste and feeling to indulge in extravagance for its own sake, but the unhappy atmosphere of luxury in which he lived would too often cause him to make an excuse for what a strict censor would have called waste, on the ground that it was necessary for his social position, his duty as a leading member of his profession, or that he could do no other as a gentleman and man of taste. With all its vanities and its vices, its dark crimes, and gigantic baseness, the age of Charles II. had some characteristics which we of latter times have lost with little advantage. The Stuart kings mingled in the society and sports of their people, and their palaces were open for harmless glee and merry-making, as well as for vice, in a manner to which we have not been accustomed since the accession of the line of Hanover.

Skirlaugh and his wife were sometimes at Court.
They often mingled in Court society, and their most
intimate and valued associates were among the warmest
friends of the Duke of York. He was, in fact, a kind
of connecting link between the City and the Court—a
man of too good blood and too high character to be
insulted by the profligate wits of the one, and too
much sense to despise the sterling qualities of the
other. Hence it followed that he was on many occasions the channel, with great gain to himself, of those
pecuniary transactions in which courtiers often find it
needful to engage with the trading classes. If we add
to the above sketch that Mr. Skirlaugh did not, like
many of his companions, injure his health and character by drunkenness and other low vices, but that
he did sing a good song, and was suspected of dabbling
in poetry with his own pen, that he played deftly at
cards, and like his friend, Mr. Pepys, of the Ad-
miralty, had a passion for the theatre, and consequently thought John Dryden the greatest of dramatists
and poets ; we have, we think, given as full a picture
as is necessary of a man who died many years ere our
history begins.

Mr. Skirlaugh's first wife, the daughter of his
partner, died about five years after marriage. Her
only child was the gentleman who now conducted the
business. The father was an affectionate husband, and
mourned deeply for his lost wife. All the hopes of
his life now centred in their boy. In this youth, as
he grew up, he hoped to see those qualities, which he

valued in himself, shown forth in a higher degree, and
as it were idealised by the tender love and cautious
training that he showered upon him. The best masters
of their respective crafts were engaged to teach him
to dance, sing, and fence; the best tailors to make
his clothes; the most cunning hairdressers to torment
and distort his hair; but all this labour was of no
avail. As the boy grew up, his father became sorrow-
fully aware that he inherited only one side of his own
nature. He saw that he would be at least his equal
in moral and business-like qualities, that he would
never flagrantly break the decalogue or neglect his
cash account, but that of the graces of society—the
song, the dance, the revel; nay, even those courtesies
which give half the pleasure, and surely some of the
poetry, to life he would for ever be as profoundly
ignorant as if he had been born the heir of a highland
drover. This was a severe disappointment to one who
believed that what we now call " success in life " was
at least as much the result of good manners as of
plodding industry. Notwithstanding these great draw-
backs, he could not as a parent resist a feeling of
pride and pleasure at the high moral tone of the lad,
and his sturdy though stolid industry. He gave profound attention to the dryest details of his education,
mastered the Latin Grammar with readiness, wrote a
clerkly hand, and was careful and penurious of his
money, his clothes, and his words. He had read
" Glanville " and " Fleta " ere he was twenty, and
mastered the intricate forms of feudal tenure (it was

then necessary for all lawyers to know something of the history of their profession) before the age most youths have settled what their profession is to be. " Father," he said, one day when he was suffering rebuke for being unlike other young men, and neglecting their accomplishments, " I can learn my business and do my duty, but I cannot dance and sing." And truly the son was right. No one save an over-fond parent would ever have thought that those long, angular limbs and the harsh voice that accompanied them were ever designed to make their way in courtly revel. The father was deeply mortified. He consoled himself, however, with the reflection that taste and position go by destiny, and that his son might peradventure be born to be a mere lawyer, even as a learned divine of the Church of England had proved in his own hearing that the Protestant martyr, Sir Edmondsbury Godfrey, "was born to be a justice of peace."* "And after all," soliloquised he, "what matters it? England is not now what she once was. Song has died with John Dryden, and innocent mirth fled away with my royal master to the Court of Saint Germains." When Robert Skirlaugh was one-and-twenty, his father, now far past the prime of life, contracted a second marriage with a lady much younger than himself. After three years she died, leaving two children—a son and a daughter. Her death was a severe shock to her husband, who soon followed her to the grave.

---

* William Lloyd, Dean of Bangor, Funeral Sermon on Sir E. G., p. 14.

What Robert Skirlaugh's feelings were on his father's second marriage we may surmise, but no one ever heard him utter a word of blame. It is perhaps rash to judge him by what we may think our sensations would have been in his circumstances. If there were bitterness in his heart, his father, who knew him best, had good reason for believing that it soon passed away, or was kept under strong restraint by high moral principle; for when arranging his affairs a little before his death, he left his eldest son sole executor of his property and guardian of the infant children. The rest of the family history may be told in a few words, sorrowful ones they must be, like most other chronicles of domestic life. The boy as he grew up to manhood showed signs of a disposition the reverse of his guardian. Gay, thoughtless, frivolous, with little of the stern devotion to the realities of life which had guided his father through a long and intricate career : he plunged into wild company with the recklessness of one who had no idea of the uses of money or the value of character.

It will be easily understood that such conduct was not only highly displeasing, but well nigh incomprehensible, to his guardian. He reasoned with the youth, after his dry formal manner, more than once paid his debts, and gave him what he called a new start in life, and at length, when he found that all hope of checking him in his wild chase after ruin was over, cast him off for ever.

With his sister Henrietta it was far otherwise.

Her smaller knowledge of the world, or deeper intuition into human character impelled her to take a far more lenient view of the scapegrace who had been her only playmate and companion. They were always warm friends. More than once, out of her own resources, slender always, and at the time we speak of rigidly under the control of her elder brother, for the girl was not of age, she had taken what were then considered long, and what certainly were expensive, journeys to nurse him in illness or soothe him in affliction.

The career of the wasteful is not, in the middle classes, of long duration. The black sheep sunk lower and lower, until at length Robert Skirlaugh was compelled to exercise his authority as his sister's guardian to prevent her from holding any communication with the reprobate. A violent quarrel ensued— the only one they ever had. It ended in a lifelong separation between the brother and sister. Under all provocation Robert Skirlaugh was as kind a relative as his hard and sunless nature could understand how to be. As Henrietta could no longer dwell happily with him, he made arrangements for her living with her mother's sister, a widow lady, whose home was on a little freehold property on the banks of the Yore— having first extorted a positive promise that she would see the face of her degraded brother no more. This vow was made very unwillingly, and with a reservation that it should terminate as soon as she was of age, but no such proviso was needed. On the

evening before the day on which it had been arranged
that Henrietta was to set out on her tedious journey
to the North of England news came that her unhappy
brother had grievously wounded a certain Mr. William
Brierley in a duel. A large reward was offered for the
capture of the culprit, but it was never claimed. For
upwards of a fortnight Robert Skirlaugh was in hourly
fear of hearing of his brother's capture. The police
of those days were neither skilful nor vigilant, it would
seem, for during the whole of that time Frank Skirlaugh
succeeded in hiding himself in London or its immediate
neighbourhood. One night after it had become dark
the unhappy young man entered the room where his
brother and sister were sitting. He bore a sleeping
infant in his arms. His face was far more haggard
than his relatives had ever before seen it, but his step
was steady and his voice firm. " Brother," he said, " I
bring you the youngest of our race! Care for him
as you fear God.—You, Henrietta, will love him for
his father's sake." As he said this, he placed the little
child on his sister's knee, and left the room.

> " All was so quick, that it might seem
> A flash of lightning, or a dream."

Robert Skirlaugh was never rapid of speech or
motion. When he found the use of his limbs he
rushed to the street door to discover that it was locked
on the outside. Some time was lost in running round
to the other door which afforded egress into the small
court that divided the dwelling-house from the business

office. Ere he had got beyond his own premises, Frank
had dived into the labyrinth of low streets and alleys
that lay on the west.

Robert Skirlaugh never heard anything further of
the criminal. Some persons surmised that he had
taken ship for America and been lost on his passage
or murdered by the natives; others that he had
enlisted in the French army. Brierley recovered,
and it was a sad reflection to those who believed
Francis Skirlaugh dead, to think that his would-be
murderer had passed away without the satisfaction of
knowing that the wound he had inflicted was not
mortal. Degraded as he was, his friends knew that
he had the remains of many good qualities, and could
not but hope that he did not die with the feeling that
he had blood on his soul.

The most searching inquiries were made after
Francis Skirlaugh, for the double purpose of saving
him, if possible, from punishment for his last criminal
act, and of gathering particulars as to the history of
the infant. Nothing, however, could be made out,
except that Henrietta was aware of the baby's existence, and that she said—and her word could be fully
relied upon—that she knew her brother could prove
the child he had left in their charge to be born in
lawful wedlock. She had herself seen the documents
in his possession. It was suggested that the hurry of
flight and the agony of mind which the culprit must
have suffered in being the means, as he thought, of
sending a man who was once his friend to an early

grave, might have made him forgetful of the duty of furnishing the necessary evidence. Many were the grave discussions on this difficult case that Robert Skirlaugh held with his friend Serjeant Morvill. We shall, however, not afflict our readers with an abstract of them, as the interest of the following tale, if it chance to have any, depends in no degree on the legitimacy of its hero.

CHAPTER II.

"My uncle was a scrivener,
　　That dwelt in Bristol city,
My father was a roving blade,
　　The more for me's the pity.

"My mother died when I was young,
　　My aunt on me attended,
If I turn out a decent chap,
　　They'll say the old stock's mended."
　　　　　　　　　　　　Street Ballad.

WILLIAM SKIRLAUGH was soon seated with his uncle at their evening meal. Tea it was not, for the old lawyer was a conservative in matters of meat and drink, and that decoction was then almost unused in houses where women's influence was not in the ascendant. When taken at all, the tiny quantities in which it was doled out were unfit for those to whom eating was a matter of business, not a mere pastime in an idle round of pleasure. Bread and cheese, a round of cold spiced beef, and a trencher of oat cakes,—these last a present from the Yorkshire dales,—formed the provender for a substantial meal. A silver tankard with a cupid on the top, holding a promegranate in his hand,

and with another and larger pomegranate for the handle-knob, contained the fragrant hot ale with which the repast was seasoned. The room was neatly furnished in the style of Queen Anne's days, but stiff and cold-looking. The walls were covered with cases mostly filled with law-books, a map of England graced a recess on one side of the fire-place, and a plan of London, done with the pen, the corresponding compartment. Three oil paintings hung opposite the windows, and a pair of prints, in narrow sham-ebony frames, occupied the place of honour and dust over the chimney-piece, whose shelf was ornamented with a pewter tobacco-box, two clay pipes, three battered conch shells, a rusty silver-mounted horse-pistol, and a pair of boot-hooks.

The young man devoted himself assiduously to " the sustentation of his animal functions." The legal work that had occupied all the day, except the few minutes he had snatched at noon for a hasty meal, had made the repast an object of very serious interest to him ; not so the elder Skirlaugh : his food lay all but untasted on his plate, while his small and piercing grey eyes wandered around the apartment, now glancing from the well filled bookshelves, whose contents he at one moment seemed counting, to the ' Vera effigies viri clarissimi Edoardi Coke equitis aurati,' a print cut from the fourth volume of that knight's 'Institutes,' and occupying one of the before-mentioned black frames; then gazing vacantly at the window, and at length resting with a look of contentment on the opposite picture.

It was a portrait of a young lady, long dead, who had in youth won the heart of the now grave old bachelor. Death had separated them, and he, unlike most of us, had remained faithful to the memory of his first love, a companionship of forty years unclouded by the troubles of family life, unbroken by failing sympathy. The contemplation did not last long, an uneasy glance towards the place where the fire should have been, and a fidgeting and twisting about in his chair, showed him impatient for the conclusion of the meal. "Come, my boy, haven't you done?—I want my pipe," were the first words with which he had enlivened the repast.

A careful observer might have noticed a slight family likeness between the uncle and nephew, but this only made the contrast between the handsome young man and his then hardfeatured relative the more striking. There was the same general cast of features in each. The head and face were modelled on the same proportions, but there never could have been anything more than a faint resemblance. Could the seams and furrows that now puckered the senior's countenance like the skin of a melon have been smoothed out as they were in youth, we should have before us a set of features almost as hard and unprepossessing as now, but without the repose of expression which age gives to all but the unhealthy or the abandoned.

The supper was now removed, but the ale tankard remained on the table, and one solitary candle bore it company. Mr. Skirlaugh proceeded leisurely to fill

one of the pipes from the contents of the tobacco box,
to light it, and seat himself in his leathern armchair
by the fire-place.

" Have you again counted all the deeds and compared them with the schedule ? " inquired he.

" Yes, sir," replied the nephew, " and folded all,
except the present conveyance, in papers properly
labelled, and put them with the fines and escheats into
the leathern bag. The present conveyance with the
schedule I will bear about my own person."

" I would have sworn it," rejoined the uncle. " As
if thine own work were better than all that had gone
before thee. Why, man, dost thou value thy precious
handy-work, which is at present mere sheepskin,
having no more weight, force, or virtue than the cover
of a ledger or the cheek of a battledore, so much that
thou thinkest it more to be cared for than the records
which evidence the title of the estate ? "

" I have heard you say, sir, that a lawyer is in some
sort regarded by the care he shows in the small things
of his business which belong to him as a scrivener
rather than as a member of a liberal profession. I
thought our cousin would ill like to see that which
shall cost him not a little tumbled, and maybe, frayed,
by jolting on the back of our nags from London to
Lincolnshire. New deeds are bigger than old ones,
and don't pack so well."

" It seems George Shelley, when he taught you
penmanship, had an apt pupil. Did that coxcomb
make you believe that all the world set as much store

c 2

by quips and cranks, flourished swans, dragons, and butterflies as the fellow that gets his living by teaching his most foolish art? You will find, as you go out into the world, that these vanities affect not the minds of men. I have bidden you be neat in writing and apparel, but for the crumpling of a deed that has to go a hundred and fifty miles on horseback I have never told you to have care. 'De minimis non curat emptor.'"

"I have an idea, sir," rejoined William, "from what little I have seen of our relative, which is, as you know, long ago, that he was a man likely to take heed more than most men of these trifles."

"I would advise you then to dismiss, ere you go from this city, that and all other ideas you may have formed of Ralf Skirlaugh; they are sure to be foolish ones, and mayhap bring you into trouble. Bethink you that you have seen him but twice; once when you were but a child—a schoolboy—an infant, incapable in law as in fact of coming to right judgment—ex ætatis defectu ; and another time when, though somewhat more advanced in wisdom, you saw my honoured client but for five minutes," said the elder lawyer, with a tone and manner that seemed intended to make a deep impression.

Young men of William's age and position, in our own days, would probably be not a little ruffled if an address such as we have repeated were delivered to them by an elder, in however close relationship. The stiffness of past ages has as entirely gone as hair powder and dress-swords. All three were commonly worn then, and it probably did not strike William for a moment that his uncle's speech was wanting in courtesy. He knew it was kindly meant, and therefore replied gaily: "I am not likely to forget the earlier interview, when I was a lad with my aunt in Yorkshire; for he put more silver pieces into my hand than I ever conceived would pass into my pocket during the whole course of my life. It is from that meeting I mostly gathered my ideas of my cousin's character. When he was a prisoner in the Tower in 1746 on that absurd charge of treason I saw him, but in a most transient manner."

"Absurd charge do you call it?" exclaimed the Uncle. "Well, of course it was absurd, because levying war against the Elector is not treason, but loyalty to king and country; but, on my conscience, Willy,—I may speak freely to you now that we are in partnership about office secrets,—on my conscience, my boy, the charge was so far from absurd, that I feared for Ralf Skirlaugh's life more than I can bear to think of. If his business had not come on late, when the blood-hounds were gorged, I don't think we could have saved him. If he had not had very powerful friends in the Government, it would have gone very hard with him as it was; thank God, I'd got the estate made safe in any case; trust me for that. I am afraid even now that his indiscretion may get him into trouble some day. But mind yours does not land you there. Don't dwell on any conclusions you may have come to about Ralf Skirlaugh ; he is a kind and good man, but as full of twines as a sheep track, and as angular as a Flemish fortification. If you don't please him, he will—though he has been a courtier—let you know it in such rough language as will put the memory of the half-crowns you talk of out of your head for many a day ; and the likeliest way to offend him is to talk, as you will, if I don't tether that rambling tongue of yours, of the cousinship that is between you. Why, you've mentioned it three times since last I lifted the tankard."

" Our relationship, sir, is a fact for which I am not responsible ; and of which I am not aware that either he or I need feel shame," said William, with a touch of pride in voice and manner.

" Well, of course it is. Nobody but a fool ever forgot the fact that he came of noble ancestry, and no one but a knave ever pretended to disregard it ; but there is a difference between cherishing a sentiment and using the facts on which it rests as a ladder to scramble over other people's heads. Ralf Skirlaugh has as much family pride as any man. Now, if he saw any in you, the chances are one to ten that he might like it ; but they are ten to one that he might think it the vulgar assumption of an attorney who wanted to put himself on a level with one whose direct ancestors have held of the crown *in capite* from the reign of Henry III. This sort of assumption has not been uncommon of late. We shall find something of it in the history of England and the Statute-book," said the elder, re-lighting his pipe, which had gone out during this latter speech.

His companion did not smile at the feeble sarcasm, if indeed satire or wit were intended by the last remark, but, with a slight tone of irritation in his manner, replied,—

" I see your meaning, sir; and will endeavour to act as you desire. If, however, Mr. Skirlaugh is what you describe, he will hardly blame me for cherishing the memory of his own ancestors."

The Uncle felt from the last reply that he had given pain, 'and tried in his homely fashion to set matters straight again.

" Look you, my boy," said he ; " you are, as usual, letting that hasty head of yours run to all sorts of wild conclusions. I never said of Ralf Skirlaugh what you try to make me say. I do say he is an honest and true man,—wise, resolute, even sometimes wary ; one who has not wasted his life in Court vices, or sunk into a foxhunter and a sot; but he is unused to town life and manners ;—has never had to work for his bread, and associated little with those who have—us of the middle class, at least. I would not have him think ill of you, my lad ; not only because he is rich and may employ you when I am gone, but because he is the head of our family, and has that about him which in these hard days wins something more than respect."

" I think we agree, sir. I, with the inexperience of

youth, use less becoming language," was William's laconic reply.

"No doubt of it—no doubt of it; and I, *durus atque infelix*, am a crabbed old man of seventy. Let us, however, talk of our work, not of ourselves."

As the kind-hearted old man said this he knocked the ashes from his pipe and drew towards the table, which he speedily covered with papers from his own pockets, and from drawers in the adjoining bookcases. The conversation that followed might, perhaps, interest a legal antiquary; but is, under present circumstances, hardly worth reporting. It was interlarded far more freely than lawyer's talk is now-a-days with scraps of Latin. Of its spirit, those may judge who have had the pleasure of talking after office hours with a modern conveyancer whose heart and soul are in his business.

CHAPTER III.

" What, not my dinner ?   Why, you have dined well,
And I will dine, in spite of any lord.
Oh, I love dining ! "—*The Thorpiad.*

AT an early hour the next morning our hero and
his attendant mounted their horses, and set off on
what was then considered a very long journey.   Why
did William Skirlaugh make his pilgrimage into Lincolnshire on horseback ? our readers will ask.   Why
not by the coach ?   Does not all the world know that
in the year of grace 175— the Mercury Flying Express
took its departure (God willing) at six o'clock A.M. on
each Monday morning from the Golden Cross at
Charing, and arrived at the Angel Inn in the City of
Lincoln—roads, highwaymen, and weather permitting
—at ten o'clock on Wednesday evening?   And is it
not a fact that is understood of all men, that a similar
vehicle, called the True Fly, departed on each suc-
ceeding Wednesday from the Bull and Mouth in
Aldersgate, bound on a like errand ?   Were not these
things duly recorded in the advertising columns of the
London and provincial newspapers of the time, and

does not the manuscript department of the British
Museum contain among its stores more than one bill
receipted by Mr. Cox or Coe—we cannot make out
the signature with certainty, and are particular as to
our character for accuracy—for the sum of thirty
shillings, being the fare from town to the capital of
Lincolnshire? All these statements are, no doubt,
true beyond shadow of cavil; and yet Mr. William
Skirlaugh, notwithstanding the temptations to "swift
and expeditious travelling" —the tautology is that of
Mr. Cox or Coe, not the author's—preferred the more
old-fashioned method of transit. We are not bound
to explain to our readers why he did so, such of them
as know the sensation of having a good horse under
them, and of being able to wander at will along the
tree-shadowed lanes of the midland counties, will not
wonder that a young man, going out into the world
almost for the first time as his own master, should
prefer this means to that of lumbering along the highway at the rate of six miles an hour, outside—or, still
worse, inside—a machine as rudely constructed, and
much worse fitted to keep out heat and cold, dust and
rain, than are the carriers' waggons of the present day.
We are not contemners of past times—we sometimes
look back with longing to the days of our youth, when
life was not so fast, when men travelled slower and
saw more; we shall not readily forget the pleasant
chat with the coachman, or the smiling visage of the
landlord. We would have our readers believe that
we can call to mind, as vividly as though railways

were not, each hostelry on the northern road from
the Green Man at Barnet to the Queen's Head
at Newcastle ; but it must be remembered that coaches
as people who are now alive knew them, were in the
height of their perfection. Mr. Palmer had worked a
reform in English travelling, the most important that
had then been known, or could be conceived ; one
that would have handed his name down to posterity
among the great benefactors of his country and mankind, had it not been eclipsed, or rather extinguished,
by that social change which brought about the English railway system. His is not the first great name
that has gone down unrecorded in a revolution ;
we fear it will not be the last. When, however, the
time comes to gather up the memorials of those who
but for the seethings of the popular cauldron would
have been famous, let a small corner in the reliquary,
or a line or two in the biographical dictionary, be
spared for one who, through no flaw in his own genius,
fell short of popular greatness. Stephen Harding,
Jordano Bruno, and Samuel Hartlib will not object to
his company. The coaches, as we lament them, were
as different from the Despatches, Mercuries, Flying
Posts, Transits, and Eclipses of the last century, as
the slowest mineral train is from the London and
Holyhead Express, things which only the poverty of our
mother tongue compels us to call by the same name.

We are fond of topographical gossip, and would
gladly ride beside our hero and tattle with our
readers concerning every village, footpath, and mile-

stone that he passed on his way. We should like to
tell them who lies buried in that church, of the
horrible murder that took place near this pollard elm,
and of the hoard of silver pennies which a drainer
unearthed in that meadow; but such tediousness is
not tolerated now, even in county histories ; so we can
indulge no hope of being permitted to oppress our
readers with it here. We will, therefore, pass on at
once to nearly the end of the journey.

The afternoon of the fourth day was about half
spent when William Skirlaugh rode into the last inn-
yard which it was to be his fortune to enter before he
arrived at his cousin's home. The highway on which
he had travelled was straight as an arrow—it was, in
fact, one of the great Roman thoroughfares which had
done duty for fifteen hundred years as one chief means
of communication between Southern England and the
Border Country. This road had been carried by its
contrivers on the eastern side of the slope of one of
those long, low hills, which make the map of Lincolnshire look almost as rigid as a geological section. By
so doing he had effectually hindered the wayfarer from
refreshing his eyes with the beautiful scenery of the
western slope and the wide valley of the Trent below ;
but he had found that which was all important in his
eyes—a platform on which to lay out a good level
pathway, a thing he could by no means have discovered, either in the marsh where the Ancholme
stagnated, or on the rough brow of the hill. A more
uninteresting piece of ground to travel over could

scarcely be found in England. Large sheep walks, separated from one another by low stone walls, with here and there an enclosure of eight or ten acres for a "coney garth," or of a large tract of land for a rabbit warren, without a tree bigger than a whitethorn or an elder-bush, or any other shrub but furze, was all that William Skirlaugh could see to admire. The slight depressions in the way had not even brooks in them, for the porous oolite rock sucks up the water as fast as it comes, except during periods of great rainfall.

After riding for a couple of hours over an uninteresting region like this, it was pleasant to the traveller on gaining the brow of a small hill to see in the hollow beneath him, by the side of a little lakelet, a cluster of trees, a large rambling house, and some white-washed cottages. The village was Merespital; the large, heavy-looking house, the St. George and Dragon. As he rode through the little street, if the collection of huts standing at every possible angle on each side of the way be worthy of that name, he could not but be struck with the picturesque situation of the hostelry. The lake was formed by an artificial mound that had been thrown up ages ago, over the course of a little stream that welled up out of the limestone on the western side of the hamlet, a natural artesian well which let out the waters of the Sheffield moors upon the cliffs of Lincolnshire. On the banks of this little lake—its detractors might have called it a pond, it was so small—shaded on all sides but the west, where it faced the road, by large elm trees, stood the inn, a building telling a tale to those who chose to listen, of many times, and the strange doings of many men.

Merespital had been, before the Reformation, a hospital or lazar-house, governed by Franciscan friars. The founder, a Vipont, who had lost his three sons by the plague during the crusades, had endowed it, with the intention of providing for the sick—no idea of establishing an hotel had ever entered into his head. He fixed upon this site because there was water, shade, and rich feeding land. It happened, however, that at this point one of the great tracks across the western lowlands of Lincolnshire fell into the Roman way, and the friars who tended the sick often found it a duty incumbent on them to give food and shelter to benighted wanderers. It would be a question of some antiquarian interest to discuss, whether these worthies did, as time went on, in reality turn their new buildings into an inn, or whether the food and fare—

> "The brown ale for the peasant,
> Red wine for the lord,"

which they dispensed so freely was left unpaid for. If it was not made a matter of direct traffic, the transaction was as like it as a counsel's honorarium is to a lawyer's charge for consultation. When the church property fell into the hands of the king, Merechapel was granted out—sold, that is, to the highest bidder— to a certain speculative lawyer—we shrink from mentioning his foul name, even though three hundred years have passed away since he went to his place—

who pulled down a great part of the monastic buildings, turned the poor sick inmates adrift, and converted
the spacious guest-house into a real inn. There was
no mistake about its destination now. He did not
even remove the statue of St. George, the patron, that
stood over the gateway, nor efface the inscription
underneath, which set forth in all the illegibility of
black letter that

> Meat and drink as I kan
> Giff I to beaste & eke to man
> For ye lof of God I pra
> Say pater noster and aue
> For the saull of brother Raulf
> Wha biggid this for theyr behaulf.

This first purchaser was a parsimonious, Plutus-fearing
man. With the aid of some red and white paint for
the saint, and some blue, black, and yellow for the
dragon, he made a reasonably good sign out of the old
image. The neighbours did not take to the device
readily at first, but continued to call the place the
Spital as in times past, but travellers soon learned to
speak of the house as the St. George and Dragon.
Why should they not? After all, the change was not
greater or more incongruous than that of Jupiter
Capitolinus into a certain fisherman of Galilee, a
transformation that has taken place "permissu supe-
riorum" in one of the churches of Rome.

The land jobber did not keep the place· long in his
family—such vermin as he do not thrive. It changed
hands very frequently during the next hundred years.
When all England was aflame with the great Puritan

revolution, it happened on a certain day in 1643 that
a troop of Sir John Hotham's guerillas from Hull
garrison having passed over the Humber on an expedi-
tion for reducing malignants to obedience "to the
King and Parliament"—so the phrase went in the
governor's despatches, which, being interpreted, meant
that they had gone forth to pillage the homes of all
persons who were not strong enough either in force of
arms or social connection to overawe them—stopped
at the hostelry to refresh themselves. They saw the
papistical emblem, though they could not read its rude
legend. Their pious hearts were moved by the beer
and strong waters with which the landlord had supplied
them, to such deep commiseration of his unhappy state
in having an idol for a sign, that they forthwith plucked
it down and flung the fragments into the lake.

From that time to the day on which William Skirlaugh entered the village little change had occurred.
The sombre-looking building from which he now heard
voices of revelry and snatches of loose song was the
same, and bore almost the same aspect as when the
lawyer turned the friars out of doors, or when, a century
later, cavaliers and roundheads refreshed themselves
with meat and beer and the new luxury, tobacco, under its
roof. What little change there had been had of course
taken the direction of degradation. Some of the Gothic
windows had been divested of their tracery and fitted
with sashes. The niche from which England's patron
had been dethronèd was still untenanted save by
martens' nests. A new sign, where some village

Titian had given an eighteenth century version of his beautiful legend, swung from a gallows-like erection near at hand. The work was not lovely, but it was highly symbolic. The saint, whose face bore a striking resemblance to that of George the Second on a five-shilling piece, had a very red rose in his button-hole and a black cockade in his Roman helmet. The dragon was expiring upon a parterre of white roses; in his death agony he vomited forth a ribbon inscribed

REBELLIO.

William's long ride made him desirous of refreshment. He at once threw the reins of his horse to his servant, slung the saddle-bags, in which were the papers, over his arm, and entered the hostelry.

Signs of riotous festivity appealed to more than one of his senses. The chorus of a drinking song rung along the passages. The scent of roast meats and mulled wines pervaded the whole house, the kitchen tables and several of the chairs were loaded with dirty crockery, cooking vessels, and the remains of courses that had not been consumed or found their way back to the larder. A fat old woman, who might perhaps fill the office of cook when awake, sat fast asleep in a wanded chair near the fireplace. Two dapper-kirtled servant-maids and a dirty, ill-clad middle-aged woman were engaged putting things in order. A thin wiry man of middle size was warming himself at the fire. He had divested his person of his coat, and his hands were stuck deep in the waistband of his breeches. He was not good-looking, but his face indicated honesty and jolly good-humour. A phrenologist, if there had been quacks of that description in those days, would certainly have found a very large bump of self-esteem on his cranium, after but a short term of acquaintance.

"Nell, my lass, th' horn's been empty this quarter of an hour. Is th' barrel dry, or wearn't th' tap run?" observed the man before the fire to one of the hand-maidens.

"Thoo may fill it thee sen as thee can, Mr. Robert. I've summuts else to do besides runnin' efter thee noo, besides yer noan so civil, do yer think I'm a gooin' to be call'd Nell by every cadger 'at comes to warm his sen at our fire? Here, Nan, draw him another pint out o' th' far barrel, I'll ha' none on him," said the damsel, repenting, as more distinguished orators have been known to do, of the earlier part of her speech before she had got to the end, and endeavouring to soften things down in the final sentence.

"Whew—w—w! That's it, *Mistress Ellen*. Why noo if I wasn't a very patient man an' a very humble-minded man, I should gie ye the rough side o' my tongue for callin' me a cadger; but it's all th' same to me, Mistress Ellen. I'm not a prood man, an' you'll be glad to be call'd Nell again when ye want owt," said the coatless man, with the slowness of mock humility.

"Why, ar'n't ye a cadger, an' nowt else? Ar'n't ye runnin' aboot th' whole country side at all hours o'

days an' neets, not stoppin' at home an' eatin' yer
victuals an' seein' yer understrappers do their work as
ye should do ? I don't call ye a groom at all ; I'd
sooner say ye was a ratcatcher, if it wasn't for that
greasy green coat ye mostlins wears." The arrowy-
tongued maiden's pretty eyes sparkled as she finished
the sentence, for at the same moment she produced
from a corner cupboard a bottle of strong waters, *alias*
Hollands, and a handsome stalked glass to aid in its
consumption, adding as she did so, " Here, you good
for nowt, that's more in your way, I'm thinkin'."

" I'd be a ratcatcher all th' days o' my life if I could
be like oud Nicky Peart, an' hev a well of this kind of
stuff in my back yard, if I had to be plagued with thee
for a wife into the bargain," responded the gentleman.

" For shame o' thy sen to say so, Bob," replied the
pretty kitchen-maid, with one of those half-frowning
half-smiling expressions that artless women use when
the producer thereof is not quite sure whether it is the
proper thing to cry or laugh. Hesitation did not last
long ; a bright smile succeeded. " Tak' that for a
drinkin' good for nowt," and so saying she administered
a sharp box on the ear, and retiring to the other end
of the apartment, busied herself, or affected to be
busy, in what she would have called " siding away the
things." Mr. Bob bore the blow with the equanimity
of a philosopher. The Hollands were plentiful,
and he probably thought he could administer retribution on another occasion. Silence reigned for
a few seconds ; at length the young woman's curiosity

got the better, and she asked, "What old woman's tale have you gotten hold on now, about Nicky Peart?"

"It's no old woman's tale, or I shouldn't be talking about it to thee, Mistress Nell, but as true as Scriptur'. I heard our Squire himself talkin' about it to Mr. Callis—that's our chaplain, ye knaw—and the priest, Father Tempest, as they call him, that goes to those papist folks at Scalhoe, and they both believed every word on it, and said it was aweful, and Mr. Callis's a goin' to put it in that big book he's alus a writin', and Father Tempest said it must be true, for he'd seen something just like it wi' his own eyes i' forren parts."

"And what is it, Bob?" inquired the girl, now really interested.

"Well, I'll tell ye the tale just as I heard our Squire tell it not a week sin'; but I've heard it ower and ower again ever sin' I was a bairn. You knaw there's a little square hoose, thack'd wi' reeds, just at Yalton Lane end, where Billy Peart, the mould man,* lives. Now, this Billy—thoo knaws him very well, he's a lame man, and alust hugs about wi' him a little spade wi' an iron point at t'other end estead of a hilt— hed a granfather just such an another man for all the warld as he is, nobut he wasn't lame, thoo knaws, an' he wasn't a quiet, steady goin' man like him as lives there noo, but a real randy good for nowt, alus

---

* A person who kills moles.

drinkin' an' feightin', an' warse, for noos and thens he would steal our owd Squire's rabbits an' hares, an' may be an odd time by chance pick up a sheep if it suited him, an' nobody was gain hand a lookin'. Well, it was one Wivilby t' Andra' fair, reight i' middle o' winter, may be fifty years sin', an' Nicky hed been drinkin' at th' Black Swan wi' a lot o' nor' country horse-cowpers. Hoo long he would ha' staid I don't knaw, may be a week if his brass hed lasted out, but just when twelve o'clock struck he remembered he hed to be at Whitton town end next mornin' about some smugglin' concarn, an' may be summut else as well. So up he jumps, saddles his galloway, and off he sets home along th' top road. It was strange an' cowd, but as leet as day, for th' moon was at full. Nicky was used to hevin' a good mess of drink o' board, and jogged away all reight, sometimes thinkin' about nowt, sometimes may be laughin' to his sen at the lees he'd been tellin' to them Yorkshire peppers, for Nicky was a strange leein' chap. Howmswever, just when he got about a hundred yards past Mottle-Esh turnin' he hears summuts whistling i' th' dikin. 'What's that?' thinks he; 'may be it's a hare in a snare,' and he pulls up the galloway to listen, and he hears it ageän directly, a sharp, ask squeal, just for all the warld like a hare. 'I'll hev it,' thinks Nick, and off he jumps, and runs to the place where the noise came fra, and there he sees, not a hare, but what do you think? Why, a little man, not six inches high, all dressed i' green, with a little red cap on his head wi' a feather in it, and

the poor little feller had got one of his legs fast in a
rabbit trap. Nicky wasn't a bad-hearted feller at
bottom, though he did lee and swear and steal things
parlous. So he lowps down into the dikin boddom
where the little chap was, may be never givin' it a
thowt what sort on a creatur he was meddlin' wi',
and helps th' little man out o' th' trap. 'Thank ye,'
says he ; 'you've been a rare good friend to me. If it
hadn't ha' been for you I should ha' been froze to dead
afore mornin'. Now, what can I do for you ? Though
I am nobut little, I can do a deal.' 'Well,' says
Nick, 'there's so many things I want I hardly know
what to say. Let me see ;' and off Nick goes into a
study like. But the little man soon wakken'd him up
wi' that sharp voice o' his. 'Nicky,' says he, 'I can't
wait. Tell me now what it's to be. Ye shall hev ony
single thing ye've a mind to ax for, but there can
nobut be one axin', and you mun hev it out directly ;
an' mind an' never tell nobody about it, for if ta does
thou'll loss it altogether, an' may be get summuts else
then ta bargain'd for to boots.' Well, I tell'd ye Nicky
hed been drinkin' all day at th' Black Swan, an'
though he could walk midlin' straight an' talk fairish,
he wasn't altogether square in his head, an' he did feel
par'lous dry, so says he, may be wi'out a thowt, may be
to get time for thinkin', says he, 'Dang it, I wish I'd
a well i' my hempgarth o' th' best red wine Squire
Skirlaugh hes i' his cellar.' 'That's sattled,' says th'
little man, and away he bolts into th' hedge boddom.
Nicky gets on his galloway an' gallops home, an' there

sure enough in the hempcroft aback o' th' hoose he fun a well o' as fine red wine as ony man ever laid lip to. He'd no mug to drink out'n, so he laid his sen down up o' th' mou'ds all his length, an' drunk, an' drunk, an' drunk till he could swallow down no more, an' then he run into th' house an' begun to holler to his wife about it, but she never heard a wod he said, for as soon as he begun to shout he fell down clean dazed like, and knew no more about owt at all till nine o'clock next mornin', when he wakken'd up an' fun his sen laid i' th' middle of a snaw reak by the dike side ommust agean Mottle Esh, just at th' place where he'd seen th' little man, wi' his galloway stanin' agean him. When he got home he looked all ower for th' well, but he never could find it nowhere, though he said there was fair to see in the new dug molds the print of his body where he had laid hisself down to drink."

"What an awesome thing, Robert; but you don't really think it's truth?" said the girl, evidently strongly inclined to believe every syllable of the narrative.

"Why, yes, of course I do, it was a fairy. Fairies are common enough now. There used to be scores on 'em then. Why, when I was a lad, one real rainy neet when it was as dark as soot, I was walkin' by my sen ower Brownlaun Hill, and just when I was passing that big stone wi' the readin' on it——"

At this point in Mr. Robert's youthful reminiscences, William Skirlaugh's entry interrupted him. The cook, as we have said, was asleep. It was her usual habit to dose by the fire when dinner had been served up. The dirty slattern, who might from her wretched clothing, head-gear and shoes, have passed for a gipsy, and Maggy, the other servant, who was the groom's sister, were the only persons on duty.

"Can you tell me where the waiters are?" said he, after a moment's glance at the situation.

"Yes, they're upstairs wi' the quality, or else down stairs wi' the qualities' gentlemen," responded the groom.

"Where shall I find some one to wait on me? I must have some dinner, and be off."

"They're all throng upstairs an' down—we've no room in the house for travellers; you'll be like to ride on."

"This is very extraordinary—very. They have strange manners in Lincolnshire," thought William Skirlaugh. "See here, my good girl, I have to go further on. You can give a traveller some dinner, however busy you are," said he, addressing the maid servant, whom the reader knows as Nell.

"We can't indeed, sir; we're quite full, and all the servants has more then they can do already," she replied.

"She's right, th' house is as tight as a dog-tick," chimed the man without his coat, oracularly.

Nell left the kitchen. William Skirlaugh, however, continued firm. He would not go without his dinner if it were possible to procure it.

"See here, my man," said he, "addressing the

person who seemed to be the self-constituted commander of the garrison, " you seem well known here, I am a stranger; can you contrive that I may see the landlord, or someone else, that will help me to some refreshment ? "

" Bless yer heart, no ; you mun live a long ways off, or you'd know that when Jemmy Sargisson's gotten good company, he's alus as drunk as a lord by two o'clock,—and there's a real lord in the house, noo."

This last piece of information did not seem to strike so much awe into the wayfarer, as a similar announcement has been observed to do at hotels in more recent days. The speaker, therefore, proceeded :—

" You'd better ride on, for I can't say when ther'll be ought to be gotten here. The folks they hev are a random lot, an' mak' the sarvants as bad as theirsens. It isn't far to Wivilby or Brigg. You'll be goin' to toner on 'em, I'll uphoud you, so you'd better ride on." As he finished the sentence he took a long pull at the beer-horn, and stretched it out with a smile of good-humoured impudence to the new comer, adding as he did so, " Tak' a drink o' this ; a man may do without beef and bread who has plenty of good beer."

Young men may know the world instinctively, many who have lived a life of close seclusion do so better than those older children who have been knocked about in it for years; but very few of us, under thirty, have such command over ourselves as not to resent hastily anything that seems like the presumption of an in-

ferior, least of all can one bred in London do so,
where the vast congregation of men who have no ascertained place in the social pyramid makes persons
ever on their guard to repress wanton familiarity.

"You are mistaken in me; I have come into the
kitchen to give my orders. I am a gentleman travelling
northward, not what you take me for, a kitchen guest,"
answered Skirlaugh, haughtily.

"Kitchen or parlour, you'll get nothing, so you'd
better be off," replied his adviser. "Here's to your
good journey and prosperous trading. I think Bob
Drury should knaw a bagman when he sees him, if he
hedn't his pokes about him, as you hev." Saying
thus he raised the rejected horn to his lips, and
after emptying its contents, clattered the vessel down
upon the dresser with a report that was probably intended to give additional emphasis to the expression
of comic conceit and self-satisfaction into which he
twisted his features.

"This is unbearable," exclaimed the traveller, as
he strode out of the kitchen in high dudgeon.

While this dialogue had been going on, an almost
similar scene had been transacting itself between Mr.
Skirlaugh's servant and the people in the yard. The
ostlers assured him that there was no stable room, and
gave ocular demonstration of the fact. Every stall
was occupied by the horses of Lord Carlton, his
friends, and their attendants. The man, however, was
a person of resource; it was not his first visit into
these parts. He soon discovered an empty shed, and

extemporized two corn cribs out of washing-tubs to
which he helped himself from the adjoining laundry.
William Skirlaugh made some hasty inquiries of the
servants in the yard, missed seeing his own, who was at
the moment busy about the tubs ; but ascertained that
what he had heard in the house was true, and that
there was not the slightest hope of getting anything to
eat or drink, except by sitting down in the kitchen in
the society of the groom. In another part of England, or on another occasion, he might have done this ;
but so near his relative's house, and in close proximity
with a man like Lord Carlton, it was impossible. He
had no desire of encountering again the menial who
had insulted him in the kitchen, still less of falling in
with Lord Carlton, whose habits and character were
not unknown to him : so he strolled forth to pass
away the time (the blasphemous phrase to kill time
had not then been imported) by a leisurely survey, on
an empty stomach, of what there might be around of
interest. The eastern gate of the stable-yard was
open, a footpath, on which a large white pig was basking in the rays of the evening sun, led through an
enclosure, which was either a very grass-grown court,
or a very foot-worn paddock upon the margin of the
lake, where several swans sailed in royal dignity at a
considerable distance from a large flock of geese ; a
pike now and then darted forward—struck is the
technical term—and marked the water with a thousand
tiny ripples. Two or three black water-hens were to
be seen running timidly hither and thither among the

thick weeds of the margin, scared by his approach. In the far-off distance were the wold hills, on the north a large mass of woodland, on the south the quaint old buildings of the hostelry, and on the west the stately trees, the straggling cottages, and a rude chapel of ease. As he gazed on the scene, whose stillness was only broken by a stray note of song from the revellers, which lost its words, and therefore its evil, in the passage, he could not but think that he had seldom looked upon a more peaceful or calmly picturesque spot. If this were not an inn, but a home, mused he, how happily might a man dwell here for ever?

So think all town-bred men. Your citizen—because the big wilderness of walls in which he lives is to him, at times, a prison, and he seeks the country with a desire for which thirst is scarcely a figure of speech—fancies that the scent of the meadows and the cawing of the rooks will never pall upon him—that the eternal freshness of Nature will be ever fresh to him.

Experience teaches otherwise. To the happy few the world without is a treasure of beauty, because of the light within. To ordinary dull souls, when the novelty has worn off, Ben Nevis is as stupid as Fleet Street, the Lago di Como but a bigger Serpentine, transparent to the bottom.

The path widened as he skirted the water. At the point where it fell into the Roman road, stood the little chapel of the village. It was ruinous and deso-

late, a gable cross yet stood at its eastern end, and
a dilapidated wooden hutch, like a chicken-coop without ends, still held a small bell. Something might
possibly be here that would interest him, or at least
help him to while away the quarter of an hour that
the horses would yet require to consume their provender. Happy beasts, they were getting their dinner.
The door was open, it did not seem to have a lock.
Some stained glass, with the coats-of-arms of now
forgotten donors to the hospitium, yet shone in the
windows ; a few half-worn-out inscriptions, which he
could not read, were visible on the green, mouldy
floor; a rickety pulpit, a few deal benches, and one
very large pew completed the furniture of this neglected house of God. The lead on the roof—church
restorers had not stolen that as yet, but it is gone
now—had cracked, so that in many places the light
of heaven came through. He was about to go
forth, with no very elevated idea of the religious
fervour of the inhabitants of Lindsey, when he observed in the darkest corner of the building, under a
low arch, an effigy in mail armour. A mere passing
glance would have been all that he would have bestowed upon it—for he, like most people of that age,
had little knowledge of such things—had he not seen
the Skirlaugh arms on the shield which the warrior bore.
This was interesting ; like many an antiquary, who
has since become as notable as such obscure plodders
are permitted to be, he was aroused to some degree of
attention by what appealed to his personal feelings.

He took from his pocket-book a letter, and began making a sketch of it on the blank part of the sheet.

William Skirlaugh was a good draughtsman. The maligned George Shelley had taught him drawing as well as penmanship. Sketching a monument in a place nearly dark, with no table but the knee, is not rapid work. Considerably more than a quarter of an hour had gone before the drawing was complete. He was just folding up the paper and putting his pencil in his pocket, when another object—this time not a visible, but an audible one—attracted his attention. From the highway arose the sound of three or four human voices singing, he could not catch the words, in a most unmusical fashion. There was, however, something in the manner, the roll of the verse, and the solemnity of the cadence, which indicated that it was not the chant of drunken revellers. It seemed earnest, and was therefore attractive. His curiosity was excited, he stood by the door, hidden in its shadow, and looked out upon a scene such as was then a subject of much laughter to the thoughtless, but has now become to us who view it through the perspective of the past a matter of great moment.

An old man, of perhaps sixty years of age, dressed in the garb of a peasant, with long, thin, gray hair, reaching to his shoulders, was standing on a large square stone by the roadside, his little shaggy pony tied to a neighbouring gate. Around him were gathered a few labouring men, who had left their work in the adjoining fields, and most of the women

from the surrounding alms-houses. On one corner of
the stone sat—or rather crouched—the poor drudge
whom we have before seen.

William now observed what he had not noticed when
in the kitchen, that the whole of one side of her
face was disfigured by a frightful burn. The sermon
had not begun. It was the preparatory hymn that
had attracted the attention of the sketcher.

> " Come hungry, come thirsty, come wretched, come bare,
> Come filthy, come starving, come just as you are,
> Come sin-stained, come blighted by Satan's dark curse
> And cast yourselves down before Jesus's cross,"

were the words of the first rude verse the preacher
sung, and they were taken up by his auditors with a
fervour that might have put to shame many a refined
congregation. Psalmody formed a great part of the
religious exercises of the early Methodists. The
hymns they sung were, many of them, not the verses
now found in the books published with the sanction
of the body, but rough poetry which had shaped itself
in the minds of unlettered farmers and mechanics,
whose hearts were filled with " the glad tidings," but
who had little power of expressing themselves in that
comely style of verse which was alone popular in the
eighteenth century. The realistic teaching of Holy
Scripture projected itself sharply upon their uncul-
tured minds, and produced fruit both in word and
action such as the literate classes were in no degree
prepared for. Hence the absurd charge of Popery
which was freely brought against John Wesley

and his disciples. Silly as this seems to us, who know more of Latin Christianity than our great grand-fathers, we can easily see that the physical imagery in much of the poetry of the early Methodists was well calculated to encourage such an illusion. On the present occasion many more verses followed the speci-men we have given, each one calling on sinners in hard but spirit-stirring words to leave the joys and sorrows of this world and cast all down at the foot of the Cross. As each fourth line was repeated, with marked emphasis on the final word, the feelings of the congregation became more and more moved; when the last stanza rolled forth several of the women were in tears.

The simple-minded preacher—like many of the preaching friars of former days, whose place he oc-cupied, for he was standing on what had ages ago been the pedestal of the village cross—was a natural orator. He saw that the hymn had done its work. Almost before the last sounds of song had died away he gave out his text,—

" Why will ye die ?".

And in fluent, but as his only educated auditor thought, in strangely exaggerated language, began to discourse on love to God. His delivery was low and sedate at first—so low, indeed, that Skirlaugh missed the purport of some of the opening sentences, but as the preacher went on, warmed with his own fervour and encouraged by that of his hearers, his utterance became harsher and more emphatic. His whole soul was bent on converting those who heard him to his own high ideas of religious duty.

"Oh, why will ye die? Why will you turn away from the only heart that loves you? We all of us hanker after love enough; there is not one of us here who has not felt that somebody's love was the greatest thing in the whole world to him—was all that was worth caring for. Tell me, my poor brothers and sisters who stand here, if the happiest thing you have to think of in your whole lives is not somebody's love? Perhaps it was your father's, when he used to take you on his knee in the chimney-corner after work was done, and let you play with the big buttons on his coat whilst he told you some soft tale, maybe about fighting and murder or fairies, bargests, and such like kelter, or mayhap sung you some wicked old song about things that men and women should not hear of, let alone a child. Perhaps it was your mother's love—ah, there is no mere worldly love like that—how she would cuddle you to sleep upon her breast, and call you darling, or how in long winter neets, when the winds were high, and you felt scared for dread of boggles, she would sit by your bedside and comfort you, when perhaps, the good woman was nearly as much afeard as you were. Or perhaps it was some other sort of love. I don't like to speak about that, there's so much that's dark about it—so much of the Devil in it. Perhaps the strongest love you ever felt was for some man or some woman who seemed everything to you, and yet was a thousand times worse than nowt. But what is all

this to the love of Jesus? Nothing! nothing! Your
father and mother are dead. Perhaps they didn't
behave none so well to you after all, when you'd grow'd
up, and them that you thought on for a husband or a
wife, if it *was* of marrying you were thinking, turned
out worse than nowt. We spend our lives in running
after love, in trying to get something to love us, and
some of us are so hard up at last that we would fain
treat dogs and cats as if they were Christians, sooner
than not have some love of some sort; and yet it is all
nought, doesn't last so long as the big rain-drops that
run after one another down the window-panes in a
thunder shower, that are dried up with the first glint
of sunshine, leaving the glass muckier than it was
afore. But if it didn't dry up in a day, as we may say,
if the love of father and mother, brothers and sisters,
wife and husband, lasted all our lives, what would all that
be to the love of Jesus? What is the least leaf on yon
trees to him that made them? Do you know where
all the love in the world comes from? Do you think
your father and mother would have loved you if *He*
had not put it into their hearts? Would your husband
or your wife have cared for you if He had not bidden
them? Oh, there is no love in the world but His.
He is all in all, and the love that every created thing
gives you was first his before it was theirs. It is His,
not theirs, and He is loving you through them, and
trying to draw you through their love from the filthy
desires that you wallow in, as a sow in a crew-
yard sludge-hole, to the joy of heaven, to heaven upon

earth, the love of Jesus. My dear friends, you all of you know that you can't live without love of some sort. We have all of us tried it again and again. I tried it on and off for fifty years; but we can't, we can't — our hearts would break. Come with me, then—come all, come now, to-day, this hour, this moment, to the fountain-head, where all the love in the world comes from. Come, come, come; throw your past lives behind you, and don't look at them any more. They are filthy rags; they have the plague —the plague of everlasting death, of hell-fire in them; but come and cast yourselves down at the foot of the cross of Christ—come and be sprinkled with the blood of the Lamb."

How long the words of the itinerant might have continued we have no means of judging. The villagers who formed his little flock were thoroughly in earnest. The sermon, however wearisome to a cultivated ear, was music to those whose intellects had never been instructed nor their feelings touched by religious teaching. It was, however, destined to an abrupt termination.

CHAPTER IV.

" Hinc via Tartarci quæ fert Acherontis ad undas :
Turbidus hic cœno vastâque voragine gurges
Æstuat."   *Virgilius, Æn.* vi.

THE words of the preacher had attracted the attention of other persons besides the draughtsman. Lord
Carlton and his friends occupied the large upper room
over the archway. They had already finished their
dinner, and sung most of the loose songs which their
memories contained ; their favourite anecdotes had
all been told, and the various cock matches, horse
races, and intrigues in which they had been engaged
worn threadbare. Wine and punch had been consumed freely, but even wine and punch, however libe-
rally administered, will not in stupid natures produce
conversation. It can only stimulate, not create.
If there be no sunlight, a prism will show bright
colours no more than a pair of tongs. So his lordship
and his following were very dull, notwithstanding all
their endeavours to the contrary. Their attempts,
however, to amuse themselves had been very various
and laboriously ingenious. One of them, a fine-

looking, middle-aged man, whom the others addressed
as Mac (he was understood to be the heir of a Scotch
baronetcy), was evidently considered the humorist
of the party. He had told more and dirtier tales, and
had been guilty of more impudent badinage to the
waiters, than any of his convives; at last, seeing his
associates becoming hopelessly dull, and knowing that
nothing of an intellectual nature would have a chance
of amusing them, he struck out the bright idea of furnishing entertainment at the expense of a large gray
cat that reposed on the hearth-rug; it was a happy
conception, calculated most accurately to suit the
taste of his friends. We regret, however, to add that
it was only in a very small degree successful. The
plot had in it all the simplicity of genius, it consisted in grasping the animal tightly with one hand,
while he burnt her tail with a red-hot poker which he
held in the other. A scream of applause greeted the
suggestion ; the laughter that followed was, however,
far more at the operator than the persecuted beast, for
the animal, when she felt the burn, instead of darting
forward as Mac was prepared for, scorning igno-
minious flight, sprung with the energy of a tiger
directly at her tormentor's face, causing him to drop
the poker upon his own foot, and indenting two long
and curiously jagged furrows to a considerable depth
in each of his cheeks. In a second the victor was
through the open door, out of the house, and high up
in one of the elms. Mac sunk into silence, among
roars of laughter, which he at intervals seasoned, but

did not interrupt, by a small dribble of heartfelt oaths.
Lord Carlton must, however, be amused at any sacrifice, all the company fully realised that, for he paid
for the dinner, and there were many other good
dinners in prospect, not to mention other and far
higher gains to be got from a nobleman, who, if poor
himself, was nearly allied to one of the most powerful
Whigs in England. A fat, pursy man, whose figure
indicated that he was on the less enviable side of fifty,
but whose pasty face seemed to show that he was considerably younger, and that his ungainly habit of body
was the result more of good living than age, tried to
raise a smile on his patron's face by drawing—the
fellow had a low kind of artist knack—men and
women with a burnt cork on the white stone chimney-
piece. While they were mere attitudinizing figures,
not a smile could be evoked, but when the brilliant
thought occurred to him of representing the scene
between Mac and the cat, Lord Carlton again deigned
to be amused, and the room was once more in a
roar.

"By Gad, Smyley, that's the best thing you ever
drew; you shall do it again on paper, and I'll have it
framed."

"Your lordship shall have it engraved on copper, if
you will," said the artist.

"No, brass, Smyley, brass! that will be capital;
and then we can give it to all our friends. Do you
hear, Mac?"

The gentleman addressed, who was busily employed

bathing his scored face with the corner of his pocket-handkerchief, looked up and made a feeble attempt to laugh—

"Your lordship had better let Smyley publish, under your patronage, a pictorial description of our tour."

"By George, it's a good idea! you're a Scotchman and a poet, you shall do the writing and Smyley the pictures."

"You will give your workmen leave to select their own subjects?"

"Scribble what you like, only make one laugh over it. If it's half as good as your cousin the Scotch lord's song book, I'd praise it if you made folks laugh at me in every leaf," responded the peer.

"That's the only book I ever heard your lordship quote," said Mac.

"It's the only one I ever read since I left college. I read few enough there, but I've given up the bad habit entirely since. I never read, it makes me think," rejoined his lordship.

"What a strange circumstance!" remarked a hard-headed man, with a strong north-country accent, who seemed to be the only one of the party quite sober. "I wish it had the same effect on other persons—most of the reading men I know never think at all."

"You know what old Hobbes said, about reading —'If I'd read,' said he, ' as much as you have, I should have been as great a fool.' That was a hard hit, Brotherton," said Mac, with patronizing familiarity.

" No fear of any one pelting you with such hard sayings, Mr. Mackenzie. I heard you charged with many follies and vices, but never with over study," replied the hard-headed man.

" Come, the book—the book! will you two boys do it for me as soon as we get to town ? You know what it's to be like. If you do it well I'll reward you handsomely—I will, by Jove," said his lordship, on whose clearness of articulation the wine was having considerable effect.

" I'll make my part like enough, my lord," responded Mackenzie.

" Like which, the book, or his lordship ? " inquired the retainer, feebly.

" Both, you blockhead. It shall be as witty as the one and as shameless as the other. By-the-bye, Brotherton, it won't do without a spice of learning in it. Dirt won't go down by itself. My Edinburgh education is fast running away, you must help me with a few scraps of Latin, and a tale or two from Ovid. What say you to this for a motto from old Tully ; it's no worse for being in Adam Littleton's dictionary—

' Qui canem et Felem ut Deos colunt.'

I shouldn't have remembered it if I hadn't once had a licking anent the said."

" I hardly understand its application," replied Mr. Brotherton, gravely.

"Dear, dear, not see it! why, ar'n't we to do a book setting forth the adventures of my lord here; and is there, when he's sober, anything in the world he likes so well as sport with dogs? Whether it's stag-hunting or hare-hunting, rabbit-hunting, bull-baiting, rat-catching, or dog-fighting, isn't it the same to him? And as to cats, don't my cheeks show the application of *felis;* besides, don't you know how Plautus uses it?" answered Mac.

"Perhaps I do, perhaps I don't. But for shame of yourself for dragging your High-School education in the gutter to please a drunken rabble."

During these latter sentences Mr. Smyley had been thinking, as well as he was able, how he was to show his resentment at the liberty Mac had taken in calling him a blockhead. He had come to no conclusion clearer than that of the Ripon tradesman who, when told over his glass at the Unicorn that his back shop was on fire, replied, "Well, then, I suppose sum'uts must be done somewhere, sometime, somehow." His ideas on the matter would probably have remained always in the nebulous stage, had not the words "drunken rabble" struck upon his ears; of their ap-plication he was not quite certain, but they sounded insulting, and he was not in a state of mind to exer-cise the critical faculty with much caution.

"I'll tell you what it is, gentlemen," said he, "nei-ther my lord nor myself are accustomed to such lan-guage as this. If Mr. Mackenzie and Mr. Brotherton expect to associate with English gentlemen, they must leave their bad words on the other side the Border. It should be sufficient for a Scotch fortune-hunter and a schoolmaster to get a seat at an English nobleman's table without presuming to vent his impudence to him and his friends. Blockhead—drunken rabble —I never heard such shocking language."

The case was becoming alarming. A Scotchman, however debased, is seldom quite dead to the honour of his country; and it is rarer still to find one who will permit that country to be insulted in his own person with impunity. Mackenzie had himself taken too much wine to see that Smyley was so drunk as to be utterly below notice. He sprung from his seat, and the answer that the artist would have received would have assumed a physical form of very impressive character had not Brotherton caught him by the arm and whispered in his ear, "Don't mind him, he's drunk as a pig now; settle it to-morrow, and I'll help you."

Mac had a very high opinion of Brotherton's judgment, but he was in a passion and prepared to resist calm counsel, had not Lord Carlton at the moment, without knowing the good he was doing, made a diversion. That nobleman, who had been sitting for some time gazing on space, the picture of half-drunken listlessness, suddenly sprang from his seat, shouting, as he did so, "Lord's sake, look here! Here's the devil of a joke, and we, like fools, nearly missed it; wouldn't have lost it for a hundred pounds, wouldn't, upon my soul." As he spoke he threw open the

window, and the hard clear tones of the Methodist's
sermon were distinctly audible within.

"Did you ever see the like of this, the canting
snivellers?" exclaimed his lordship.

"What are they after?" inquired Mackenzie, who
had probably never heard of Methodism.

Smyley endeavoured to explain; his articulation
was not clear, nor his views accurate. He was understood to say, "Damned new religion, like Puri-
tans—Noll's days, you know—won't fight cocks, don't
drink and sing, but pray like the very Devil."

"Another bumper, and then we'll squander the
hypocrites," cried Lord Carlton, who, tossing off the
punch with no very steady hand, rushed downstairs,
followed by all but the hard-headed Scotchman.

"There go fools too swinish to enjoy themselves,
and knaves too rascally to succeed in their own small
intrigues." So saying, he selected the most comfortable chair in the room and placed it near the open
window in such a position as to be able to watch the
result of the affray which, he doubted not, was about
to take place. The staid Scot was not mistaken.
With a yell, such as the Mohawks of London gave
when they attacked some peaceful citizen, they burst
in among the congregation. The preacher paused,
but moved not; most of his hearers fled at once, two
or three of the men only remaining at a very safe
distance. The woman, whom we have had occasion
to mention before, continued sitting on the corner of
the stone in the same attentive attitude as if the

sermon were still going on. The silent gaze of the
Methodist was fixed on the leader of the rioters, who,
pouring out curses and threats, menaced him with
instant punishment if he did not "come down from
his perch." His only method of resistance was remaining passive. When, at length, a lull came, so
that he had a chance of being heard, he said, in a
voice almost as calm as if no interruption had startled
him, and he were still pursuing the thread of his discourse, "Young man, I came to preach the Gospel to
the poor and ignorant. The Lord hath sent me those
who need it more. Listen; I have a message for
you."

"A pretty message you have, you sniveller. If you
don't come off your pulpit, I'll pull you down by the
ears and roll you in the gutter," screamed the leader
of the party.

"There is a pond near," suggested the more ob-
servant Mackenzie.

"So there is, by Gad. To the pond with him,"
cried the peer.

"To the pond, to the pond!" echoed his companions.

And so saying, all three dashed at once upon the
preacher, crushing, as they did so, the one unfortunate
member of his congregation who had remained faithful,
beneath their feet. The threatened ducking seemed
inevitable. The old man was, by profession and sincere conviction, opposed to violence. If he had been
sufficiently powerful it is improbable that he would

have aided himself by physical force; but had he
put forth all his little strength, it could have been
of small avail against three active men. Their
evil design, however, was not to be carried into
effect. William Skirlaugh had been attentively watching the proceedings, and knew the characters of
Lord Carlton and his friends by report, sufficiently
well to be quite sure that, heated as they were with
wine, they would shrink from no atrocity to which
their brutal sense of the humorous might prompt
them. His voice, calling on the rioters to desist, was
most likely drowned by their own hideous laughter, as
they dragged the preacher from the stone. None
seemed aware of his presence until he knocked Mr.
Smyley down with the butt-end of his riding whip, and
seizing hold of Lord Carlton by the collar, proceeded
to drag him from his victim. A well-delivered blow
from Mac, which almost levelled William by the side
of the recumbent Smyley, forced him to let go his
hold. He retained his balance, however, but only to
be the object of the united attentions of the peer and
the Highlander. He had learnt the art of self-defence,
and could easily have made good his position against
either of his antagonists, though he would probably have been at length overpowered by the two.
Their victory was rendered more speedy if less glo-
rious by the intervention of Mr. Smyley, who, still
prostrate on the earth, at a moment when Skirlaugh
was delivering a blow with his full force, grasped his
legs and stretched him on the road beside himself.

William was now entirely at the mercy of the victors. The cry of "To the pond, to the pond!" again arose, and the three ruffians proceeded to drag their captive to the margin of the lakelet. In a moment more he would have been floundering in its waters; but, at this juncture, another person appeared upon the scene.

CHAPTER V.

" All this being done in such a godly, grave, solemn, and substantiall manner, as would extraordinarily have affected any truly honest and godly heart to have beheld it."—John Vicars' *Jehovah-Jireh*, i. 424.

CALL up before your eyes a human figure, upwards of six feet in height, thin, muscular, and trained to exercise by twelve hours of daily toil; clothe this figure with neat but work-day raiment of Quaker-like complexion—drab coat, drab waistcoat, drab small-clothes, and gray worsted stockings, buttons cloth-covered, not shiny metal, as the use then was; place on his head a brown felt hat, steeple-crowned, like those worn in the middle of the preceding century, but with a narrower brim; put a heavy ash cudgel in his right hand for a walking-stick, and you have the every-day costume of John Stutting, the Wivilby Tanner, a noted man in his neighbourhood, the leader and chief spiritual and temporal adviser of a small and scattered remnant of Independents, who had remained faithful to their conception of truth through the per-secuting times that followed the Restoration, and per-formed the still harder task of confessing their faith

during the days of toleration which followed the Revolution, when fines and imprisonment were replaced by
social contempt and obloquy. John Stutting was a
sworn foe to all ungodliness and tyranny, under which
comprehensive words he included not only most of
the things which with us go under those names, but
also such venerable institutions as a titled aristocracy,
country squires, horse racing, game laws, a hireling
ministry, and even the institution of monarchy itself.
Add to this that he had travelled much, had lived
and fought in America, and visited the Mediter-
ranean and the Iberian peninsula as a sailor, was well
off in this world's goods, could read and write "as
well as the parson," and was esteemed on all hands
to be a thoroughly honest, upright and downright
man, whom no one could intimidate, and King
George's exchequer could not bribe, and you have a
sufficiently accurate limning of a person who contrived
to make some few of his poorer neighbours reverence
him almost as a superior being, while most of those
outside the narrow circle of his influence looked on
him as a dark and dangerous fanatic.

As we before said, the rioters had already reached
the margin of the water; to souse their victim in its
depths would be scarcely the work of another second,
when Stutting's tower-like form intervened. His
stick was in his hand, but there was little menace of
voice or manner in the words he spoke—loud enough,
however, to be heard by all present—"Let that man
go." Mackenzie and the peer replied not; the greater

part of the physical labour of the row devolved upon them, for Smyley, since he had performed the feat of putting William Skirlaugh *hors de combat* by a process not inaptly described in the old ditty :—

" It was na' varra bold,
It was na' varra canny,
It was na' gude for braggin' on,
But it was varra handy,"

had reposed upon his laurels, adding to the glory of the victory, only by the noise he made, and to the humiliation of the conquered by an occasional kick in the ribs. He judged by the new-comer's dress that he was a peasant; his experience of persons of that order had been limited; such as he had was gathered almost entirely in the southern counties. A brazen face, and a few fierce oaths will make him run off like a rat, thought he; so, without any real intention of violence, brandishing his clenched fist in the immediate neighbourhood of the tanner's nose, he begun an address, the exordium of which was, " Damn you, you clodhopper." We regret that we cannot report it further; like the *Faerie Queen* it has come down to posterity but a fragment; for John Stutting, seizing the artist by the shoulder, whirled him round until his body was between himself and the water, and then with one blow on the chest sent the unhappy gentleman backward into the lake. This was the work but of an instant. Before Lord Carlton knew what had happened to his sycophant, he was himself prostrate over the body of his intended victim.

Mackenzie was a ruffian, but neither a coward nor a fool; he probably would not in any case have deserted friends at a pinch. In this instance he knew well that it would be to his advantage, however the affray turned out, for him to stand stoutly by his associates. He was strong of limb, and therefore by no means so contemptible an antagonist as the others had been. The fight was, however, not destined to come to its natural termination. The hubbub had at length attracted the attention of the people belonging to the inn; Lord Carlton's own retainers, William Skirlaugh's servant, and the groom; Brotherton, too, seeing the course matters were taking, had reluctantly disturbed himself. He gathered information on his way to the scene of warfare, that showed him it was high time to interfere. The whole bevy bore down on the rioters in a body. For a moment it seemed as if the great increase of numbers was only to lead to a battle on a larger scale.

At first, the groom was the most important personage. He elbowed his way to the front, shouting out to Stutting, "Stand to him, John; I'm here, and will soon sattle ony three on 'em."

The most demonstrative of Lord Carlton's servants was the coachman. To this person our friend at once offered the courtesy of the duello. "Come on," cried he; "I've told yer afore now, yer lord would dee in his boots; dust thow want to go where he's gone to, 'cause if thow dust, smell o' this, it smells o' dead men," and he shook his fist in the face of the noble lord's menial.

The decisive battles of the world—fifteen of them, that is—have met with a knightly chronicler. The battles that might have been decisive, had not fate hindered their being fought out to the bitter end, have not yet found a historian. When one arises, he will have to describe several less hearty turns-to than the one we have feebly sketched.

Brotherton was but a pace behind the coachman. He pushed him on one side to prevent further mischief; flung himself between his countryman and the tanner, and endeavoured with all his force to drag the former from the field of conflict.

"For heaven's sake be quiet. Do you know what you are doing, and where you are?"

"Helping my lord in a row, not looking at him through a window," responded the belligerent, angrily, making an effort—but by no means a very determined one—to turn again upon his antagonist.

"You're a fool, sir. If you don't settle this matter, you'll all of you be in gaol within twelve hours, and besides, ruin his lordship's prospects. The fellow you've knocked into the puddle is a relation of old Skirlaugh's—nephew or cousin or something—going to see him this very day."

A deep ejaculation of "Good Gad!" was the only sound that issued from Mac's lips for the space of a quarter of a minute, during which interval he seemed from the direction of his eyes to be attentively considering the form and make of his silver shoe-buckles.

" We're wiped out, and no mistake : what is to be done ? " at length ejaculated he, still gazing on the ground.

" Done ! why pick up your drunken leader; take him upstairs, and scare him half to death, if that Hercules has left him any brains to work upon, and leave the rest to me." The Highlander slunk off in no happy frame of mind. Brotherton's words had conveyed to him much more information than they will at present do to our readers.

Lord Carlton had already been picked up, and was being supported to bed by two of his own people. So Mac turned into the dining-room to refresh himself with the remains of the punch. His sorrow, deep as it was, gave way rapidly before what he saw when he entered the apartment. There lay stretched on the hearth before the fire the form of Mr. Smyley, a mass of mud from the lake, and not mere common mud, such as any pond or streamlet might produce, but slime as black as the dregs of an inkstand, and as fœtid as the deposit of a sewer. The unhappy gentleman had been hurled just into that spot where the drain of the kitchen sink deposited its filth in the clear water. Mr. Smyley was somewhat of a fop. His coat but an hour ago was bright blue; his waistcoat buff, picked out with lavender flowers ; his small clothes, a rich chocolate : now all were sable as the hangings of a hearse. No word escaped that gentleman as he re-

turned Mac's provoking gaze with a scowl which would
have been frightful but for its imbecility. This was
too much for the Scot; he burst into a yell of uncon-
trollable laughter.

"Sir, sir! dem you, sir! What do you mean by
deriding, sir—ridiculing and insulting a friend who
has stood by you? You're a cowardly, a dastardly
sneak; and I'll be damned if I don't have satisfaction!"

"Peace, peace, my good fellow," gasped the Scotchman, with a convulsive effort, but there was no peace
for him. The storm of invective still pelted him from
the hearth-rug, only now and then modified by deeper
and more fervent curses against Lord Carlton, who
had led him into mischief, and the redoubted champion
by whom he had been overcome. Laughter cannot
last for ever, even when fed by the stimulus of imbecile
rage. When Mackenzie came to himself, he hastened
to assure his companion that no harm was meant, but
that if it had been "Lord Carlton or King George
himself, by gad it must have been the same." He
had quite forgotten what had happened before
the fight. Smyley, however, thought good to remember it.

"It's all very well, sir; but I am a gentleman, not
accustomed to receive such treatment as this from any
one; and I remember, too, the shockingly abusive
language which you were using towards me just before
we left the room. Upon my honour, I believe the pain
it gave me to suffer thus at the hand of a friend un-

nerved me, else how could that low fellow have struck down a master of self-defence like me ? ''

" Upon my word, Smyley, I had forgotten all about it, my good fellow, and must beg you to do the same. . Said after dinner—after dinner, you know. Why, my head still swims with this fellow's brandied port (they had been drinking punch) ! If I could have thought anything I had said could have offended you, by Jupiter I'd have kept my mouth shut as tight as my old father's purse strings, and that's the fastest thing I know. But I couldn't help laughing if it were to save my soul, that's poz."

" Your soul's nothing to me, Mr. Mackenzie : but to persecute with scorn a poor fellow like me, suffering from blows and unable to defend himself, is a matter I can't look over ; I can't, indeed."

The Scotchman's amusement was not lessened by this conversation, but it was diverted into another channel. He had now no tendency to laugh, but a curious—almost scientific—interest in watching the action of Smyley's mind. It was clear he was " after something," but that something was not quite so obvious. Mackenzie knew him far too well to suppose that he had any serious desire to quarrel with him. When you are studying any natural phenomenon, whether it be the circulation of the blood in the back of a spider which you have imprisoned in your microscope, a transit of Venus, or the contortions of face of a popular orator while he harangues a mob, you will observe the best if you are silent and calm. This has been pointed

out in divers manuals of natural science, and a friend
of ours happened to see nearly the same thing repeated
in a useful "Handbook to the Manners of Good Society," which he observed the other day on the table of
a newly-elected borough M.P. Hence we conclude
that this simple generalization has now penetrated
down considerably below the surface of society. It
was not taught in Mackenzie's time, as those who are
acquainted with its scientific literature well know. We
must, therefore, give him some credit for originality,
when he filled a glass with punch, sat down by the
fire in perfect silence, and gazed intently between the
bars. There were no sounds from the prostrate one
for some time. At length, in a voice of stage heroism,
he exclaimed, "Are we friends or enemies?"

"Don't be silly, Smyley—why friends, of course.
What is there to have a fuss about?"

"My feelings are far too much hurt not to require
reparation."

"Your feelings be damned! Now I'll tell you what
it is: I never meant to insult you, and you know I
didn't. You don't want to fight me, and you know I
know you don't. Therefore come to the point like a
sensible man; but before you do anything else, for
goodness sake, get into some decent clothes. Wash
your hands and face, and put a clean wig on your poll.
Did any man ever talk about satisfaction and hint at
pistols and rapiers, think you, laid reeking before the
fire like a big black poodle. You're a disgrace to
Lord Carlton's equipage. If you don't go I'll fetch

the fellows who carried off his lordship to act as valets
to you."

" Oh! don't, don't!" cried the prostrate form,
piteously.

There was silence for about a minute. During that
brief space Mr. Smyley, like other generals, had changed
the plan of his campaign.

" I can't be friends with you any more. To insult
the unfortunate is a stain on a man's honour. I didn't
think it of you."

" Don't talk in that whining voice, but go dress
yourself, and we'll make it all right, old fellow," rejoined the Scot.

" I won't stir from where I am till you have made
reparation, Mr. Mackenzie; I won't, indeed."

" What am I to do? I don't want to quarrel; you
don't want to fight, so we are friends; but pray, for
heaven's sake, get rid of that miserable snivel, which
is more like that of a whipped schoolboy than a
man."

" Then you do wish us to be friends—firm friends
again, do you?"

" Yes, of course I do."

" And you will, as a proof of friendship, sacredly
revere a secret I wish to communicate?"

" Yes, yes! of course I will."

" It is a very serious affair, I assure you—one that
I would not communicate to any living soul but your
own; and had I not the greatest confidence—"

" Well, well; we understand all that. What is it

you want me to do ? By jingo, I have not a guinea in my purse, if that's your aim."

"It's not money I am thinking of, Mr. Mackenzie, but the tailor. I left all my clothes in London, and I haven't a rag except these, which are now spoilt for ever."

"Nonsense ! Why, there's a portmanteau as big as a meal-bin in your bedroom."

"Ah ! but it hasn't clothes in it. I left everything I had at home, except two shirts and these damned black things I have on. What shall I do ? It will take a week to get them down, and we are going to Lord Burworth's to-morrow."

A dark shadow passed over Mackenzie's face, his eyes only showed signs of merriment, which he suppressed with the greatest fortitude.

"Why have you brought that empty coffin lumbering along with you, then ? Now, no nonsense. Tell the truth, if I am to help you."

The prostrate form replied not, except by a stifled groan.

"You are such a touchy fellow, and I really like you, demme I do, or I would tell *you* why you left them, and call you a damned sneak into the bargain, but it's no use. What can I do for you ? My clothes won't fit ; they're too big one way, and too little the other."

To this address there was no response from the hearth-rug. After a moment's thought, the Scot continued—

"I've a great mind to believe, Smyley, this is all a trick to deceive me!"

The abject suppliant swore he was never more truthful in his life.

"Then there is no time to lose," said the Highlander, "not an instant. If I am to help you, it must be my own way, and that way is to send to Lincoln for some more; but then you must go to bed at once, strip off those stinking garments, and send them over for patterns. There's no time to be lost by a snipper-snapper coming all the way over to measure that round carcass of yours."

"I can't lie in bed till they're made."

"You must."

"You can't send to Lincoln without Lord Carlton and Brotherton knowing."

"Lord Carlton's in bed, and will be God knows how long. Brotherton must know. I can't send a servant away without him."

"Oh, Lord! oh, Lord!" ejaculated the sufferer, almost moved to tears.

"It's no use moaning. Trundle off to bed, I tell you, and fling your things outside the door."

Suiting his action to the advice he had given, the Scot dragged the unfortunate into an upright posture. His next duty was to seek out Mr. Brotherton, who was a kind of guide, companion, friend, book-keeper, and sycophant to his lordship. Brotherton was grave from nature and design; but even he could not suppress a chuckle at Mackenzie's description of the unfortunate Smyley.

"Gad, I wish I had seen him!—the fool!—the vain fool! We must help him; it will only delay his lordship for a day. We must help him; he's very useful. Will lie like a Jesuit and swear like a fishwife, when we want him. Poor Smyley! His lordship must pay for the clothes, if they ever are paid for."

A servant was despatched with the mud-stained garments to Lincoln.

We have sufficiently discoursed on Mr. Smyley's dress, and will now go on to other matters.

CHAPTER VI.

" A building of brick, varied by stone copings, and covered in a great part with ivy and jasmine."—Lord Lytton, *Paul Clifford*, xi.

BEFORE William Skirlaugh had collected his scattered senses, so far as to comprehend the novel situation in which he found himself, he was alone with his servant. The tanner had seated himself on the old stone where the action had begun, and, with as calm and unconcerned a manner as if nothing had happened to interrupt his rural musings was, or seemed to be, watching the flight of the swallows over the water. He ordered the horses without a moment's delay, and going up to Stutting thanked him for his timely aid.

" You are called Skirlaugh," abruptly broke in the tanner, " a kinsman to Ralf Skirlaugh, whom men here call the Squire ?"

The traveller assented.

" There is then no need to thank me. Ralf Skirlaugh and I know each other. He is a child of darkness. I am a child of light. He would if he could, even as his fathers did aforetime, imprison, scourge,

yea, even hang such as I am. Yet from mere carnal
tenderness of heart, which profiteth nothing, he will
help the poor and the suffering, yea, even when they
are of the household of faith. You, too, are no doubt
like minded. Say, therefore, no more of what has
been done through my means. I profess I was not
sorry to use my stick about the sides of these sons
of Belial. If you are not like unto them, I would
bid you avoid their company. They will know you
now and hate you. They are powerful through the
influence of the man whom they call Lord Burworth,
who is one of the tribe of Whigs which as yet sit in
high places."

After thus delivering himself, without salutation or
farewell, he strode away in a direction different from
that in which William Skirlaugh was about to travel.

If the reader has ever, in early days, when the intellect and character were formed, but the manners as
yet imperfectly developed, found himself on the point
of being introduced into a new sphere of life, and that a
socially higher one than his own, he will understand
our traveller's feelings as he stepped from the autumnal darkness of the court into the hall of the
Squire's mansion.

William Skirlaugh had, from childhood, been
prompt enough in action, but quickness, firmness,
and their allied qualities, though they go far towards
making a noble character, are of little help to a
person just about to pass into a circle of whose
thoughts and tone he knows little, but whose position

and importance have been a frequent subject of
conversation and eulogy. His education had been
just of the kind calculated to foster this weakness.
His bachelor uncle never went into society, and saw
no one at his own house but on matters of business,
except two or three lawyers like-minded with himself,
whose professionally learned talk was the most treasured relaxation of his life. The nephew cannot be
supposed to have delighted much in listening to the
conversation of these friends; it may be doubted,
however, whether, to his imaginative temperament,
their ponderously learned talk, interspersed as it now
and then was with a word picture—in very neutral
tints, it must be confessed—of days different from his
own, was not more pleasing than the insipidity, noise
or flaunting profligacy of such society as he might
have entered. Two worlds he had seen : the sombre
one of legal London, and the quiet rural one into
which he had glided on his occasional visits to his
Yorkshire relative. Both were pure, the latter calmly
beautiful.

Whatever shyness there might have been passed
away almost instantly. The warm reception given the
traveller by his host, and the kindly manners of the
ladies, soon put the young man quite at his ease. A
certain school of novelists, and that not the most
despicable, are wont to give their readers a description of the furniture, animate and inanimate, of the
apartments into which they conduct their readers,
almost as elaborate as an auctioneer's catalogue. We

will spare ours this affront to their imagination, simply observing that the summer parlour in which the guest was now seated formed one of the smaller of a suite of apartments occupying the whole of the western side of the building. The persons making up the family party were the Squire himself, a tall slightly-built man of about sixty, his wife, a portly dame, perhaps five or six years younger, whose Scottish accent—the old court Scotch, not the barbarous peasant dialect—slight though it was, indicated that she came of northern lineage; their only daughter, Isabell, her friend and companion, Mary Morley, and Mr. Callis, the non-juring chaplain. The last was the only one who did not join freely in the conversation. His mind was completely absorbed in the contents of a folio volume in some one of the less known Teutonic languages, whose very characters would have been well nigh unintelligible to the visitor, had he glanced at them over their reader's shoulder.

The ladies and the divine retired at an early hour. When alone with the Squire, William felt it to be his duty to introduce the subject of the law affairs which had been the excuse for his long-contemplated journey.

" A truce, a truce,—an old soldier cries truce,—and if that may not be had, fairly throws down his arms and begs for quarter, any terms, however hard, to be rid of feoffments, leases for a year, deeds of bargain and sale, final recoveries, entails, and suchlike ill-

omened words. Surely my good cousin, Mr. Robert
Skirlaugh, has not filled your young head so full of
law jargon that you cannot spare a relation the first
evening you spend with him on the old homestead;
besides, you come here to-day not as a lawyer, but as
a child of chivalry, a knight-errant, a true son of Sir
Ingelram de Skirlaugh, who saved the Breton damsel
from the Sallee rovers, and whose picture, painted
three hundred years after his death, but a striking likeness, I will show you in the gallery to-morrow. True,
you fought for a wizened old methodist preacher, he
for a noble maiden : but the spirit was the same. So
I must have a full and circumstantial account of this
last act of heroism from the chief actor, that Mr.
Callis, who is not only the chaplain but the historian
of our house, may add it to the family chronicles."

William gave a modest narrative of his day's adventure, suppressing the passages which related to
the head groom.

"Capital, capital!" exclaimed the Squire, when he
had done. "Capital! By Jove, we'll pay them off
for it some day. A brave fellow, that Stutting. A
stout, trustworthy fellow; but cracked—cracked—mad
as a March hare—believes in the New Jerusalem
coming down from Heaven somewhere just hereabouts, on my domain, I fancy, all ready built, streets
paved, chimney-pots on, knockers ready fixed, and
lighted up day and night from within, without sun,
moon, or stars, or any expenditure in tallow dips,
wax lights, or oil lamps. Preaches, too, to lots of

people who go to hear him, and tells them it is of no
use to keep the Ten Commandments, but that they
may all follow their own fancies, so that they don't
contradict him. He is a sort of Protestant Pope,
just such a fellow as John of Leiden, whose bones
yet hang in an iron basket from the big church tower
in the market-place at Münster. I've heard them rattle
in the wind many a time."

"I hope my friend of to-day may not come to so
fearful an end as the mad tailor whom the brutal Ger-
mans tortured to death," said William.

"Trust Stutting for that. To hear him talk when
he raves about religion, and the inward light, you'd
think him as mad as the wildest of the Anabaptist
crew; but speak to him on any matter of worldly
concern, of hides or tallow, of politics even, and
you'll find him a calm, cautious, and hard headed
yeoman. If the cavaliers of Lincolnshire had risen
in the forty-five, he would have gone with us with all
his disciples. And he could have brought a following
of some two hundred men at his back. I am heartily
glad he gave Lord Carlton a drubbing. He hates all
lords, and I am very much of his way of thinking, at
least as to the new ones whose patents are written on
Dutch paper or in German text. This Lord Carlton,
now, is the grandson of a Cheapside hatter. He has
a peerage because his father did dirty work for Hanover, when the Whigs were passing their act of
settlement. He has run through all his property,
and would be a pauper if my neighbour, Lord Bur-

worth, to whose settled estates he is heir, did not help him. He is one of the same gang, but he has brains if not principle. I wonder what they are down in Lincolnshire for; Burworth told me that he had made it a condition that he was not to be troubled with his nephew's society. The rascally drunken ruffians will drive the poor gouty old gentleman out of his senses if they stay long with him. Now, there are some men of your age who, if they had been insulted as you have been, would have talked of pistols and rapiers, sent the chief fool a challenge, and perilled their own valuable lives against that of a worthless scamp. I am glad to see that you have more sense and breeding. I know the laws of the *duello*, have served in France, the country where its usages have been reduced to the strictest code, and there can be no doubt that not only are you not called upon to give this fool a chance of shooting at you, but that you are explicitly bound by the laws of honour not to do so. Had yours been a quarrel between gentlemen, you must have fought him; but it was a mere street row, in which you were not bound to be aware that your antagonist was a gentleman; besides, he was *ebrius*, drunken; and for acts so done a man may well be subject to the common or statute law, but can be by no means worthy of the chivalrous courtesy of a man of honour."

William intimated that he had no intention of fighting Lord Carlton, unless the combat were forced upon him. The strict religious principles in which he had

been educated would not have permitted him, in any
case, to give a challenge, though, under certain circumstances, he might have felt himself bound to accept
one, if offered.

The conversation flowed on for some time in the
channel it had now taken. The Squire was a great
authority on the laws of honour: his French education had supplied him with many chances of watching
such courteous passages—his semi-military life, when
he had served as a volunteer in the French armies,
had contributed not a small amount of personal experience, all of which he was ready to pour out for the
delectation of his patient listener. Ralf Skirlaugh
was a man with few friends. He had quarrelled with
most of his Whig neighbours, on account of their
politics, and had good reasons of a social nature for
seeing but little of the Jacobite gentry around. He
was consequently thrown almost entirely upon his own
resources for amusement. It was, therefore, a complete godsend to him, when he happened, as on the
present occasion, to come in contact with a gentleman
of "honest principles," who was at the same time
a good listener. On this, the first evening of their
acquaintance, he poured forth a whole volume of his
French reminiscences; and was not a little surprised
and delighted to find his hearer not only well acquainted with the geography of what was then to
most untravelled Englishmen an almost unknown
land, but that he possessed also no inconsiderable
knowledge of the lives and actions of many of the

notable persons with whom he himself had been thrown in contact.

" I am surprised, and more pleased than I can express, cousin," said he, " to find in you not only those principles of loyalty which are befitting all who bear our name, but also a cultivated understanding, which does not despise men and things different from what are to be seen at home. Now, I assure you, that among my acquaintances here, there is not one who would not have yawned long ago if I had told him half the experiences which I have communicated to you to-night. They would one and all have put me off with indecorous jokes about frogs, wooden shoes, and such like gear; and if they were of the vile Whig gang, would have added some silly gibe about the devil, the pope, and the Pretender, as they call king James; and yet, if I were to talk to them about foxes and hounds, horse-racing and cock-fighting, or even killing partridges, they would listen with open mouths and staring eyes, as if it were an oracle that was speaking, till long past midnight — as it is now, for I heard the hall clock strike two when I was in the midst of that good story about my adventures with the Cape Breton fish-wives. So enough of *la belle France* and the damned Whig crew for to-night; to-morrow you shall have a long ride with me, to see the nakedness of the land. And now to bed."

CHAPTER VII

" Lever matin n'est poinct bon heur."—Rabelais, I. xxi.

IT is a mistake to believe that the upper classes in the last century were early risers. Early of course they were, when compared with those foolish people of to-day, who breakfast in their bedrooms considerably after wise men's luncheon time, but certainly not early, as a foreigner or even a Scotchman would count earliness. It is not surprising that William was the first to make his appearance in the lower world, where only servants were stirring. The hall door was open, inviting the stranger to wander forth to survey the pleasant home in which he found himself a temporary sojourner.

Skirlaugh Manor was a large, compact house, with little claim to antiquity. The edifice, except some insignificant fragments concealed in the interior arrangements, had been built by the present owner's grandfather. The old house, a square fortified building, with four angle towers, had been so rent by the shot of the besiegers in the unhappy domestic wars of

the seventeenth century, that its owner, after many
ineffectual attempts at repair, had determined to pull
down the whole, and make himself a comfortable
modern mansion out of the ruins. This he succeeded
in doing, mainly, perhaps, because he discarded all
false antiquarianism, and set to work to make a home,
not a sham castle, a Roman villa, or an Italian palace.
Another reason may have been, that he was his own
architect. The old fortalice, like many of the latter
middle-age secular buildings of eastern England, had
been constructed almost entirely of thin dark-coloured
bricks; these, with stone-dressings for windows and
corners, made admirable building materials. The
simple plan, an oblong block, was rendered picturesque
by three gables at the northern and southern points.
The plain surfaces of the walls were a mass of jasmine,
ivy, and roses, through whose tangle peeped at intervals a carved shield, monogram, or grotesque head,
which the builder had saved from the old wreck, and
had, in defiance of all propriety, persisted in using in
his new building, in spite of the incongruousness
which, as the art critics of the neighbourhood assured
him, would entirely spoil the effect of his work.
There was one point however, the great hall door
under the central gable of the south, and the porch
protecting the same, where the designer had poured
forth all his cunning. No climbing plant was permitted to defile this elaborate piece of chiselmanship.
In the rest of the building mere comfort had been considered. Here had been found a fitting place for the

higher instincts of man to shew their superiority
without restraint. The ponderous stone work was a
mass of heraldry; every form that the Skirlaugh
coat had assumed—and like other old things, it had
passed through various stages ere it came to maturity
—every match that a Skirlaugh had made with an
heiress of blood, every shield that she had brought in
with her, was duly set forth in all the hard grotesque-
ness of that now well-nigh forgotten picture language
which our inaccurate ancestors called the science of
heraldry. The shields and crests, which seemed a
mere jumble of bad carving to one who did not care to
master the riddle, told the whole genealogical history
of the house to attentive and instructed eyes. Even
the true-love knots, scythes, death's-heads, and war-
like trophies, in which the family motto,

More Faithfull than Fortunate,

was embedded, had each their appropriate meaning. A
paved court cut off the hall from the park beyond; a
fountain, where a leaden sea-god spurted a tiny stream
of water about three feet into the air, decorated its
centre; an hydraulic contrivance almost as ugly as its
sisters in Trafalgar Square, but considered a miracle
of applied science by the simple rustics around. Two
large cedar trees stood one on each side of the
wrought-iron gates, and stone benches, much too high
to sit upon, were placed at regular intervals around
the fence wall. Not a flowering shrub, a fruit tree, or

even a weed lent its greenness to mitigate the stiff
grandeur of this prison-like enclosure. The gardener's
art was elsewhere not neglected; trim pleasure grounds
of large extent, in which flowers, fruit, and the humbler
vegetables of culinary and medical use were mingled
in picturesque confusion, not kept rigidly apart, like
nobles and burghers at an old German festival, spread
on both sides the manor. Their style would be considered by many persons of the present day repulsively
formal. The long, straight walks and trim fences of
our forefathers having gone out almost as entirely as
chain armour.

At Skirlaugh Manor this mode of producing beauty
or ugliness was to be seen in full perfection. From
the outer fence, a compact wall of hornbeam, rose
at regular intervals limes of large size, whose heads
had from earliest youth been taught to grow, not as
forest trees, but alternately into the shapes of globes
and pyramids. The interior was divided into numberless sections by smaller hedges of yew and box, the
upper parts of which the shears of the merciless gardener had tortured into the semblance of every animal
real or imaginary, which had a place in the Skirlaugh
heraldry. The same officious hands had been at work
endeavouring to improve on Nature in the lower parts.
Here texts of Holy Scripture, scraps from Horace,
and quaint mottoes of uncertain origin and very
dubious spelling, were carved by the shears into the
living walls. The contriver of this stiff pleasaunce had
not, however, wasted all his thoughts on the fences.

The flower beds shone bright with such autumn flowers
as are able to bear our climate, and almost every rich
foliaged tree that was then known in Britain, might
be seen in full beauty; nor had he been unmindful of
the duty of providing a central point of attraction.
A little sheet of water, covered with lilies now in the
full glory of their large, sleepy, white and golden
flowers, enclosed a miniature island, to whose shores
a brightly-painted lattice bridge gave access. In the
centre of the island rose an octagonal summer-house
of small yellow bricks, each of whose sides was guarded
by a molten image of a heathen deity, whose stiff
draperies and angular limbs indicated that they were
the work of the unknown artist to whom the lord of
the mansion owed the fountain in his court.

Yellow brick may not be the proper material of
which to build summer-houses; the present taste
points rather to a turf stack, a bee hive, or a stick
heap, as the type of excellence. In George IV.'s
time people of taste preferred a Chinese joss-house,
or an Indian pagoda. Greek temples, windmills, and
churches of lath and plaster, have all been tried, and
found admirers. Here convenience and beauty of a
certain low and cold sort were attained, at least, without sham. The mind, if not raised above its own
sombre brooding, was not put into a combative attitude by an ugly and soulless parody.

William seated himself in one of the comfortable
arm-chairs with which the pleasure-house was furnished, and gave himself up to a most uncritically

happy contemplation of the scene around him. It was certainly beautiful, notwithstanding its grave formality. The windows of the pleasure-house corresponded with the main alleys of the garden, and from several of them might be seen a widely extended and richly varied view. To the east the eye wandered over the long range of the cliffs, now clad in old wood, which had succeeded to the Druid forests of our Keltic predecessors, interspersed with new plantations of larch and Scotch fir, and then for miles over a mere bare expanse of rabbit-warren and sheep-walk. To the west the Trent was visible, at intervals, for the last twenty miles of its course, its banks dappled by villages, whose whitewashed cottages shone in the morning sun like snow, and running parallel with its eastern margin for nearly the whole of its course, was that strange strip of sandhill and peat bog which furnished the Yorkshire antiquary, Mr. Abraham de la Pryme, with so many objects for curious speculation. A dull, uninhabited region, where wildfowl played in the meres as unharmed and fearless as if they dwelt in a land where their great enemy, man, had not set his foot; where the red deer, children of those hunted by Roger Mowbray, the crusader, still maintained a precarious existence, in spite of the guns, dogs, and pitfalls of the neighbouring pot-hunters. Beyond the Trent, stretching far as the eye could reach, was the Isle of Axholme, a little wedge of Lincolnshire, cut off from the rest of the county by a broad, unbridged river, and from Yorkshire by wide marshes, impassable

even in the driest summers, to all but foot people,
whose inhabitants kept up an insulated existence,
almost as untrammelled by external law or custom as
if THE ISLE, as its indwellers affectionately called it,
were a little republic, like San Marino or Andorra, independent of the empire that surrounded it. The
history of some passages in the latter career of this
fierce and ignorant people, was not unfamiliar to our
hero, on account of diverse law pleas—as the Scotch
call them—much quoted in the old books, which had
afforded food for many a long talk to his legally-minded
uncle.

We have already made the reader understand, if we
have not directly told him, that William Skirlaugh
was a young man of imaginative temperament. Such
persons, unless their minds have, in early youth, received some unfortunate bias in politics or theology,
or been stained by some evil and therefore degrading
passion, are usually strongly affected by scenery and
its associations. These influences would at any time
have acted with unusual force upon the young lawyer;
but he was now peculiarly susceptible to them. For
the first time in his life he was at the home of his race,
where every village and hill top, almost every solitary
tree and patch of green sward was consecrated in his
mind by association with that family on whose dignity
in former days and goodness at the present, the relative to whose motherlike kindness his heart most
fervently warmed, was never weary of dwelling. What
wonder is there, then, that he gave himself up to the

full enjoyment of the hour, heedless of the flight of
time. He sunk into profound reverie; the new house
passed away from before his eyes; again the old castle,
such as he had seen it in his dreams, stood before him.
The old garden was again joyous with the laughter of
knights, bright dames, and fair maidens, who had been
dust for centuries. So perfect was the illusion that
his cousin, Isabell, and Mary Morley, as they tripped
down the central alley, seemed but part of the vision-
ary throng, and it was with a start, if not a blush,
that he replied when they accosted him. The dreamer
may be forgiven who for a moment thought those two
lovely forms but children of air; so fitly did they correspond with the scene around, that a more experienced observer of life than William, might have
doubted if the vision were real. Isabell was slightly
the taller of the two, and of a figure whose grace and
suppleness was shown to full advantage by her simple
morning costume, untrammelled as it was by the
hideous ornaments with which our ancestresses but
too often endeavoured to add a charm to beauty,
or to take off the full bitterness of ugliness. Her
light-brown hair unsullied by powder, fell in long
waves over her shoulders. The county dowagers,
many of whom hated Isabell for her beauty and her
father's politics, and more than all, for the well-known
Skirlaugh freedom of tongue, a blessing or curse which
both father and daughter had inherited, could only
object to her, that beautiful as she must be admitted
to be now, her form was too rounded, and that some

day or other she would be like her mother, a catastrophe which, had it been prophesied in her hearing,
would not have alarmed the young lady. Mary Morley
was of far slenderer figure, smaller, and therefore
perhaps even more graceful in her movements; her
animated eyes rendered her countenance, shaded as
it was by a profusion of very dark hair, more expres-
sive at ordinary times than that of her friend, but the
features, though lovely, were less regular; and if at
times they showed the play of thought and life more
readily on the surface, indicated much less width of
mind than those of her blue-eyed and more placid
companion.

Unconnected by ties of blood, the girls had lived
together since childhood. Though without a particle
of arrogance or self-assertion in her nature, Miss
Skirlaugh's more continuous strength of will and
higher powers of reasoning had produced their natural, though unobserved effect. No one knew, least
of all, perhaps, the girls themselves, how entirely
Mary was dependent on Isabell for the guidance of
her thoughts and feelings on all those sides of her
character where circumstance had not given her intense convictions.

"If it were night, not breakfast time, I should
have thought you were some astrologer watching the
heavenly bodies, you were so wrapped in thought when
we approached," said Isabell, laughing.

"My thoughts were of the earth, not of the skies.
I was so charmed with the beauty of the scene before

me, that I think I had forgotten everything else,"
replied the visitor.

"Do you call this beautiful? What, the barren
sandhills or the long moor, where my father's people
dig their firing; or is it this prim garden that you
mean? Why, you must have seen far better lions and
elephants at Exeter Change than these green ones we
have to show. But pray don't tell John Dent, our
poor old gardener, so, or you'll break his heart. He
thinks his holly monstrosities as far above their living
originals as my father does one of the Chevalier's
knights of the garter above those of the Elector's
making, who wear the dark-blue ribbon and sit in the
stalls at Windsor. I am surprised that you who have
seen all the glories of our polished capital, should find
anything to admire in this grim old place. The
gardens the King—Elector that is—what would my
father say if he were here?—has at Hampton Court,
are finer, in our own prim style, than these," answered
the lady.

"You do not know the craving we Londoners have
to get out of sight and hearing of our dim city, and all
that belongs to it. Hampton Court is haunted by the
buzz of the town, and by the hundreds of underbred,
fussy people, who go there for their holiday. But
above all, it is not consecrated to me by memories
such as you have here. When I look around me now,
I think of those who lived on this spot before Hampton Court was built," answered William.

" Oh, if your talk is of dead people, I must hand

you over to Mr. Callis, our chaplain. He did not speak a word last night, for he had but just received, when you came, from a friend of his whom he has never seen, but with whom he has exchanged Latin letters for some twenty years — he is a professor at Copenhagen, but what his name is, though I can spell it I won't venture to pronounce—a book in the old Frisian dialect, of which he has been dreaming half his life. If you just set him off on pedigrees he'll talk for ever," said Isabell.

"I will certainly, through your kind intervention, have some conversation on a subject which it is now the fashion to treat as trivial, but which has great charms for me," replied William.

"I will promise you that Mr. Callis shall tell you as many anecdotes of our people as would set up the printer of the 'Gentleman's Magazine' for life ; but then there is one difficulty, when the good gentleman once gets you into his study, and has fairly begun somewhere in Normandy, about a hundred and fifty years before the battle of Hastings, you are a prisoner till he has got through his whole stock, and has told you how my father escaped—through no merit of his own—being hanged in the '45, and how I, his unworthy daughter, was saved, but last year, from being gored by a bull, through the intervention of our groom, Mr. Robert Drury, alias ' Squire's Bob,' " replied Miss Skirlaugh.

"The picture you draw is not so fearful but that I am willing to run greater risks for so much instruction," replied the visitor, not a little charmed with the young lady's conversation, so different from that of the primly-set dames whom he had occasionally met in London.

"Well, I have put you on your guard, and will now proceed to discharge the mission with which I have been intrusted; but ere I do so, as I fear I have led you into a scrape, I will point out a way, if the worst comes to the worst—say if the room should take fire—how you may find a means of escape. Did you ever hear a clock strike itself down?" said the young lady.

"No; and have no idea what it is," replied William.

"Nor do I know the cause. But this I do know, from sad experience, that a few weeks ago my good mamma, who can seldom trust me or any of her other domestics to do what she thinks wants care, was winding up the great clock in the hall. You may have noticed it, or rather *her*—being a useful household drudge, our people naturally make her feminine,—she lives in an inlaid ebony case, with a stuffed heron on the top. My mother had got *her* wound up to the very last curl, when suddenly there came a click, then a buzz, and the clock began very deliberately to strike one—two—three. We hoped when twelve o'clock came that there would be peace; but no, on *she* went, loudly, slowly, but unceasingly. My father, who was in the little room he calls his office, where he keeps guns, fishing-tackle, and such things, was on this lamentable occasion really very busy in making up his half-year's accounts, and was consequently in a bad temper. When he heard the din he rushed into the hall. A hasty question satisfied him of the nature of the catastrophe that had taken place, and without waiting for his hat or walking-stick, he dived into the innermost recesses of the wood, and did not appear till dinner-time. My good mother is prompt in action. Squire's Bob was at once dispatched on the fleetest horse we have to Wivilby, for John Chubb, the clock doctor. When that functionary arrived, he took off the weight, and all was silence. My mamma, whom we are all taught to believe, is as learned in domestic matters as Mr. Callis is in useless knowledge, was abashed, and for three days did not censure either Mary or myself for not knowing what we hadn't been taught. Should you not like to have been present?"

" Very much. But how would that experience help me, if I wished to escape from Mr. Callis?"

" The case is very simple. Mr. Callis is the clock running down, you are tired and want to escape. You have got, we will say, into the middle of the Wars of the Roses, and you hear the dinner-bell ring, or you know that our weekly post has come, and you expect a letter. Or lastly, which is also barely possible, you think the society of Mary Morley and Isabell Skirlaugh who now are, preferable to that of their namesakes who flirted with Edward the Fourth. What you must do then is simply to take the weight off. This can be done the first time the good old soul pauses. Ask

him then a question, and in that question contrive to
introduce the name of the present Elector of Hanover,
or his father, taking care to call them by their English
titles.　He will be so shocked at observing such a
defection in you, that you will get no more genealogy
till I coax him into a good temper, which I will do
whenever you wish for another infliction.　But I am
forgetting the high and important errand on which I
have come.　I appear as a humble suppliant, craving
mercy," said the bright girl, putting on a comical air
of dejection.

" Your words are riddles," responded William.

" To come down, then, to the level of common
sense," replied the lady, laughing, " the groom, Robert
Drury, the hero of my deliverance from the bull—
a legend I shall leave you to learn from the historio-
grapher of our house—tells me that he met you yesterday at the inn at Merespital ; that he didn't know
who you were, and was very rude in consequence.　He
had been from home some days on an errand, and had
therefore no idea you were coming here."

William assured his cousin that latter events had
quite effaced the groom's insolence from his memory.

" I am sure he was very insulting, and that he
richly deserves the severe reprimand which I have
given him.　If my father knew of his misconduct, he
would be very seriously offended with the faithful
fellow."

" I must add my name, too, to the petition for pardon, Isabell," said Mary Morley.　" I believe the

man would die for any of us; but I hope you have scolded him very much. His manners to many people are unbearably insolent. It is evident that he considers himself on a perfect equality with almost everybody he meets, except the few persons who have the happiness to bear the name of Skirlaugh, or those whom they honour with their especial protection. He is always very civil to me; but when he goes to Scalhoe, his conversation is of the most easy and familiar kind."

"I'm sure I wish mine was. When I am there I never know what to say when the few commonplace remarks about fox-hunting, which I always keep at hand, are done. I really cannot, even to win the hearts of your relatives, show any enthusiastic admiration for the gentle arts of dog-fighting, badger-baiting, or pugilism."

The conversation was here interrupted by the thin, harsh clank of a cracked bell.

"It is the call for morning prayer," said Isabell; "come with me, and I will show you our chapel. We are cut off, at present, from worship in our parish church; but my father is determined we shall not grow up heathens, so he not only keeps us a chaplain, but provides us with daily prayer. If you want to win his affections you will not fail to be a regular attendant."

They threaded their way through the cross alleys of the garden, and soon found themselves at the chapel-door. It was a circular building; the remains of one of the angle towers of the castle, whose upper part had been battered down, and the lower, consisting of the first and second stories only, accommodated with a high-pitched, overhanging roof of blue slate. The whole fabric looked much like a small bit of candle which has been put out by a large extinguisher. As they entered the doorway, William became aware, for the first time, that Mary Morley had not accompanied them.

A modern high-churchman would be not a little startled could he see the chapel in which his representatives worshipped. The nonjurors were fervent and orthodox in faith, but had little idea of the outward and mechanical adjuncts which to some people now-a-days, make up so large a part of religion. The room, as we have said, was circular; a small segment, just big enough to contain the oblong table which served as an altar, and the desk in which Mr. Callis performed the service, was taken off from the side opposite the door by a thick red cord. The congregation, except the squire and the ladies, sat on wooden benches; for them was reserved the dignity of arm-chairs, planted immediately in front of the rope. The place was as clean as repeated coats of whitewash could make it, but there was not a single ornament to show that it was devoted to sacred uses.

CHAPTER VIII.

" Such powers in medicine she display'd,
The apothecaries rued their sinking trade.
And as their shoulders they began to shrug,
Sung the soft requiem o'er each gentle drug."
Polwhele, *Old English Gentleman,* i. 29.

THE service was very short. It consisted of certain
prayers selected from the morning office of the
English rite, with a few additions from the more
ancient service-books. No terrors of the Act of Uniformity hindered Mr. Callis from making the devotions which he conducted, truly embody his own and
his hearers' faith. The prayer for the king was not
the half-hearted form which the latter nonjurors, as
our fathers knew them in Scotland seventy years ago,
were wont to use, wherein no names were mentioned,
but direct petitions for his Majesty King James the
Third, Charles Edward, Prince of Wales, and all the
royal family.

Mrs. Skirlaugh's seat was vacant on the present
occasion, and when the family gathered around the
breakfast-table, the mistress of the mansion did not
make her appearance. A hasty and somewhat queru-

lous inquiry from the squire, drew forth the information that Dr. Chubb, the Æsculapius of Wivilby, had that morning, sent an express over to the Manor for certain medical herbs which Madam Skirlaugh was known to possess, both growing in the garden, and dried for use in the still-room, but which he had found absent from his own stores the very moment he needed their use.

Ralf Skirlaugh was an eminently good-natured man, but he had for the greater part of his life been in the constant habit of enjoying his own way in trifles, and therefore very slight things were wont to ruffle his really very easy temper; such was the strange contradiction of his nature, that the tender love he bore his wife showed itself quite as often in irritation of voice and manner, when that lady was hindered by household cares, or her own somewhat feeble health, from ministering to his amusement, as it did in the really great sacrifices he was prepared at any moment to make for her comfort. The fault, it must be owned, was not all on the Squire's side. His lady had been accustomed ere her marriage to a home where the maxims of Scotch frugality had been intensified by a mother of foreign birth, who while she widened in some respects the narrow parsimony of the Borders, had added by precept and example many an additional link to the heavy chain of household care. But it was not the parsimony of his wife that troubled our Squire; Madam Skirlaugh was not careful in any mean or niggard sense, but it was the daily, unremitting de-

votion to what she regarded as her housewifely duties
that sat heavy on his soul. The good man had no
ideas beyond his age. Had he lived fifty years later,
he would probably have felt ashamed that the wife
of one of the chief landowners of the northern part of
his county should know what was going on in the
kitchen, or be learned and efficient in the arts of the
seamstress, or the science of household surgery. Such
silly modern prejudices did not trouble him a whit,
but he was much dependent on his wife for companionship, and he felt, not unnaturally, that if the heart of
his spouse were less set upon domestic economies he
should have more of her society, and that her conversation, when she did condescend to talk to him, would
be·more lively and less in the habit of being deflected
in the direction of the pantry.

The Squire's bad temper on the present occasion
was not soothed by a servant presenting him with a
letter addressed:—

"To my honr^d ffriend,
"Ralf Skirlaugh of Skirlaugh Manor,
"Esquire."

The missive bore a magnificently large seal of
red wax, on which a baron's coronet was conspi-
cuous. The gentleman to whom it was addressed
remorselessly shattered this splendid imagery. The
perusal of the letter produced an effect far from
soothing. He glanced it over hastily, folded it up,
and put it into his pocket, took it out again, re-read

it, examined the broken seal, and then burst into a discourse, whether of the nature of a soliloquy or of an address to his daughter it would be hard to say.

" This fellow," no name had been mentioned by him, " is only equalled in effrontery and cunning by the denseness of his stupidity. Here is a man, sprung on all sides except his mother's from the scum of the people, parading on his shield as many quarterings as though his paternal forefathers had served under the Plantagenets, and putting the three stars of Hansard, the only respectable thing of the sort he has got to brag of, in a corner, where one wants a pair of spectacles to see it among the other lying frippery."

Miss Skirlaugh, perhaps to divert her father's thoughts from his spouse's delinquency, perhaps because she was really curious about such nonsense, asked to be permitted to examine the impression.

" I think, as a work of art," said she, returning it to her father, " that the coronet is far too big, it makes the whole heavy and ugly, far different from the effect produced from the French and Italian seals I have happened to see, where the coronet, however high the wearer's rank, is always of small size."

" That would not satisfy the pride of its owner, Bella. He wants you to know he is a real lord, and perhaps thinks that will give some dignity to the fantastic zoology below."

" I thought, too," said the girl, " that a gentleman should have his own coat only, or at least his own and the last grand quartering without addition on his private seal."

"Of course he should," answered the Squire, prepared, as his daughter intended, to run off on a favourite hobby. "Of course it is vulgar assumption, like a man sticking esquire or justice of the peace after his own name, for a fellow to put a picture of his whole pedigree on every letter he writes."

At this moment Mrs. Skirlaugh entered the room; she probably knew from experience that her husband would be prepared with a string of questions as to her absence, which it would be irritating if not difficult to answer, and therefore, with womanly tact, thought it well to give an account of the reasons that detained her.

"I am neither an apothecary, a herbalist, or a market gardener, Mrs. Skirlaugh, and I think it very hard that that impudent fellow, Chubb, should keep my wife from her prayers, spoil my breakfast, and throw me wrong for the whole day, just because he wants some pestilent weed which he might have picked out of the nearest ditch if he had not been too idle to look for it."

"Indeed, my dear, he could do no such thing," replied the lady, somewhat tartly, for she felt the value of her own collection of simples was being attacked; "there is not a single plant of this sort for miles around but the one in our garden."

"I will tell John Dent to root it up as soon as I go out, if you will only be good enough to inform me where it grows. Better far have one curious weed the less, than be deprived of one's wife's society," said the Squire, angrily, but with a smile as if conscious of his own folly just playing about the corner of his lips.

"I shall not tell you anything about it, and you would not do such an absurd thing if I did. It is of sovereign use in sprains and bruises," answered Mrs. Skirlaugh, evidently quoting some herbal which she had been that morning consulting.

"And so I suppose," said the irritating man, now himself in a good temper, but endeavouring strenuously to conceal the fact. "And so I suppose because some Wivilby farmer's kitchen-girl has left the cow unhoppled, 'and had her milk-kit kicked over for her idleness, and has therefore pretended to sprain her ankle, to escape a well-merited drubbing from the farmer's wife, I am to be disturbed at my devotions, kept waiting for my breakfast, and deprived of your advice when I need it most urgently."

"The doctor," replied Madam Skirlaugh, "gives a different account of the accident to yours. He says that one of the poor women at Merespital alms-house was very much hurt by those people who attacked our guest yesterday."

"Indeed, indeed; then why, woman, didn't you tell me this at once. This puts a very different face on the affair, and I should have been seriously displeased had you not done all you could for the poor thing. These brutes must be corrected. I will see some of our magistrates about it."

" Can you tell me which of the poor old creatures it is ? " inquired Mary. "I know them all."

Mrs. Skirlaugh intimated that the doctor's billet had mentioned no names. He merely said, a woman at the alms-house, probably, not supposing that any member of the family at the Manor would take any personal interest in the sufferer. If so, as doctors are wont to be at times, he was mistaken.

The Squire's mind was running on other matters.

"We are all going out for a ride that way this morning, and will make inquiries. We shall perhaps see the Doctor. But now let us put away from us pestles, mortars, simples, and broken bones. Read this," and he passed or rather flung the big-sealed letter to his wife. " Read it aloud, we may want some legal advice ere we·send an answer."

The missive was as follows :—

" DEAR SIR,—The uninterrupted friendship of more years than I like to count, makes me bold to ask a favour of you which I could never have thought I should be under the necessity to ask of any one. I have suddenly had a call for the sum of 200 libs. ; the money is wanted urgently, so that I cannot find time to send to Lombard Street for it, and besides the roads are now so dangerous that it is not over safe for the servants of a nobleman, especially one of His Majesty's ministers, to travel with much money in his pocket. I therefore make bold to ask you to lend me the above-named sum, and as I know you can oblige me, I feel sure the will will not be wanting, and have therefore enclosed with this a note of hand on stampt paper. The accompt shall be settled when the next interest falls due, either by my paying off the sum with lawful interest thereon, or by adding it to your capital, secured on the Mereflat farm, whichever you may most desire.

"I am sure you will pardon this trespass from an old friend, whom you have before encouraged by so many acts of unmerited regard. The gout makes me a stay-at-home while in this damp country, which must excuse me for not having paid my respects to Mrs. Skirlaugh and Miss Isabell, both of whom, I hope, are in good health.

"Believe me to remain,

"my dear Sir,

"your much obliged friend

"and servant to command,

"BURWORTH.

"Brackenthwaite Hall,
Septemb. 4th, 175—.

"There is no news from over sea except what you see in the public prints."

"What is to be done?" said the Squire, when his wife had finished reading the epistle.

The lady mused a moment, probably balancing various contingencies in her mind. She answered by another question: "Who has he sent for the money?"

"His agent. The man he employs to take care of that young mohawk, Lord Carlton."

"Brotherton, the Scotchman. Then the money will be all safe. He is a careful fellow, I hear, and is making great retrenchments at Brackenthwaite. He won't let anybody cheat his master but himself. Therefore, whether he is an honest man or a scamp, we may be sure he is to be trusted with two hundred pounds. You had better oblige his lordship," said the lady.

"Well, so I think; but I don't like it. I'm not a goldsmith or a banker. If I had a good excuse, I would make one."

The Squire did not like turning his attention to business of this sort, and threw the above out as a feeler, in the faint hope that his wife might furnish him with one. He was destined to be disappointed.

The money was counted out, and a short letter concocted for the peer, which was sealed with the smallest and least heraldic seal which could be found, after a considerable search. They were handed over to Mr. Brotherton, who, during the interval, had remained in an apartment far away from the master and his guests. That functionary had seen a good deal of life of various sorts in his time, and was far too much of a philosopher to be in any way offended with the cold and formal manner which the Squire thought fit to put on, and which sat on him so very badly, as he counted the money out for him.

Philosophers have often a taste for natural scenery, and still more frequently for studying those portions

of the globe where the hand of man has improved on
nature. There were several ways out of Skirlaugh
Park; the nearest for him lay in a southerly direction,
but he took, from preference, that which led to the
east, and gave him a view of a great portion of the
garden. As he passed through the gate into the lane,
he came upon "Squire's Bob," who was riding in the
same direction, exercising one of his master's horses.
The two men recognised each other; neither were
adverse to conversation, and they jogged on for perhaps half a mile in company, each avoiding any allu-
sion to the place or company in which they had last
met.

"From the size of the house and grounds I should
think your master must keep a good many servants,
Mr. Robert," said the Scot, carelessly.

"Yes, a goodish few," replied the groom.

"How many grooms and gamekeepers, now?"

"Bless thy heart, I don't know. We've as many as
we want; sometimes more, sometimes less," answered
Bob, very reluctant to throw any light on his stable
economy.

"And gardeners the same, I suppose?"

"No, we're fixtish there. There's old John Dent,
the head man, Bill Havercroft, Dick Stocks, and
maybe a threepenny lad or two in a busy time."

"Are John Dent and you on good terms?"

"Yes, fairish. He's a cross cantankerous old tyke,
but we get on midlin'. He's lame, and can't get often
to Wivilby, and I go alm'st every day, so I buy his

things for him, and sometimes gives him a bit of
'bacca. He's strange and fond o' chewin'," answered
the groom."

"Ah, well, I had a reason for asking. My eldest
brother—I come of a working family, you see, Mr.
Drury—is head gardener at Dalkeith in Scotland.
He has heard of the superb grounds at Skirlaugh, and
is very anxious for me to write to him some account of
them. Thinks he can get useful hints, you know, for
the improvements he is about to make. Now I don't
like taking the liberty of asking your master such a
favour, but I think you could manage it for me.
Here's a guinea, just see what a portion of it will do
in soothing Mr. Dent's temper, and keep the change
till I ask for it. I may, perhaps, be over at Skirlaugh
in a short time, and shall trust to you to manage this
little matter for me quietly," said the agent.

Squire's Bob had listened in grave attention to this
last speech, and drunk in not only every syllable of
the words, but the whole tone and manner. He had a
profound distrust of his questioner. There were
nevertheless obvious reasons why he should not refuse
the request point blank.

"John Dent's a queer fellow, a very queer fellow;
I a'most doubt if he'll come to. He hates Scotchmen
worse than I do small beer," replied he, pocketing the
guinea.

"He must be strangely prejudiced. Couldn't you
say it was for a friend of mine, the gardener to an
Earl, who lives in Devonshire?"

"Well, yes, I maybe could. I think I can come round the old rogue somehow. I'll do all I can for you. But might I be so bold as just to ax, by way of talk like, if them nice young men as you was with at Merespital is likely to come wi' you next time you're here? 'Cause if they do, they mun tread their shoes very straight, or there'll be a row on with our Squire."

The Scot was evidently startled at the question.

"Nay, I'm not a curious chap; don't say no'ut if you don't like. If you never tell no'ut, you know, you can't hev your tongue bent for backbiting, as my oud grandmother used to say. I'm a strange still chap mysen; that's how I've kep' my place so long," added the groom.

Brotherton had had time to concoct a reply while Mr. Drury was enunciating his grandparent's wise saw. It was to the effect that he didn't know; all depended upon circumstances.

"Well, yes, just so," added the groom; "circumstances is queer things; they are, as I say, just for all the world like stirrup leathers; if a little man wants to ride you mun draw 'em up to th' last hole, so that there is, in a way o' talkin', no circumstances at all; but if a big chap gets on, he can do wi' nearly any length of circumstances. If your chaps is big enough, it'll not be circumstances as 'll hinder 'em."

There was an unsatisfactory tone in this last remark which seemed to imply that the groom was aware of certain intentions on the part of one of his employers which he felt pretty certain had been kept a profound secret.

"Well! whether the other gentlemen come to visit the Manor or not, you may make sure of my giving you a call some day, to have a peep at the gardens," added the wily agent, carelessly.

"Honour bright," said Bob; and leaning over in his saddle till his mouth almost touched the ear of his companion, he said, in a clear whisper, "You'd better leave them other chaps at home, circumstances 'll be ower much for 'em. Our 'Squire rides wi' long stirrup leathers : " and then he added, in a loud voice, "Why, if there isn't some o' them Bozzel chaps a nippin' up our rabbits." He wheeled his horse, leaped the low sod wall that separated the highway from a warren, and cantered off gaily in the direction of the Manor. When he arrived there the party were mounting their horses in the stable court of the mansion. The house itself was, as we have said, a modern and regular building, not so the out-houses. Many of these were formed out of the castellated outworks of the old fortress, while others had been built, here and there, just as fancy dictated, to minister to the out-door wants of the successive owners of the place. Thus, whilst some had the appearance of great age, others showed by their less careful masonry, the lighter tints and greater thickness of their bricks, that their origin was due to a very recent period. Here and there, to fill up a corner, or provide for some hasty necessity, small turf-covered sheds arose, whose walls were formed of bundles of furze cut from the neighbouring moorland. Although this large collection of offices had grown up without any regard to regularity, most of the buildings stood in some sort of proximity to a large irregular court known as the back-yard. This area was paved with round cobbles. It was scrupulously clean, and free from weeds. The whole Skirlaugh family were fond of pet animals. At times this court was, as those who had no sympathy with their taste averred, more like a wild beast show than the entrance to a Christian man's dwelling. In the centre, if centre could be found for such an irregular inclosure, stood a lofty fir-tree divested of its branches, at the top and bottom of which were the town and country resi- dences of Jenny the monkey. Near, but just out of the reach of that mischievous lady's chain, were the rabbit and ferret houses; and in cages, hanging on each side of the doorway, were canaries, parrots, and other birds which had, or were believed to have, the faculty of song, or the power of imitating the tones of the human voice. Two burly ravens stalked gravely about among the plebeian rout of ducks, chickens, and pigeons, who made the place their own. They were the only animals who dared to venture within the magic circle of the monkey's chain, at whose strangely human gestures of anger even the dogs were afraid. The dogs, to do them justice, should have a chapter to themselves; their number and varieties must at pre- sent go unrecorded. It was really one of the chief amusements of the Squire to watch his pet animals;

but he had, like some wiseacres whom we have known in these days, contracted an opinion that it was below his dignity to do so. He, therefore, readily excused himself by laying the blame on his wife, who was quite able and willing to bear it.

The irritation of the morning had blown over; the Squire, and therefore the whole party, were in high good-humour. Mrs. Skirlaugh had determined to remain at home; she occasionally took horse exercise, but it was very rarely that she accompanied her husband in his excursions, for he had a wicked delight in exciting the good lady's nervous fears by conducting her on the most uneven paths, and at a pace far more rapid than was, as she said, suitable for her age and position. By which shallow equivocation she believed she kept from the world the true state of her feelings as completely as the hunted rabbit thinks it has concealed its panting body from pursuing dogs when it has hidden them from its own sight by burying its head in a tuft of grass.

CHAPTER IX.

Lusimus."   " Vacui sub umbrâ
Horatius.

"HERE is a sight for a man to see," exclaimed the Squire, as he pointed with his riding-whip to the monkey, the ravens, the birds in the cages, and half a dozen dogs which were basking in the sun beams. " Since Noah's ark cast anchor, do you think any one man has ever been troubled with such a collection of beasts, wild and tame, as Madam Skirlaugh inflicts on me?" It was his habit, when in good temper, to call his wife by the popular term Madam—the title given her by the peasantry. " She has a perfect craze, mania, infatuation for such like dumb beasts. It began with flowers; then she took to dogs :—

" ' When with Bologna's lap-dog soft supplied,
Her soul unsated for a monkey sigh'd,
And with the prating of a magpie blest,
A paroquet her longing hopes carest.'

I fear the arrival of a lion soon, and have not a doubt in the world that when the restoration takes place,

and King James asks her what favour he can grant
as a reward for her husband's loyalty, she will say,
' May it please your Majesty, I should like a couple of
elephants.' "

"You need not be under any alarm, papa, that the
king should ask such an unfortunate question, the
well-known gratitude of the Stuarts makes it quite
certain that his majesty will have ascertained, without
asking, what reward is most suitable for a family so
distinguished for its devotion," said Miss Skirlaugh.

The Squire was at this moment playing with the
monkey, and may be presumed not to have noticed the
sarcasm. Had any one else ventured on such a disloyal piece of impertinence, it would not, we may be
sure, have passed without a sharp rebuke. -

The departure of the cavalcade seemed a sign for
idleness among servants and workpeople. Trim female
heads—presumably those of housemaids and seamster-
women, with whom the place was abundantly supplied
—peered from many a lattice. The helpers in the
stable, the carpenters in the woodyard, even the weeding boys in the garden, gathered in knots, perched
themselves on the top bars of gates or on the ridges of
walls to watch what to them was no uncommon sight.
The heads disappeared, the gates and coping stones
became suddenly unoccupied, and the saws grated with
renewed vigour on the appearance of Madam Skirlaugh. Her question, " Can ye not find aught else to do
than to spend the morning gazing at dogs and horses,
Jemmy, when the pigeon-house floor hasn't been swept

for a week?" was addressed to one of the young gardeners whom Squire's Bob had called "threepenny lads;" it was felt to have a much wider application.

The retainers may be pardoned for resting from their labours to watch the riding party. It was a pretty sight. First of all went the Squire and his guest; the former mounted on a large black horse, and dressed in a half-military, half-sporting costume, his hat looped up with a white rose, not the manufacture of the artist who had supplied that needful article of dress but culled that morning from the tree. His sword by his side, silver-mounted pistols in the holsters at his saddle bow, a gold dog-whistle hanging from his button-hole, and a heavy long-thonged riding whip in his hand, he seemed the very picture of a modern cavalier, a man fit for any desperate soldierly adventure, if the rude game of war could be played, as his predecessors had so bravely but vainly tried to play it, with the mirth, dash, and wild jollity of a stag hunt, but utterly unfit for those slower, more calculating and deeper laid schemes of butchery which a wider knowledge of the science of warfare had now long rendered needful.

The two ladies followed. Miss Skirlaugh was a splendid horsewoman, her light-coloured, tight-fitting, riding-dress showed to perfection her beautiful figure. Mary Morley's habit of somewhat darker tint was looped up with white rosettes. No political badge was to be distinguished on the dress of Isabell. The girls, while loving as sisters, differed much in thought and feeling. Mary was a Roman Catholic, the daughter of a man who had given up his fortune and the whole energy of his life to the cause of the Royal fugitives, and was an exile himself, under sentence of death for his devotion. She threw herself with all the fervency of a deeply religious but somewhat narrow intellect into the cause for which her father was a distinguished sufferer. To her it was an act of duty to wear on her person the badge of the fallen dynasty, and to say or do nothing even in the lightest conversation that should seem to imply that there was anything on earth dearer to her than the hope of seeing the Roman Catholic line restored. In the eyes of such a person, the imaginative side of the contest had no charms. The half-dreamy, half-pretended chivalry, which made so many people talk treason, when no sacrifices were required to be made, was only one degree less distasteful to her ardent temperament than the actions of those sordid plotters, who by using its forms to cover their own meanly self-interested manœuvres, had done so much towards the ruin of the cause she loved.

Tales of wild adventures are ill calculated to amuse those whose early lives have been scorched by the fires of civil war. When the Squire was detailing with delight some strange accident that had befallen friend or foe in the Forty-Five, expatiating on the revels of Holy Rood, in which he had participated, or the rout at Preston Pans, stories of which he had heard from the mouths of a hundred of the heroes of that fruitless

victory, her mind would revert in sickened horror to
the butcheries of Kennington Common and Carlisle.
At such moments the brave men who had perished
there by a doom we cannot now bring ourselves to
contemplate, to gratify the revengeful lust for blood of
a terrified and heartless clique, would arise before her.
A laughable adventure, or the scrap of some Jacobite
melody, which made Isabell's eyes sparkle with
delight, only brought to her mind the martyr-death of
one she had known well—her father's earliest and
dearest friend—whose hands she could now almost
feel toying with her glossy locks as they did in childhood, when she sat upon his knee to hear him tell of
the holy and beautiful things he had seen in Rome. A
shudder near akin to physical torture would run
through her frame when some light jest called up
before her that pale heroic face, of which all that was
now left was a white skull, that the savagery of those
who ruled still condemned to remain bleaching on
Temple Bar.

Two grooms in the green livery of the family came
next, and in their charge half-a-dozen dogs, conspi-
cuous among whom was Milo, a large blood-hound,
the property of Isabell, but an especial favourite with
her father.

The path they followed was not a highway; nothing
with wheels could have travelled upon it, but for
horsemen it was smooth and level. For a short
distance their course lay under the shade of a dense
coppice of hazel, yew and maple, the low uniformity of

which was broken here and there by large oaks, the
growth of many generations. The riders soon
emerged on the brow of the hill ; with one consent all
reined in their horses, to admire what is in its own
style of beauty one of the loveliest prospects in
England.

" There, Cousin William, you've nothing like this '
to show in London. What have you to see from Rich-
mond Hill compared to what I can show you here.
See, look to the north-west. No, not there, a little
more this way, just beside the smoke ; that little
point you see in the distance is York Minster—forty
miles away—and now, if you like to venture your neck
by climbing into the top of one of these oaks, you'll
see the spires of our own big church at Lincoln, thirty
miles in the other direction. We cannot see them
down here for the trees, but I have done so many a
time when I was a boy, and could tumble about in the
branches as lightly as Jenny does when she breaks
her chain. I once prevailed on Jem Nobbins, an
Oxford scholar, who wrote a stupid book called *A
Tractate of Natural Beauty* to ascend, and I never '
was more frightened in my life. Thought we should
have had a coroner's inquest. When he got about
fifteen feet from the ground he fell down, just for all
the world like a pig of lead. *Un gross saulmon de
plomb*, as my good friend, Master François Rabelais,
would say. I am not a scholar, Cousin William,
as you must have found out, but there are three
books which I do read, my bible and prayer-book for

my devotion as a good Protestant ought, and the
Vanities of the French Doctor for my amusement. I
speak French abominably, for I am out of practice,
but I can read the old jester till my eyes water.
Addison, Dick Steele, or the dirty Dean of Dublin
were nothing to him. If you don't know French you
should learn, if for no other reason than that you may
be able to laugh with me at my old companion's
iokes. I have carried him in my pocket about with
me for thirty years, and he should be buried with me
if I did not think that Madam Skirlaugh would object
to his company in the family vault. She's a serious
person, and has no more idea of a joke than poor
Nobbins had. Well, as I was saying, Nobbins
plumped down from the second arm of this tree just
where we are, and I thought he would never have
spoken word more. We got him laid lengthwise on a
gate for all the world like a corpse, and carried him
home. My wife gave him strong waters, and administered all manner of bodily consolations in the way
of liniments, embrocations and plasters. When at
last he came round, I made Mr. Callis write a Latin
inscription, setting forth, with many a flowery twist,
that here Nobbins fell. It was to have been engraved
on a stone, and set up on the very spot as an eternal
memorial, but before the stone-cutter could get it
finished, Nobbins ratted—ratted, went over to the
damned Whig crew, took their dirty oaths, and accepted as a reward for his apostacy a fellowship at
Scrope College, Oxford. The inscription would have

been a merry jest, but I never talk about it now, for I
have a rule, which I would have you to know, William,
that I never joke any more with a person who has
seriously offended me. But I've kept the stone, and
have vowed that my very first act, as soon as the restoration comes about, shall be to have it fixed over the
gate of his own college. I will go all the way to Oxford
myself to see the thing accomplished, and will take
Barsabas Brown, my own mason, with me, to do the job.
You see those white houses over the Trent, just where
the sun is shining on the curl of the river, that's Culverness, in the Isle of Axholme, and many a stout tussle
have the Isle men had there with the French and
Dutch interlopers, who came against their will to
drain their commons and spoil the wild duck shooting.
The Skirlaughs always took the side of the natives
against the foreign invaders. The matter is nearly
settled now. Just a riot now and then, a bank cut,
and a few hundred acres of plough-land drowned,
here and there, perhaps, an annoying person of the
new order ducked in one of his own dykes; but
nothing serious, as it was in the old time, and I'm
very glad of it, for, you see, Madam Skirlaugh,
through her mother, who was heiress of one of these
settlers, is owner of some of the reclaimed—that is
stolen—lands, and I should be much troubled in my
mind whether to go according to family custom or the
way my own interest lies. I suppose I should take
the former, and have a quarrel with my wife, who has
a great affection for the Culverness cornlands. The

hollow, almost at our feet, where you see the smoke
is our brick pit.   I burn bricks there every summer."

And here the garrulous gentleman ran off into a
long account of his bricks and brickmaking, which,
diverging into numberless anecdotes of persons and
things in the neighbourhood, occupied William Skirlaugh's attention until they had proceeded some two
or three miles on their journey.   The fantastic talk of
his host was certainly amusing in itself, and to one
who was fond of studying the effects of local circumstances on human character, had the charm of throwing considerable light upon the habits and thoughts
of a kind-hearted, but somewhat selfish and eccentric
person, whom a life of affluence, cut off from equals,
and almost worshipped by his own people, had
rendered, in most of his ideas, and some of his
actions, as despotic as the kings of that weak race for
whose children he was prepared to lay down his life,
if that sacrifice should be called for in carrying out
his own wild plans of insurrection.   Entertaining as
the gossip was, while it had the charm of freshness,
William would have much preferred that the ladies
should have mingled in the conversation.   Such
was not the Squire's will; he preferred a mono-
logue, and they were far too well trained to thwart his
wishes.   There are, however, breaks of continuity in
all things.   Even Ralf Skirlaugh himself sometimes
interrupted the flow of anecdote and political vitupera-
tion for the sake of a few minutes' chat with a gamekeeper or tenant; on these occasions William found a

delightful relief in the sparkling conversation of Isabell.

The party had just crossed over a ford, where a tiny stream of water found its way to the Trent, between huge banks of sand, when a turn brought them close to the abode of a person we have met before. The nose, no less than the eyes of the visitors, were informed of the nature of Mr. Stutting's business. That person's gaunt form was to be seen to great advantage as he followed his daily work.

If the reader has ever happened in childhood to become acquainted with one of the many early editions of Paradise Lost—the ninth for instance—where a very dull artist, whose name has happily perished, has tried his best to set before him a most unpoetical ideal of the ruler of the underworld, he will, unless a very unimaginative person himself, call it distinctly to his recollection. Some such a figure as Stutting must have been before the engraver's eyes when he made his sketch of Lucifer, so like was the tanner in his outward form to that fellow's miserable work.

The ladies were requested to stay outside the gate of the home garth; the Squire and his companion carefully threaded their way among the tan-pits with which it was almost entirely occupied. By the side of one of these stood the tanner, his head covered by a tightly-fitting skull-cap, the upper part of his body clad in a coat, from which the tails had been severed, reducing it by that process to the configuration of a school-boy's round jacket. His legs were bare to considerably above the knees, and had assumed by frequent exposure to the elements a brown tint not much different in colour from that of the water in which he soaked his hides. When the visitors approached he was occupied in drawing, with the aid of a long three-pronged fork, a number of half-tanned skins from the depths of one of the pits. The stench that his territories gave off at ordinary times was far from pleasant. When however the deposits were disturbed, it was increased almost beyond the endurance of any one who had not become accustomed to it by long habit. Stutting, though evidently aware of their approach, made no pause in his labour.

"Why, John, your place gets to stink worse and worse, every time I come near you. You'll be having the plague here some day, man," exclaimed the Squire as he rode up.

"The plague's sent where it's wanted. It's not cow-hides, but God Almighty, that chastises men for their sins," replied the tanner, leaning on his trident.

"Well, well, I won't argue with you—you're too much for me when you begin with divinity. I must send Mr. Callis to you when I want to convert you. If your arguments failed to make him sound a retreat, you could soon raise such a stink as would drive him from the field. By the bye, they tell me the pond at Merespital stinks almost as bad as your tan-yard, if a body be thrown into it."

A grim twinkle of the eyes showed itself for a moment like a glimmer of summer lightning on the hard features. "I want nobody to convert me. I would gladly, how gladly God knows, convert you, Ralf Skirlaugh, and them that dwell in your house from the dark night of —"

" Yes, yes, exactly, I am sure you would," broke in the Squire, who though sufficiently unmerciful in his own prosiness, shrunk from the long Calvinistic harangues of Stutting with a dread of one who had frequently been under torture. "We came to thank you warmly for the brave help you gave yesterday when my cousin was attacked by those young curs who are kenneled at Lord Burworth's."

" Then you've lost your labour, for as I told the young man, I want no thanks for what I do. It was not to serve him but my Master that I drubbed the cowards. Do you think it would be fitting for John Stutting, when light has been vouchsafed unto him, to let those children of darkness smite travellers on the highway. God giveth not his grace in full measure to those who are loth to use it. No, no, I will not tell you as your flatterers would, that it was because his name was Skirlaugh that I helped him. I will tell you that I would have done the same for any packman or beggar that trudges on the highway."

" That's no reason, my good man, why we shouldn't be grateful. Help is help, and it's all the better when it comes from a sense of duty. You're not a flatterer, but an honest man, though hard of tongue."

" Don't talk of duty, what duty do I owe anywhere ? Talk of grace, or, carnally minded as you are, talk of

natural love and kindness such as heathen negroes,
Greeks, and Romans have shown to one another. No,
I am no flatterer, but you would like me better if I
were, if I did as other men do. If I touched my hat
when I meet you or your wife, called you squire, and
her madam. Because I tell you the truth, you say—
Ah, poor Stutting, he's a good fellow enough but
crazy, and call me a Fifth Monarchist, a Quaker, and
Independent fanatic, or by some one of the other foul,
new made names by which the men of this world have
taken of late to miscall Christians. Do you think that
the lip, the hat, and the knee service, that the poor
creatures here about give you, is worthy of a man's
caring for, who knows there's an everlasting burning
hell just under the green grass beneath his feet. No,
no, Ralf Skirlaugh, if you knew the things that I
could tell you, yea even what the letter of Scripture
says, you would be as heedless whether men called you
squire or not, as I am whether the bairns that play at
taw in Wivilby town street say when I pass—' There
goes John Stutting, or, there goes our tanner.' "

The Squire, although sufficiently gratified by the
social deference which his neighbours showed was by
no means inclined to be irritated by Stutting's freedom.
He would have shrunk from democracy with the loath-
ing of a cotton lord had it come before him in any
dangerous shape, but in the grotesque form that it
assumed in the person of the tanner, it was amusing
without being in the least degree dangerous. The
extreme opinions which Stutting held on the one side

tallied almost exactly with the extreme on the opposite. The doctrine of the divine right of kings was not more strongly opposed to existing institutions than was the Antinomianism of the peasant. Both were anxious to upset the present government; both believed such a work not only possible but inevitable; and both looked forward to building up on its ruins an edifice which should completely embody their own ideas.

" If you'd not come here this morning I should have walked over to see you after work. I must have some correction done about those young Morleys," said the tanner; "and as you know more of the laws of man than I do, whose heart has been mainly set on the knowledge of the law of God, I want you to give me some advice."

" Why, what's the matter now?" inquired the Squire in no very easy tone, for these said young Morleys were in a certain sense persons for whom he was responsible, and he knew them to be by no means amiable neighbours.

" There are two or three things the matter," said the tanner. " The old man never looks after nowt, he's getting past it, and mostly spends his time by the fire side, drinking. He leaves every mortal thing to his sons, mostly to Jim, the eldest. Now their land joins mine, there's only the beck divides 'em, but his is in Scalhoe parish and mine is in Wivilby. Just at the end of this garth, very nigh opposite the house, there was a little point of my land run out into the beck. The commissioners of sewers, when they made the beck wider, axed me if they might cut through this bit to make the watercourse straight, and I let 'em, you see; so it's now a little island not worth sixpence, for it's all sand and stones. But I've put a foot-bridge over to please my daughter Bessie, and she has set it with flower roots. Well, Jim Morley says as it lays past the mid stream, it's their land; and every now and then the fellow comes when I'm away, and treads down all the things."

"Jim Morley's a fool, John, as I will show him when next I fall in with him. When I've talked to him about it, I don't think he'll trouble you again. If he does, you've a clear case in law."

"He doesn't care two pence about the bit of a rouk o' cobble stones and sand. It's all done to aggravate Bessie, because he thinks if he plagues the lass, that vexes me. They're a bad lot, young and old, little and big, the whole name of 'em; they hate me because they're Papists," rejoined the tanner, with the conscious superiority which his unimpeachable Protestantism gave him.

"He's a silly fellow, I know, but it isn't Popery that makes a fool of him. Many Papists are sensible, kind-hearted people. He can't get on with you because you won't let him kill things on your land. It's a pity—a great pity—to see a man who should be a gentleman spending his time in doing badly the work of a game keeper."

"I won't have him or any one else killing God's harmless creatures for sport, where I can hinder 'em," exclaimed Stutting fiercely, giving emphasis to his words by digging the prongs of his trident violently into the earth at his feet.

"I don't agree with you, John, as you know, as to the sinfulness of sporting, but I do wish very much these young fellows could be taught to respect the rights of their neighbours. You are not the only sufferer. I have told them frequently that they would displease me very much if they killed or chased the wild deer, and yet when my back is turned, even in breeding time, they are continually after them," said the Squire.

"Their dogs are such heavy lumbering brutes, that they don't catch many; but they're never-easy when they're not after them, unless they're serving the devil at a horse-race, a bull-baiting, or a cock match. My daughter feeds the poor things, and they would be as tame as her hens, if it wasn't for Jim and his brothers, and the pack of Wivilby lads he has with him. It's only last Sabbath was a fortnight, when the faithful remnant who worship in my house were at prayer, that the whole gang ran hallooing close past, like so many devils chasing a damned soul, and all because they had a hare in chase. It would do a power of good if I was to drop one or two of 'em into one of these pits, and let 'em soak for say twenty minutes. I don't see why it shouldn't be as good sport for me as hunting is for them."

We presume the last remark was meant in grave irony,—the only sort of jest in which the Independent ever indulged. Mr. Skirlaugh was not sure that it was not in earnest, and took no little trouble to explain the evil results which would follow from such a course.

As they rode away by a route different to that by which they had entered the garth, they passed the island garden, where Jim Morley's taste for wanton mischief had been displayed so cruelly. It was covered with a profusion of Michaelmas daisies, sunflowers, marigolds, red and white double daisies, honesty, lad-love-lass, and those other common flowers which are the favourites of the English cottager. Signs of the depredator's hand were visible, though the damage that had been done was repaired or concealed as much as possible. Elizabeth Stutting, the girl to whom the little patch owed its cultivation, was standing in its midst; she had been interrupted in her work by the ladies of the party, who were receiving from her lips a vivid account of the ill deeds of Master Jim. She was a strong, fair-haired country lassie, the picture of good health, with face, hands, and arms embronzed by exposure to the sunshine.

The Squire greeted her kindly, listened with attention to her lamentations, promised to lecture her tormentor, and to send her some barley for the deer she was endeavouring to tame, and rode away gaily at the head of his cavalcade, leaving one human soul much the brighter for the few kind words he had spoken.

There are hundreds of men and women in this world who are prepared to make great sacrifices of time, money, or comfort for their fellow-creatures, but

how very few there are who will divert themselves
from their own thoughts for a minute or two to talk
kindly to another person, who may be suffering keenly
from one of the minor sorrows of life. The Squire was
quite unconscious that he made any sacrifice, or that
he was doing an act which would add to his popularity
by his few seconds' chat with the tanner's daughter;
yet it was such acts as these, far more than the hospitality of the Skirlaugh kitchen, or the cheap rent at
which he let his farms, which made him the popular
hero for ten miles around.

CHAPTER X.

" Beyond participation lie
  My troubles, and beyond relief :
  If any chance to heave a sigh,
  They pity me, and not my grief."
                                Wordsworth.

WIVILBY, though a market-town, is not much larger than many a neighbouring village. Its claim to importance rested, firstly, in the fact that it had the honour of possessing one of the prisons of the shire; and secondly, that it was in former days the centre of an extensive feudal jurisdiction. At the time of which we are writing the fictitious importance with which the manor courts of its lords had invested it, had become a mere shadow. The terrible penalties that the steward of the franchise could once inflict almost at his pleasure, had been reduced, first by custom, then by statute, until the great man, who had been accustomed, when he held the court leet, to be attended by a lordly retinue of trumpeters, javelin men, and standard bearers, had sunk down into the portly person of Mr. Howell, the Wivilby lawyer, whose duties consisted mainly in accepting the surrender of

copyholds, enrolling title deeds, and inflicting infini-
tesimally small fines on persons whose cattle strayed
into other people's corn.

The rights of pit and gallows, *furca et fossa*, as it is
called in the law jargon once so frightfully real, were
only kept in memory by the Gallow Hill on the north
side of the town, where the Wivilby crones still saw
unearthly sights, and heard noises such as belonged
not to this world, when they passed at nightfall.

In the market-place, which stood on the brow of the
hill, and whose regular outlines suggested that it had
grown up around the entrenchments of a Roman camp,
was the dwelling of Dr. Chubb, or rather of two persons who went by that name ; for Dr. Chubb, who had
taken his degree in medicine at the University of
Leiden, occupied a house jointly with his brother,
also called Dr. Chubb, but whose art consisted not
in mending or marring the physical economy of his
fellow-creatures, but in superintending the health of
their clocks and watches. Neither of the brothers
had ever married, and they lived amicably enough
together, occupying the same room, which answered as
a surgery for the one, and a workshop for the other.
Each confined himself strictly to his own line of business. It would not be easy to say whether the good
folk of Wivilby had more confidence in the doctor,
on whom they were dependent for their somewhat
vague notions of time, or on his brother, by whose
skill they were aided in their passages into and out of
this world of shadows, which to most of them, as to

their successors at the present, was the only reality for which they cared.

The party paused at the door where the doctors carried on their respective employments. The clock-maker alone was at home; a little man clad in a dressing-gown, perhaps a quarter of a century old, whose chief ornament was a running pattern composed of peonies and sun-flowers. Thinly scattered grey hair clothed his head; his nose was bestridden with a pair of horn spectacles, the elasticity of whose spring kept them firmly on the bridge of that organ, without the aid of the lateral supports now in use.

The loud call of the Squire at once brought the Doctor to the door. With a very low bow he explained that his brother was from home.

"I want some information," said Mr. Skirlaugh, "about the woman who was hurt at Merespital yester-day. Which of the poor creatures is it that has been wounded, and what is her name?"

"Of the patient's state of health, honoured sir, I can give no information; but her name I can tell, if I may but be permitted to return into the surgery for a short space," said the little man, disappearing to consult his brother's day-book. He returned in an instant with the information that the woman's name was Anne Mason.

"Which of them is it, Mary?" said the Squire, turning to Miss Morley.

"The poor woman whose face has been burnt? I know her well; she is a good creature, who has seen much sorrow. I hope she does not suffer a great deal."

"It's only a short ride to the place. You would like to see her, I know. I want the Doctor. I must have full particulars, for I keep an account against these fellows which will call for quick settlement some day," said the Squire to his companions. Then turning to the clocksmith, he inquired whether it was probable that his brother was to be found at Merespital.

"Indeed, honoured sir, I cannot tell. My brother is a close man. He never says when he returns where he has been, nor when he sets out where he is going. All professional matters are secret. The sciences we follow, Squire, are different. He is a physicist. I am a student of the mathematics. Unless he has seen something new in chronometers, clocks, watches, or hydraulical machines, or unless one of the gentlemen or ladies who reward my devotion to science by their unsolicited patronage have sent me a message, he will keep silence. Of an evening we talk of the sciences, but not of our own empirical practices therein," replied the horologer.

"Indeed! Well, I wish your brother had been sufficiently communicative to have told you where he was going."

"I think, if I might be so bold as to make a suggestion," said the mathematician, with a bow more profound than ever, "that if you and the ladies took the bridle-road to Merespital, you might not unlikely meet him on his way from thence. He did tell me that he should call at Mrs. Nicholson's to-day, and took a message from me about her eight-day clock. She's a new one, by John Wheeler of London, a sweet piece, that tells the day of the month, and the moon's age, and is adorned with a sculpture of Eve giving Adam the apple on the top, most artfully done; but she requires great care, very great care. It's astonishing what humouring even the best clocks want. They're like children, Squire; to treat a clock like a dumb machine is surely a great error."

"Certainly it is, that I can vouch for. You re-member what happened to the big one in my hall? I'm not likely to forget it."

"Ah! a matchless piece; a sublime piece of me-chanism. She was produced long before we mathe-maticians were compelled by law to put our names on our poor works, but it was surely marvellous modesty in so great an artist not to leave his name on what must have been his chief work. I have often surmised that she was made by none other than the great Anthony van Leeuwenhoek himself."

"Not improbably. It belonged to my wife's mother. But I must lose no time, if I am to catch the Doctor; so, good morning." The Squire, as he spoke, turned down the narrow street that led eastwards.

The Merespital almshouses were but hovels. If there had ever been better accommodation for the inmates, centuries of neglect had ruined it, for now the huts of " stud and mud" where the alms-women lived

were precisely of the same character as the adjoining
cattle pens, except that they possessed the luxury of
glass in their windows.

In one of these dwellings the poor woman whom we
saw yesterday was stretched upon a bed of suffering.
Her thigh had been broken. The house, though miserable in outward appearance as neglect could make
it, had something of the aspect of comfort in its interior. The walls were clean with lime-wash, and here
and there a rude print illustrating the career of the
Prodigal Son—a young man dressed in the fashionable
costume of Queen Anne's days—relieved their extreme
plainness; a few common plants bloomed in well
rudded pots on the window-sill, and a glossy black
cat sang her monotonous song of happiness on the
hearth!

The sufferer was not alone. The girl, whom
"Squire's Bob" had on a former occasion called Nell,
was by the bedside administering to its inmate's
necessities.

The English poor have many vices; they are at
times hard, unsympathising; cruel in their hatreds,
and harshly exacting in their love; but they possess
one virtue in a far higher degree, as it seems to us,
than those above them. Their kindness to physical
suffering knows no limit. True, it is sometimes unwise
—often directed to unworthy objects—but there it is,
a bright ray of light shining from heaven on their dull
and unhappy lives. Soothing the lot of the sufferer by
kind words, and calming the heart of the giver not by

a consciousness of virtue, as some shallow persons would say, but by the action of the kindly deed itself upon the soul.

The door opened and Doctor Chubb entered. He was a fine-looking, rosy-faced man of some sixty years old, one on whom age sat lightly. His dress and manners were far removed from those of his mathematical brother. Foreign residence and some years' practice in London had made him a man of the world. Finished gentleman he was not, but his manner and tone showed at once that he had been in the habit of moving in the society of refined people.

" You will take care, my good girl, not to leave the patient," said he, in an under-tone ; " her condition is very critical."

" I don't know what I mun do, sir. I wouldn't hav owt happen to her at nowt through me not being here, but I belong to th' George, and they'll not be for sparin' me long, I reckon," replied the girl, in a troubled tone.

"Ah ! true, true; it's a sad business—a sad business. We must see—stop to-day, I'll talk to Mr. Sargisson about it." Then, turning to his patient, he inquired which of the rioters it was who had caused the accident.

" I can't tell what she says, poor thing, can you ? Well, Lord Carlton was at the head of them ; he must do something. I'll ask him to pay for a nurse."

The patient, who had seemed in a doze, roused her-

self to consciousness, and said, feebly, " What did ye
say, Doctor?"

" I only said that I would ask Lord Carlton to pay
for a nurse for you. It's only fair, you know, as he
was the cause of your hurt. I shall see him perhaps
to-day, I'm going to Brackenthwaite."

" What's he doing at Brackenthwaite? Lord Burworth lives at Brackenthwaite," asked the sufferer.

" Yes, Lord Carlton is his nephew, and will get his
property, so he might do something for you. He'll
have plenty before long, and he shall, Nanny; I'll see
to that."

" No, no, you'll do no such thing. I'll hev none on
his money, no, not a penny. I'll soon be better,
and work again for my sen. Nelly 'll stop wi' me for
a day or two—won't you, lass? Don't ask him,
Doctor."

" Yes, Nanny, I must; you'll be two or three weeks
before you are better. And it was all his fault, a
damned scoundrel. I wish I'd been there with my
horsewhip. Zounds! he shouldn't have got off so
easily. I don't know what John Stutting was about.
He's not generally over tender of Lords."

" Did you say he was Lord Burworth's son, Doctor?" inquired the sick woman, now aroused to vivid
consciousness.

" No, no, his nephew. His sister's son, not his
own. But he'll get all there's left when Lord Burworth dies, and that won't be many years first. I'm
going to see him now; he's got the gout again."

" Poor thing. It's hard to bear, Doctor, to be badly and hev' nobody about you except them as is paid for it. Ah, poor thing! he can't bear pain as I can, he hesn't been so used to it."

The patient seemed to sink into a troubled sleep ere her attendant left her. He had not gone many yards from the door before he met the riding party.

" Well met, Doctor," exclaimed the Squire, shaking the practitioner heartily by the hand, " well met ; I feared we might miss you. I want to know what you think of this accident."

" I think," said the Doctor, looking grave, " that the woman will never recover the use of her limb, and that probably she will not survive many weeks."

" And what do you think of a country and a government that permit brutal assaults on women in the public highways to go unpunished, so long as they are done by a lordling, while if a poor cottager snares a hare in a hedgerow for his Sunday dinner he's sent for God knows how long to Wivilby jail ? "

We need not record Doctor Chubb's reply. It led to a long conversation on the demerits of persons who are already sufficiently odious to our readers.

The ladies dismounted and entered the cottage. Isabell had never been there before. The place was familiar to Mary. It would have been interesting to watch the two girls in the presence of suffering. Isabell, who had never known acute sorrow nor seen dangerous bodily pain, though her kindness was manifested by every word and action, was evidently constrained in

the presence of a grief which her bright smile could
not dispel, or her charity relieve. Mary, though far
more diffident in ordinary life, with much less trust
in her own resources in all those matters where
Isabell was conscious of power, was at once at home.
A few words from Nelly revealed the whole state of
affairs. She saw at a glance what things were wanted
to render the sick woman's life as comfortable as circumstances would permit, and gave the needful directions with a promptness which showed that Mrs.
Skirlaugh's domestic training had produced far more
hopeful results on the character of her guest than on
that of her daughter.

"You will not leave the poor thing, Nelly. If they
can't do without you at the inn, arrangements must
be made to find someone else in your room. I——
that is, Miss Skirlaugh will take the responsi-
bility."

"I think, miss, Doctor Chubb will ask Lord Carlton or Lord Burworth to give summut for a nurse.
He said as he would, but she is strangely again' it,
poor thing," replied the girl.

"Yes, of course she is. Isabell, this must not be.
Go at once, Nelly, to the doctor, and tell him to say
nothing about her to any one at Brackenthwaite. We
shall do all that is required. Do you think she will
know me?"

"Oh, yes, miss. She has asked for you a many
times sin' I've been with her. Nanny, Nanny, here's
Miss Morley some to see you."

The patient's eyes slowly opened. She had caught the meaning of what had been said to her but imperfectly. " What are Morleys to me, all the lot of 'em. Go thy ways, lass; they're no good to thee, nor to none of us."

Ellen hesitated, blushed, and looked down as people do when some question they have asked has drawn forth a peculiarly unfortunate reply, and then, throwing her apron over her head, darted across the road to deliver her message to the doctor.

" She is thinking of some others of my name, not of me, I believe," remarked Mary; and, quietly sinking on her knees by the side of the bed, she said, in a low tone, so low as to be inaudible to Isabell, " Nanny, have you forgotten me ?"

" No, how could I, darlin' ? God bless you for coming to see a poor thing like me. I have wanted you bad ever since I was took. Let me look at you," and she gazed with grateful affection on the face of her benefactress. " I want to talk to you about a sight o' things, but I'm clear dazed now along o' that nasty drink the doctor's bin a giving of me. Where's your father; I mun see him when he comes this way next time."

Mary responded, but in an inaudible voice.

" Oh, ay, I see. Well, gentlefolks must fight, and head, and hang one another, I reckon. Is it for religion, then?"

" Well, yes—for the Catholic king."

" They do say, the father of the man they've set

up now for king in Lunnon used to be nought but a
turnip-hoer, before he came over sea.

> " Geordie was hoeing his turnips,*
>   When the sun went down,
>   And up there came an English Lord,
>   Wha gave him a golden crown,
> Wha gave him a golden crown,
>   And gave him sceptres three,
>   Now am I king in London town,
>   That once was silly Geordie.

" I've heard my mother sing that, and some more
like it. Was it so?"

" Nearly, but not quite. Let us not talk of such
things now," said Mary.

" Ah, well, we'd a brewer once for king, they do
tell. But I should like vastly to see your father again.
Do tell him, if ever he comes, Anne Mason wants him
bad."

The poor woman paused, her eyes wandered half
vacantly around the room, and fell on Miss Skirlaugh,
of whose presence she had not, till then, been aware.

" Nelly, Nelly! there's Miss Skirlaugh come to see
me; give the young lady the chair. Dust it for her
wi' your apron, lass, first. Do sit down, miss. It's
very good o' you to come and see a poor crëatur' like
me. I thought I'd summat to say, but that kedge he's

---

* At Norwich Assizes, 2nd August, 1716, " Mr. Matthew Fern was
. . . convicted of drinking the Pretender's health and calling King George
a *turnip-hougher*, for which he was sentenced to pay a fine of forty marks,
to be imprisoned for a year, and to find sureties for his behaviour for three
years."—Salmon's *Chronological Historian*, p. 364.

given me put it all out o' my head, till Miss Skirlaugh
put it in again. They say," as she spoke, she sunk
her voice once more to a whisper, inaudible save to
Mary, " they say you're to marry the young Squire,
Mr. Ralf. Is it so, ay ?"

Mary hesitated; the poor peasant was not by any
means the sort of person she would have chosen to be
the recipient of love secrets; but her simple nature
and her religious training alike precluded equivocation. She at length whispered something about the
gentleman being abroad at present, and that many circumstances might have occurred of which she was
unaware.

" Oh, yes, I know. God bless you both. They're
a good house; but they do say, them that knows 'em
best, that they're strange, and huncht, and proud. Is
it so, miss ?"

" Oh, no, no ! not to poor people, nor those they
love; only to——"

" Ay, I see; but you're all alike for that. No
gentleman or lady was ever good for aught that was'nt
full o' pride. I get proud mysen wi' thinkin' about
'em, though I never was a lady no more nor I am
now. That young Skirlaugh, who was here yesterday, he's just for all the world the same. I seed
him twice. He'll be for marrying Miss Skirlaugh, I
reckon."

Mary preserved her equanimity admirably, while
questioned concerning her own love affairs. The
novel suggestion now made was more than she was

prepared for. The extreme improbability of the foretold event caused an almost irresistible tendency to laugh ; while the knowledge of the very embarrassing results that the remark might have produced had it reached the quick ears of Isabell, made her blush to the tips of her fingers. No prisoner, on liberation from captivity, was ever more relieved than Mary, when one of the grooms brought a summons from Mr. Skirlaugh, saying that he was impatiently awaiting the ladies' return.

CHAPTER XI.

" A very venerable man, who is ever with Sir Roger, and has lived in his house in the nature of a chaplain above thirty years. This gentleman is a person of good sense and some learning. . . . . He heartily loves Sir Roger, and knows that he is very much in the Old Knight's esteem, so that he lives in the family rather as a relation than a dependent."—*The Spectator*, 106.

WE need not tell our readers that William Skirlaugh's time passed happily among his new friends. A week glided away almost without observation. The life of the household was very regular, but full of pleasant change for one to whom a residence in the country, away from the restraints of business, and in constant intercourse with refined people, was of itself an intense pleasure. As the weather was fine, most of the days were spent out of doors and on horseback. The Squire's stores of topographical anecdote were inexhaustible, and the company of the ladies was seldom wanting to add a charm of a far higher kind.

The young man found a delight in their society which those of our readers who have formed their ideal of female excellence exclusively on what we

commonly see around us at present, will find hard
to realise. They were certainly well educated women
according to the opinions of the time, had no inconsiderable knowledge of the lighter literature that
was then popular, and had even read some grave books
which young ladies of our time would not contemplate
without a yawn; but they were, it must be confessed,
almost entirely deficient in several of the accomplishments which are now thought absolutely indis-
pensable to female education. Pianos were unknown,
but the spinet or harpsichord, of which they are a
development, was common in the houses of wealthy
people. Although not insensible to the charms of
music, none of the Skirlaugh family had learned the
use of that then fashionable instrument. Though
both the young ladies had good voices, their natural
taste for song had remained so far uncultivated that
neither Isabell nor Mary would have dared to delight
their guest by attempting to sing the most simple
melody. When evening closed, conversation, reading
aloud in French or English, and a game at quadrille
or whist filled up the vacant hours till bed time. If
the reading were some light tale, one of Richardson's
novels or a play of Shakespere, the office usually fell
on one of the ladies; but if, as was not unusual, some
grave book, such as Carte or Clarendon's histories,
were selected, the post of lector devolved on Mr. Callis,
who, not content with the information afforded by the
author, frequently broke off when he came upon a congenial topic to pour forth his own stores of knowledge

in illustration of the more meagre details of the historian.

Ignorant as a little child of the world in which he
lived, William had never met anyone who knew half so
much of the times that were past. A life devoted to
the study of the minute details of history, much of the
latter portion of it in the quiet seclusion of Skirlaugh
Manor, though eminently unfitted for developing the
very few grains of worldly wisdom with which the
chaplain had been endowed by nature, was exactly
calculated to insure the happiness of a shy, deeply religious man, whose sole desire, next to the duties which
he conceived he owed to his Maker, was to be of service
to the family of his patrons, and to store his own
voluminous manuscript collections with facts illustra-
tive of the social and domestic history of the eastern
shires, and to accumulate knowledge concerning the
various branches of what was then called the Gothic
tongue.

In early life the old man had taken orders in the
English Church, but as time passed on, and his antiquarian tastes cut him off more and more from the
main current of public opinion, he became troubled in
conscience for having taken oaths of fealty to what he
considered a usurping power. When this conviction
was firmly rooted, with simple-minded consistency
he threw up the small London living which he held,
and became an outcast, earning a precarious pittance
as a hack author or translator for the booksellers.

He was of Lincolnshire extraction, though born in

another county. An ancestor of his had produced that memorable book on drainage law, which, notwithstanding the labours of Serjeant Woolwrych, yet makes the name of Callis familiar to the fen men.

On one of his rare visits to the Metropolis, Mr. Skirlaugh was introduced to the unhappy scholar. His connection with his own county, and his sufferings in what the Squire considered the cause of righteousness, opened at once his heart and shortly after his purse.

The good soul was asked to come for a few weeks to the Manor, for the purpose of arranging the library. That hospitable roof was from henceforth his home. Isabell and her brother were children at the time. Mrs. Skirlaugh was anxiously looking out for some one who could communicate to them solid knowledge in the shape of languages, penmanship, and the properties of numbers. She was greatly taken with the retiring manners of her guest. A suggestion on her part that Mr. Callis should be retained as chaplain and tutor was readily acceded to by her lord, who wondered greatly that so obvious an arrangement had not occurred to him in the first instance.

The base of the round tower was fitted up as a chapel, and the apartment over the same turned into a school-room and study. Here the recluse spent his days. Regular at meals, still more regular when his patron required him as a listener in an evening, the rest of his life, except an hour now and then spent on fine days in a sunny walk in the garden, was

passed in a minute analysis of local history or the
study of the northern languages.

It was a foggy morning. The ladies were engaged,
and the Squire busy with some agricultural matters.
William, therefore, accepted the student's invitation
to spend half an hour with him in his study. He had
never been there before. An invitation to visit that
sanctuary was a great honour reserved by Mr. Callis
only for very favoured guests. There were not half a
dozen persons in the world, beyond the family at the
Manor and the old woman who occasionally " put
things to rights," who had penetrated into that upper
chamber since the student set up his staff therein.

If any imagine such a man surrounded with costly
folios and preciously illuminated manuscripts, they
have greatly misunderstood him. Valuable things
there were in abundance among his collections, but
few that would have attracted attention except from a
person interested in similar pursuits to their owner.
Cases covered the walls of about a third of the room ;
in these were arranged the few printed books which
were Mr. Callis's own property, and a larger number
that he had from time to time brought for temporary
use from the library in the Hall. The rest of the
shelves were occupied by piles of his own manuscript
collections, bundles of charters, rolls, letters, and other
documents which he had gathered in a life devoted to
picking up wrecks on the shore of the ocean of time.
Here and there a chalk or lias fossil showed that the
owner of the apartment was not entirely uninterested

in natural science. The room was not quite without ornament. A very pleasing picture of Miss Skirlaugh, taken when, at eighteen, she ceased to be formally his pupil, was his most treasured possession. In rivalry with it, and curiously contrasting in feature, was the grave, sharp face of Serjeant Callis, to whose "Readings on the Law of Sewers" we have before alluded.

Two or three small miniatures, which his visitor did not particularly notice, completed the catalogue of ornaments. Such of the walls as were not hidden by the bookshelves or pictures were painted by his own hand with a running pattern of green and chocolate, in very bad taste if we judge it by the canons of Greek or Gothic art. Miss Skirlaugh, however, the only critic in whose opinion the artist had any confidence, pronounced his handiwork to be very pretty.

"You led me to hope, Mr. Callis, that you would favour me with a sight of the curious vellum roll in which the Skirlaugh pedigree is emblazoned," said his visitor, after he had attentively examined several curiosities, in which he found little to interest him, for the sake of giving pleasure to his entertainer. "You will remember that when Mr. Skirlaugh asked for it the other evening to show me, you discovered it was here, not in its place in the library."

"Ah, true; so I did," answered the student, with some hesitation of manner. "I will get it. It is really valuable as a work of art as well as a curious genealogical record. The arms down to the time of my patron's grandfather were all emblazoned by Gregory

King, the prince of heraldic artists. Those that follow, which are of very inferior workmanship, are by my own hand."

This was said while Mr. Callis was engaged in disentangling the roll from a heap of superincumbent papers, and divesting it of the various wrappers in which it was carefully stowed away. William could not help noticing that there was something of reluctance in the old man's manner, which was very unusual.

Whenever the reader has occasion to consult for the first time a guide-book, county history, or directory of that part of the world in which he lives, he will have observed, if he be an introspective person, that he instinctively turns, in the first place, to the part containing an account of the spot where his own home is situated. Why is this? It can hardly arise from a preconscious exercise of the critical faculty, for it is agreed by all competent psychologists that most of us possess that organ only in its most rudimentary form. It may spring from vanity, the pleasure that is given us by finding a record, however slight, of anything with which we are personally bound up. The same habit certainly has attached itself to those far fewer persons who con pedigrees. Naturally, unless indeed we have purchased a Norman pedigree (price five shillings per generation; two-and-sixpence for collateral lines), like some of our wealthy neighbours, and ancestry has the fascination of entire novelty, we glance first, not at the Crusaders, knights, or cavaliers

whose names grace the upper portion, but at the
bottom, where our own name and that of our brothers
and sisters, their wives and husbands, form the con-
cluding line. So did William Skirlaugh. It was the
fear of this which gave pain to the kind-hearted
chaplain. He knew that William, though not, like
himself, learned in genealogy, had a romantic venera-
tion for the race from which he sprung. He believed,
and with good reason, that much of the purity of his
young friend's character was to be traced to that
mystic feeling of race, which it had already become
fashionable to despise and endeavour to make ridicu-
lous by confounding with a certain sort of vulgar pride,
the noxious offspring of an entirely different class of
intelligence. He therefore feared that the dubious,
or rather imperfect way, in which the entry of his
own name appeared would give pain. He was not
mistaken. It was, however, for the very reason of
seeing what the record testified on that head, that
William Skirlaugh had asked to examine it.

"I see," said he, suppressing a sigh, "that my
father is the only one in the long catalogue since the
reign of Edward III., whose wife's name is not
recorded. I had a hope, a mere fancy, that it was
just possible you might have possessed information,
which, from a feeling of kindness, my uncle and aunt
might have kept from me. Of course it is mere
dreaming, but will you tell me, do you know who my
mother was, or where my parents were married?"

Mr. Callis declared his entire ignorance. He said

that he was in London at the time of the duel, knew his father, aunt, and uncle well, but that he knew nothing further of William's parentage than has been already recorded.

" You will, I am sure, excuse me for troubling you, Mr. Callis, with these personal matters, the interest of which is to me so deeply painful," continued William.

" Most gladly will I. As a priest of God, it is my duty to give comfort to all who ask for it, and surely a man of proper principles cannot but be glad to see one of your age, now so many lax and evil principles are abroad, anxious, yea even if the anxiety causes pain, to clear his birth from any supposed blot that in the eyes of the world might cling to it. Truly the love of ancestors is one of the most sacred feelings we possess. I doubt much if the sanctity of the marriage tie will itself continue to be venerated if men get to think as lightly as some now pretend to do on this almost sacred subject."

" Although you, as was natural, know no more than I do, your experience in genealogical researches may be able to point out some means of clearing up a mystery which hangs so heavily upon me. I have determined when I go back to town to leave no stone unturned to dispel the darkness, even if disgrace should be behind the curtain," said William, earnestly.

" Disgrace,—in the sense of illegitimacy, that is,—I am sure you need not fear. I was one of the persons who were consulted by your relatives at the time, and I distinctly remember your aunt asserting that she had

positive knowledge that you were born in lawful wedlock. No one who knows that lady could have the
temerity to doubt her word."

"I feel certain," added William, sadly, "that my
uncle did all he could to clear up the doubts. It is
scarcely likely that what so acute a lawyer failed in
doing at the time, I should succeed in now."

"Are you absolutely certain that your aunt has
communicated all she knows?" inquired the genealo-
gist. "I remember she left London at once, having
had a quarrel, which, as my duty was, I vainly tried to
reconcile. Her statement may not be the whole truth,
there may have been a secret marriage between your
poor father and some lady of high rank. Your aunt
may have promised or even sworn secrecy. Such a
promise or oath would clearly not be binding at this
distance of time, as I could demonstrate to you on the
authority not only of the most approved casuists of the
Latin communion, but also by the far higher authority
of Bishop Taylor, our own great moralist. You may,
I think, feel pretty certain that whatever the marriage
was, it was not in a genealogical sense disgraceful. I
knew your father, poor Frank, as we called him, and I
don't think he would have married beneath him. Of
the morals or character of the unknown wife we can
predicate nothing, but you are yourself a living testi
mony of her gentle birth; would you have been what
you are if she had been ignoble?"

William Skirlaugh, though sad at heart, could with
difficulty repress a smile at the last remark, which,

coming from any one else, would have been fulsome flattery, but from the unworldly student could only convey the idea that the little courtesies which he had almost unintentionally shown him had caused the withered heart of the old man to open towards him.

"I have no reason to think," continued William, "that my aunt suppressed anything. Still it is certainly strange that she could be positive of what she did assert, and not know more. Is there a chance, do you think, of some hideous mistake on her part? I have great hesitation in questioning her on the matter."

"My dear friend," exclaimed the good old chaplain, touched with William's dark forebodings, "there is no fear—none whatever—of what you imagine. I knew Henrietta Skirlaugh well, and if any human being may be trusted to tell God's truth, it is she. I do not wonder you shrink from asking what might possibly offend her. I never saw her equal."

"Miss Skirlaugh slightly reminds me of my aunt, but has more animation," added the visitor.

"Not more than she had five-and-twenty years ago. I see not a slight likeness only, but a very strong one. They are two of the best creatures the earth affords, but Miss Isabell has never known sadness. Let us pray that she never may," said the chaplain, with an earnest gravity which almost startled his guest. "Let us pray that one so good may never undergo the discipline of sorrow. It is fit for hard sinful hearts like mine to pass their days in sadness, and I often wonder that God, who knows me as I am, has given me this comfortable home and these friends and books to make me happy. But it does seem that your aunt or Miss Isabell are too pure to need it, as I am sure they are of too Romanlike nobility to let the world see them bow before it."

The latter part of this speech may not, to modern ears, seem consistent with the piety of what went before. Those who know the noble spirit of much of the High Church theology of the seventeenth century will think differently. There are few points where the modern Anglo-Catholics differ more from the school of Laud or that of the higher-toned Nonjurors than in their notions as to the virtue of humility.

CHAPTER XII.

"Hyt is not al for the calf
That the cow loweth,
But it is for the gode gras
That in the mede groweth,
By my hod ! "
'—Poem, temp. Edw. II.

THE conversation was interrupted by the advent of Mr. Skirlaugh. That gentleman, after a long and not quite harmonious interview with his wife, had come to seek Mr. Callis, for the purpose of requesting him to write sundry letters of invitation to dinner.

A dinner party was of rare occurrence at the Manor. The Squire, as we have intimated, was on distant terms with most of his neighbours, and with those whose society he did at times seek he was not very intimate.

Ralf Skirlaugh was emphatically not an unsocial man. He would spend a whole day in gossip with his tenants or work-people ; would ride over to one of the neighbouring villages, or to the rural metropolis of Wivilby, ostensibly, it may be, on some trivial matter of business, but really for the purpose of having a

pleasant chat with the people whom he might chance
to meet. He was delighted to have William staying
with him in his house, and had really begun to look
forward to the time of his departure as a great personal loss. Nor was he by any means backward when
called upon to meet on matters of county business the
three or four great titled magnates who towered above
the rest of Lincolnshire mankind, heavy and louring
as the great rock of Königstein towers over the valley
of the Elbe ; but to those of his own rank, or of that
immediately below it, he was rarely hospitable. Circumstances of position, politics, and education might
partially, but not wholly, account for this. The real
truth lay much nearer the surface. He did not care
to put himself out of the way to entertain those who
did not contribute to his amusement, or in whose
society he could not give a loose rein to his garrulity.
The company of the great nobles was so seldom to be
had, that the very change gave him a certain amount
of pleasure, mostly of the sarcastic kind. He liked to
feel, and to remark to his wife and children, that he,
who was at least the equal of the best of them in
blood, and far superior to the majority in brains, was
only a simple untitled gentleman, because he and his
ancestors had remained faithful in their allegiance,
while the Earls and Dukes, whose names he mentioned, had purchased their position by subserviency
to what it pleased him to call " the foul cabal of
scheming plotters, who had disinherited their lawful
king and enslaved their countrymen." A long course

of indulgence in the feelings generated by the here-
ditary royalism which had come down to him with the
Skirlaugh estates, had made the good gentleman believe—not as a figure of speech, but with real conviction—that the land in which he was living, in the
daily habit of talking treason against the king *de
facto*, was really held in abject slavery by a few great
nobles, who had succeeded by violence, bribery, and
cajolery, in depriving the lesser aristocracy, and
through them the common people, of that share in the
government which was their natural right. This
opinion, wild as it may seem to us who were born
after the destruction of the tyranny of the great
houses, had in it a very large amount of truth. The
extreme form in which Mr. Skirlaugh held it can
scarcely be called irrational in one who had witnessed
the despicable meanness and reckless bloodshed, by aid
of which the members of a few families—under the
shadow of the name of a German king—had tried to
build up an oligarchic government, as exclusive as that
of the worst days of the Venetian Republic. How
near the plot was in being successful, those who gain
their ideas of history from certain popular Whig books
are not likely to know. It would be well, however, if
such of us as have no sympathy with the traditions of
the Revolution houses would sometimes consider who
they were that hindered the despotic ideal of that
small faction from being realised.

The conversation of the peasantry pleased our
Squire, for reasons very different from those which

made that of the few peers with whom he interchanged occasional courtesies attractive. He liked their free manners, racy, provincial dialect, and, perhaps more than all, though he was quite unaware of it, he was attracted by the deference they paid him. Devoid of the common and meaner forms of pride, whose frequency has caused a noble virtue to be branded in sermons, catechisms, and such like literature, as a vice, it really gave the possessor of Skirlaugh manor no little delight to be addressed by the title of " Squire "—a half-affectionate, half-courteous term, that our poor never use to any or of any. but those for whom they entertain a sincere respect.

On the other hand, Mrs. Skirlaugh was of a decidedly social turn. The gossip of the day interested her much more than it did her husband; and, being of a far less retrospective and more practical cast of mind, she felt that he lost no inconsiderable portion of the kind of influence he most highly prized by neglecting a few social courtesies. Though a lady, not only by education, but by birth on the side of each of her parents, her mind had been formed in early years among a far different class of influences to her husband's; and, therefore, the very slight matters which in many cases ruffled his temper when in the society of his equals, passed over hers without notice. There was, also, another motive—some will say a higher one—which had much weight with the good lady. Deeply skilled in all those sciences which we, who know them not even by name, must generalize

under the one inadequate term—cookery—she knew the
effect of her ever vigilant superintendence. She was
quite aware that the power she could communicate to
her domestics over the forms and flavours of things,
was well-nigh unlimited; and with a feminine vanity,
for which such of our readers as enjoy a good dinner
will readily pardon her, she was at times, like many
other ladies of the period, exceedingly anxious to
show her skill.

"I find," said Mr. Skirlaugh, addressing his conversation, as it would seem, both to his friend and the
chaplain; "I find that I cannot get those deeds
signed and the balance paid over, without asking the
whole Scalhoe kennel to dinner. So we've fixed next
Thursday—Friday won't do, you know; Papists can't
eat my wife's good things on a fast day. Will you,
Mr. Callis, be so good as to write the sort of letter to
them that they are likely to understand?—say we dine
at two, but they're to be here at one, that we may get
the law matters done before dinner. They'll be drunk
after."

"Signing the deeds won't take five minutes," interposed William.

"Won't it? You don't know what numskulls
you'll have to deal with. If you get it done in an
hour, you may safely attribute their brightness of
intellect to a special Popish miracle worked in their
favour, unless you can believe that the scent of
Madam Skirlaugh's Protestant kickshaws and my
nonjuring claret has superseded the necessity of such

intervention. I'll have the business done in a room nigh hand the kitchen, so that the needful stimulants may not be wanting. And while we are doing," continued the Squire, now addressing the clergyman, "we may as well let things go off handsomely, and clear off old scores ; so write also for Jordan and his wife, they'll do to amuse Bella and Mary; and we'll have Dr. Chubb, for my wife's special entertainment."

"You told me to remind you, too, that when you next asked any friends, Mr. Tempest was to be invited, if at Scalhoe. I believe he is there now," added the chaplain.

" Certainly, certainly, we must not forget the good father. The only one of the lot that's got any brains or religion, except the Doctor, and he only has the former ; besides, he is Madam's guest, not mine. All the rest will merely eat and drink like my pigs ; he's a good Christian, though a Papist. Mary will like it, too."

" Mr. Tempest has had the misfortune to have been brought up, and to have taken upon him holy orders in a schismatic branch of the Church, but he is a learned and good man. I doubt not his presence will be a restraint upon those who, but for him, might indulge their appetites too freely," said Mr. Callis.

" Not a bit. Not a jot more than yours is to restrain me from swearing at the Whigs. They'll all be as drunk as bagpipers of a Sunday e'en, if I can't devise some plan to hinder 'em, but I think I've arranged a way by which we may play off one passion against another. They most of 'em love sporting more even than drinking. We'll have some night-fowling for the double purpose of keeping them steady and amusing William, here. They'll all go except the parson, and we can find a bed for him or send him home in a barrow if he can't walk, as they did Dicky Stevenson of Wivilby. But what is yon? I could swear I heard a carriage drive into the court."

William, who stood near the window that had a southern aspect, said that a yellow coach, drawn by four horses, had just gone up to the door.

"It's old Burworth. Gad! Can the money have been wrong?" exclaimed the Squire, as he shot down the newel stair.

The coach stopped at the great door and two persons descended therefrom; neither of them was Lord Burworth. They were guests of that nobleman, whom Mr. Skirlaugh would much less readily have received than their host.

One was a slim, fair young man, with sharp eyes, the lid of one of which drooped considerably. Drunkenness, almost continual, and other bad habits attendant on a loose life, were writing upon his features the characters of premature age. It was Lord Carlton; his companion was the stalwart Highlander who had aided him in the mêlée at Merespital. The countenances of both showed them to be

"Deep-mired in vanities and low desires,"

but the face and figure of the Scot, partly from natural constitution better calculated to resist the effects of foul living, and partly because he was more circumspect in his sinning, showed fewer mud stains than that of the peer.

They had not long to tarry for the coming of their host. When he appeared he had put on his most reserved manner. No two things in life could be more different than the recklessly free conversation of Mr. Skirlaugh when in a good temper, and in the company of people who understood him, or who he thought did so, and the distant reserve which was also quite as natural to him when compelled to interchange courtesies with those whom he had good reason to dislike.

" To what am I indebted, my lord, for the honour of your visit?" said he, with a frigidity that would have made the fortune of an actor.

" To several circumstances, my dear sir," responded his lordship. " I have been greatly hurt at an accident that happened, partly, as I fear, through a childish folly of mine, to a gentleman I have since learned was your relative, whom I chanced to fall in with at an inn, near here. May I beg you will think no more of it, as it was quite unintentional."

" I have never thought of it since I heard from those who were present the end of the catastrophe. As far as my cousin is concerned the matter was, of course, perfectly trivial. As trivial as I imagine the suffering you have caused to the poor woman whose leg you have broken, is to yourself," answered the Squire.

"I never heard of that; upon my word I didn't. Did you, Mackenzie? Of course we will make all right with her. I'll send my servant over to-day," said the peer, with a not very badly simulated sorrow.

"That I would beg you not to do. She is, I find, in the alms-house, on my presentation. I am in the habit of maintaining, and, if need be, of seeing justice done to my own poor," replied the obdurate Mr. Skirlaugh.

"Indeed! Believe me I am very sorry, especially so, as she is one of your people. I hope you may be able to point out some means by which I may make amends without trenching on your private charities. But I am forgetting, absolutely forgetting, while talking to one whom I have not seen for so long, a duty of courtesy. Let me introduce you to my friend, Mr. Mackenzie. He's the son of Sir Robert Mackenzie, of Newbiggin, in Perthshire."

"I have met Mr. Mackenzie before. The last time that I saw him was at Edinburgh in a house he knows well, and you may have heard of, called Holyrood. We once had a common friend named Corbet. I shall have no objection to renew the acquaintance with Mr. Mackenzie elsewhere, but not here," said Mr. Skirlaugh, pointedly refusing the offered hand, and uttering his words with the slow deliberation of one who wished to say as little as possible, but that every syllable should tell.

The Highlander gazed on the Squire with a look of real or very well feigned astonishment.

"Indeed, sir," said he, "you must be mistaken ; you are doubtless thinking of some one else who bears my name. We Scots have many cousins by blood, and far more by service. It is too bad to blame a man for the acts of every knave who abuses his surname."

"The question is hardly worth discussion now," responded the Squire.

"Not at all. But I'm sure if you've heard or seen anything bad of anybody called Mackenzie, and you may have, for as far as I can hear they haven't above half a dozen names in the whole of their country, it won't have been my friend Mac. I have brought him with me on a very delicate errand, because he's the best friend I have," said his lordship, evidently trying to seem quite at his ease.

"I once knew another person who thought as you do ; his introduction has rendered yours superfluous," replied the Squire, with his temper under complete command.

A very small thing would often irritate Mr. Skirlaugh. A slight domestic jar, such as dinner being late, or his wife not seeming to give some plan of his the sympathetic approval he thought due to it, would cause his temper to ruffle, and curl itself about in all the various forms and hues that the wattles of a

turkey-cock are wont to assume at the presence of a
shred of scarlet cloth; but he had the power of meeting the more serious crosses of life, in whatever form
they might present themselves, with a degree of calm-
ness which those who saw only his weak irritability
in ordinary life found hard to understand.

"Mr. Skirlaugh will admit he does me injustice
when I assure him that he is mistaken; that I have
no knowledge whatever of the persons or things of
which he speaks. I must add, however, that if my
presence, which your lordship hoped might in some
slight degree be useful to you, is in any way a
hindrance in the matter on which you have sought
an interview with Mr. Skirlaugh, I will at once
retire."

"No, no, Mac; for God's sake, no!" the nobleman
ejaculated, as the Scotchman made a move towards
the door.

"The presence of no one can possibly be an impe-
diment to any business Lord Carlton can have with
me," said the Squire, arranging himself in an attentive
attitude in his arm-chair, with the grave air with
which a judge of assize may be seen to settle himself
ere he charges the "gentlemen of the jury" in a trial
for murder.

Lord Carlton would have given all he possessed,
had he been so fortunate as to own anything, to be
enabled to cut the interview short. Had he calculated on the reception he had met with, no hopes of
success could have lured him on. His experience of

Mr. Skirlaugh had misinformed him on several important points in that gentleman's character. His
own coarse and vulgar mind entirely incapacitated him
for putting himself in imagination in the position of
one whose feelings were of such an entirely different
mould. There was, however, it must be confessed,
some slight excuse for his want of judgment. When
he had hitherto met the Squire he had only seen him
in his jovial and amusing moods; and, therefore, could
form little idea of the character that was natural to
him when his feelings were roused. There was a long
pause ; at length the Squire broke it by saying,—

" My lord, will you tell me the object you have in
seeking my society ? "

This was the very thing that the nobleman was most
anxiously endeavouring to do, but, alas ! the reception
he had met with was so different from that which he
had hoped for, that notwithstanding the careful prepa-
ration he had gone through, the nicely turned sentences
which had been invented for him by the joint efforts
of Brotherton and Mackenzie had all come to pieces
in his head, and left only an unconnected jumble of
pretty sayings. His pale face flushed, he rose, seated
himself, changed his position, stood up again, and,
holding on to the back of a high chair, delivered
himself as follows,—

" I come," said he, gasping—" I come, moved by
the strongest, deepest, most disinterested affection, to
solicit, to—to—to—that is, to beg—I should say, to
ask—of you the hand of your daughter."

This was evidently only a small portion of the speech that was to have been delivered according to the " perfect platform" laid down by his friends. It was the whole of it that was spoken. No interruption on Mr. Skirlaugh's part caused it to terminate abruptly. That gentleman sat as grave and apparently unmoved as the marble caryatides that supported the chimney-piece. Unmoved he really was not; but had seen too much of the world to give outward signs of being easily startled. His astonishment was none the less because his command of temper was unshaken. Had a miracle been worked before his eyes in confirmation of the theological doctrines of the Wivilby tanner, had the Lords and Commons of England waited on him some morning to offer him the crown, or the sun and moon been both eclipsed at the same instant of time, he could not have been more filled with wonder than he was that the grandson of a Cheapside hatter, a man of a life as foul as he held his lineage to be base, should make a proposal of marriage to his Isabell. After a moment's consideration, in which several modes of action presented themselves to his mind, he replied,—

" And I positively decline to grant your request."

" I beg—I do beg, dear sir, that you will reconsider this. It cannot but be for your daughter's happiness. You are, perhaps, not aware that by the entail I succeed to my good uncle's estates. For Miss Skirlaugh's sake, if not for mine, pray—do, pray, reconsider your hasty decision."

" This is too much," said the Squire—"too much, young man;" and, walking leisurely across the room, he rung a handbell. " Conduct these two persons to their carriage, James," said he, as, without salutation, he walked out of the apartment.

CHAPTER XIII.

" There is scarce any virtue incident to a man, but there are singular
sparks and resemblances of the same in sundry kinds of dogs."
                              Guillim, *A Display of Heraldry*.

THE excitement of surprise or anger acts very
variously on different temperaments. Probably Mr.
Skirlaugh had never in the course of his life been
more enraged than on the present occasion, but the
higher feelings of his nature only were aroused. He
felt that he owed it to his own dignity not only to
keep his temper, but to conduct himself as if nothing
serious had happened to ruffle it. "If I stay in the
house I shall be making a fool of myself," thought
he; so he strolled leisurely out into the gardens.
He had not gone far before he saw Isabell and
Mary sitting on a rustic seat, with Milo, the blood-
hound, couchant at their feet. His daughter had
been engaged in reading the few dry scraps of foreign
news that in those days filled nearly the whole of the
small sheet called the *Stamford Mercury*. Her interest

in foreign affairs was, perhaps, not greater than that of English young ladies at present, but she took pleasure in reading about the motions of continental armies, and the splendours of foreign courts, because she connected those things vaguely with her brother, who was engaged in performing the grand tour. The newspaper of course threw no light on his individual career, but it suggested, or at least she thought it did, the sights he had seen, and some of the ideas which might be passing in his mind. Persons who have been long separated from those they love, especially in times distracted by war or violent crime, know how tender hearts seek after any thing that can bring to their ears an echo of an echo of the absent. In one country of continental Europe Isabell had foreign relatives, on her mother's side, with whom she was well acquainted; their names sometimes appeared even in the dry columns of the Stamford newsman. Mary was perhaps unoccupied. Her eyes were fixed on the ground, her fingers seemed to be playing with the beads of her small ebony rosary.

" I cannot make out anything from what I see here as to our chances of receiving letters," remarked Isabell, as she laid down the sheet. " If any had come by this last mail, we should have had them before we got the paper. I think when Ralf writes he will, as he has done before, get some English envoy to enclose his billet under cover to Lord Burworth."

"My father," replied Mary, "will, I fear, hardly try that again, though the audacity succeeded once; but I shall hear soon, very soon, I hope, by some channel or other. His last letter seemed to say so, if I understood it; but it was, as they now always are, written by a secretary, and I cannot be quite sure of the meaning. The cypher we used to correspond in was much clearer to me than the letters which are written in plain English, but so composed as to appear to relate to entirely different things from their real purport. It is hard to be deprived of the pleasure of possessing even his handwriting."

"Ralf will very soon be back, not to leave us again, and will certainly bring you not only a letter from your father, in his own writing and natural style, but volumes of messages such as he dare not trust to paper, in however safe custody it might be. I do wish Ralf were back with us again. For my part I do not see why because a man is born a gentleman, he should have to waste a large slice of his life in wandering about in foreign countries, when his old father and mother, his sister, and, more than all, his lady-love are pining for him at home. I want him very much just now that he may see my cousin William. I shall be sadly disappointed if he doesn't return before he leaves. I am sure this new friend of ours is a person Ralf would take to instantly."

The Squire joined them, humming as he sauntered up the gravel walk a verse from *The Sale of Rebellion's*

Household Stuff,[*] very inappropriate to the times in which he lived, unless he believed that the jingle was redeemed from utter nonsense by having a prophetic meaning.

"I have had visitors," said he, "two persons of distinction."

The ladies inquired who had been, with the eagerness of people not in the habit of being jaded by callers.

"No less a person, fair dames, than that distinguished nobleman, Lord Carlton, son of Dick Carlton, who got a peerage for the Act of Settlement business, grandson of old Carlton, the hatter, and a great grandson of a puritan knave who helped to supply the rebel army of 1642 with clothes, cheated his masters about the soldiers' breeches, and got hanged for it. You see, my dears, there are other people who study pedigrees besides the learned Mr. Callis."

"What could such a person want here, papa? I should have thought he knew you, indeed all of us, too well, to suppose his society would be desired even if he had not insulted our cousin," exclaimed Isabell.

"So should I, but he didn't. I may possibly have made the fact clear to him. I'll tell you both sometime or other what he came for, but not now. Who do you think was my other guest? Well, you won't guess, I'm sure. Do you remember a certain person who was the chief witness against poor Corbet, Mary?"

[*] " Percy's Reliques," 4th edit. vol. ii. p. 342.

"I can never forget Kenneth Mackenzie," said she, her face flushing, and her eyes flashing.

"Lord Carlton brought that person here, and did me the honour of introducing me to him."

"And did you, could you stand on your own hearth, Mr. Skirlaugh, and receive the miscreant in friendship?"

"I told him we had met before and might meet again. I could not, you know, Mary, fight him here; but as sure as there's a heaven above us, if ever I meet that fellow outside my own doorstep, I'll send him to join Judas Iscariot and Titus Oates, or another Skirlaugh shall die with three inches of steel in his body. I am thankful Ralf was not at home. I doubt whether the good breeding he has picked up, *outre mer*, would be strong enough to have kept his hot blood from boiling over."

"And has the cold-blooded, calculating murderer of Richard Corbet, and of half the other martyrs, partaken of the hospitality of a friend of his victims?" said Mary, deeply agitated. "Received what he will call his friendship, and gone away to tell those who hired him that the Jacobites have sunk so low that for the sake of enjoying their own acres in quiet they will receive into their houses one that even——"

Mary was about to say much more. Unwise her words certainly would have been, for the deepest feelings of her heart were aroused. We do not think that anything of hers would have made Mr. Skirlaugh seriously angry; on the present occasion his feelings were far too nearly of the complexion of her own to cause the wild outburst, as far as it had yet gone, to produce any other sentiment than admiration. "I wish I knew no more of the world than the dear child does," thought he. Isabell, whose temper was calm, perhaps because she had not suffered so bitterly, pressed the hand of her friend beseechingly, and Mary, accustomed from long habit to obey the dictates of a stronger will, left the sentence unfinished. Stooping to hide her emotions, she caressed the hound at her feet, who, as his large loving eyes gazed into her face, seemed to respond to what was passing in her breast much more fully than, as she for the moment unjustly considered, the cold and calculating hearts of her friends.

It is happy for those who can thus translate the language of brutes. Where there is a fellow-feeling of love between us and the nobler animals, it rarely springs from those motives by which certain philosophers, now in the ascendant, have endeavoured to explain it. If we loved them merely on account of the good we got from them, the dung-cart that assists in the manuring of our fields, or the umbrella that shades us from the rain, would have a proportionate place in our regard. Such persons as are able to feel joy at the affection of a dog, have in them, whatever their lives may be, qualities too noble to be influenced by mere utility. The true ground of our love is that their sympathy is never lacking. Your dog, if he once loves you, loves you for ever. No act of yours in the

N 2

outer world, no cruelty towards himself even, will turn
his affection into carping criticism. He has no ambition to satisfy, no higher or lower motives to divert
him from you, the one object of his regard. The
hackneyed words of the poet, so untrue of most
human love, are true of his—

> " I know not, I ask not, if guilt's in that heart,
>   I but know that I love thee, whatever thou art."

Therefore in whatever mood we may be, this sympathy gives pleasure or relief, not so deep nor so last-
ing, perhaps, as that which some few beings of our
own kind afford at rare intervals, when, by something
approaching to a special providence, they happen for a
few moments to stand exactly on the same plane with
ourselves, but far more really valuable, because certainly within reach. We know not when entering our
own doors, depressed by sorrow, or filled with joyous
excitement, whether those within will be in a mood
that does not clash with ours, but the quiet, mute love
of our dog, gazing into our eyes, as if longing to tell
his affection in human words, or licking our hand in
token of submissive devotion, is sure to touch the
right chord, because, as distinctive expression is wanting, we translate his symbols into the words that
soothe us most.

In the middle ages this must have been deeply felt,
though we are not aware that the idea has found a
place in the literature which has come down to us.
There are, however, remains, among the most touching

that time has spared, which show how deeply our ancestors realised such thoughts. The writer has before
his eyes a certain alabaster monument in a north
country church, where, blended in an embrace no
human hands will ever sever, there rest the remains of
a great feudal lord and his spouse, dame Maud, a lady
who brought to him wide lands, and, if we may trust
chronicle and sculptured stone, a peerless gift of
beauty. On the tomb the husband and wife are represented as they lived, and with such skill as the best
fifteenth century artists could produce. Angels swing-
ing censers, and playing on harps, support the cushions
where their heads are pillowed. The figures lie side
by side; the lady gazes not on her lord, who seems
calmly to await the judgment, with no sign of hope or
fear on his noble features, but upwards, as it were
trying to catch a glimpse of the celestial visitants who
shed around the heavenly music. Her hand seems
but a moment since to have been locked in his, but
she has withdrawn it; a sign, it may be, that the choirs
of the blessed have more charms for her now than the
love of her knightly lord. But the hound on which
his feet rest; he, poor brute, sees no angelic throng,
listens to no heavenly harpings, but gazes mournfully,
wistfully up into his master's face. The lesson that
these images convey is a sad one. Some, perhaps, will
be more touched by the affection of the dog for his
master, which death could not destroy, than by the
lady's longings for a spirit world she could not
realise.

At this moment of awkward pause in the conversation, a flock of startled pigeons came hovering over their heads, and settled on the walk within a few yards of them. The birds were quite tame, and it was no unusual thing to see them picking about almost close to the feet of the servants in the court, but none of the party remembered a sudden descent like this upon the garden.

" This is very strange, Isabell," said the Squire, glad of a chance of changing the subject of conversation. " You know the old woman's fable, that when pigeons suddenly become tame it is a sign of death, or great misfortune to some one in the house. Of course it's all nonsense, a remnant of the Pagan notion of augury by the flight of birds ; but it is odd that they should fly to us in this startled manner ; I never noticed them do so before. I have heard my aunt Mary say that my grandfather was sitting in this very garden on a summer's evening, when suddenly the pigeons, which were not tame then as they are now, came and picked about almost close to his feet. He was struck with an apoplexy, and died that very night."

CHAPTER XIV.

" Post equitem sedet atra cura."—Horatius.

IF Mr. Skirlaugh had known as much of what was going on in his own domain as our readers will shortly do, he would not have had the least inclination to believe that the birds conveyed any preternatural warning.

They may not have forgotten that Mr. Brotherton had expressed a strong desire to feast his eyes upon the beauties of the gardens at Skirlaugh Manor, and that Mr. Robert Drury was under something not very unlike a promise to aid him in gratifying that inclination.

The carriage which brought Lord Carlton and Mackenzie, contained the agent also. Instead of entering the house with his patron, he walked round to the stable-yard, where he discovered the groom leisurely engaged in platting a whip-thong. He was seated on a corner of the saddle-room table, near a large fire, whose heat he seemed to enjoy, although the weather was mild. A horn of ale was at his elbow, thongs of white leather, balls of twine, and a curious assortment of knives, pincers, and other tools strewed the table.

" Glad to have found you, Mr. Drury. I've not forgotten my appointment, you see," said Brotherton, in his most friendly manner.

The groom raised his eyes. " Oh, ay, about th' gardins, is it ? Well, this mun be kept very squat. It'll never do for our maister nor madam to know. She's warse about them sort o' things then he is. I really omast think I'd better hev nowt at all to do wi' it. It's a tickle job, I can tell ye."

" Well, really, Mr. Drury, I'm very sorry. I quite depended on you. You promised that you'd do me this little favour next time I came, and I've written to my brother already about it. He'll be as much dis-appointed as I am," said the agent, in a coaxing tone.

" Promise, did I ? Well, I'll see then ; but I mun get this little job for Squire done fost. He'll be wantin' it, maybe, when th' company leaves. Will ye just give us that there lump o' bees-wax off o' the shelf yonder, it's agean the colic drink bottle ? I hev said a word or two to oud Dent. He tuk the ginney like a man, he did. If he'd been as much used to pocketing ginneys all his life as thoo hes, he couldn't hev done it no better. We'll hev no bother wi' him now, but you knaw our gardins is strange an' big, there's acres an' acres on 'em, and then there's the wood, all like a Gillian bower, wi' walks, and rides, and seats, and things. Now what is it ye'd like to see ? You can't tek it all in at a view no more then ye can th' four sides o' a chetch steeple all at once."

" Oh, I shall be satisfied with seeing far less than you have described. My brother is not particularly anxious about any other part except that on the east wing. The Morning Pleasaunce, I think it is called," replied Brotherton.

" Come, then, let's be off," exclaimed Bob, who, seized with a sudden fit of energy, jumped from the table, rubbed the new made thong with pipe-clay, drank off the beer, bundled his various tools into a drawer, stuck a stable cap on one side of his head, his hands into his pockets, and strode off in the direction of the garden with an energy very disproportionate to his former apathy. Their route lay along a devious path among the out-houses. They soon reached a small gateway, whose lower portion was furnished with two doors studded with nails, waifs from the demo-lished castle, one communicating with the offices, the other with the Morning Pleasaunce. Between them was a little dark room, some eight feet square, sup-porting a chamber where the tame pigeons resided.

" Noo thoo sees this is th' road, but t' other door's locked. I'll run round and oppen it. Afore I do, though, thoo mun go in here and let me lock the door, for feerd madam should come, she's alm'st alus pychin' about."

The agent was reputed to be a subtle man, he cer-tainly considered himself to be so. He had however no suspicion on the present occasion. He entered the little windowless cell without a moment's hesitation; Bob turned the key and walked jauntily away. Brotherton was as ignorant of the topography of the premises as the good monks of Ferrieres, concerning whom Robertson and Maitland have discoursed, are said to have been of the geography of Flanders. He surmised that the distance the groom would have to go might be considerable, and was therefore not at all uneasy at his captivity until perhaps ten minutes had elapsed. When a quarter of an hour had gone over his head, he really began to be fidgety, but still the idea that a trick had been played upon his credulity did not strike him. " The fellow has been called off by his master," thought he.

At length the doubt loomed darkly on his mind— " What if the man has been playing off a rude practical joke upon me. His manner is repulsively familiar. He evidently has not that respect for superior station that he should have." A ready answer seemed to be furnished to this dark suggestion, by the fact that a trick of this peculiarly senseless kind (all practical jokes do seem particularly foolish to those who suffer from them) could afford no amusement to the operator, because it would be necessary to keep it quite private, for fear of the wrath of the Squire and his lady. Jests are made to be laughed at. It did seem therefore very improbable that the menial would take the trouble of concocting one where this result could certainly not be obtained. How long Mr. Brotherton would have continued balancing probabilities in his mind without coming to any definite conclusion, we do not know. His speculations and suspense were alike cut short by the rumble of the carriage wheels as Lord Carlton drove away. The reception he had met with put everything else out of the nobleman's head. He ordered the coachman to drive off without a thought as to how Mr. Brotherton was to get home. Even had it occurred to him that that gentleman would have to take a long walk in consequence of his own impetuosity, he certainly would not have delayed his departure for an instant.

The sound of the wheels had hardly died away ere Bob's heavy footsteps clattered on the path which approached the gateway, not on that side to which he had promised to come for the purpose of opening the garden door, but on that at which he had entered.

" Oh Lord, oh Lord !" shouted he, " we're in for it. You'll be killed, and what's warse I shall lose my place, all a long o' you and this offil old gardin. If ye speak a wod, or if ye so much as move yer toes inside yer shoe leathers—whatever on earth's the matter I doant knaw, but I never i' all my born days seed our Squire in such an a tackin'. He's bundled them two chaps as came wi you out o' th' house, as thof they'd been a couple of dogs as had gotten th' maunge, clodded 'em into th' carriage, an' teld Reuben th' coachman to drive wi' 'em to Hell an' tell oud Nick it was him as hed sent 'em, an' noo he's rampagin' up an' doon wi' his gret horsewhip i' his hand,—you seed me a mendin' on it this mornin', Mr. Brotherton—an' swearin' by all 'at's good that if he can nobut leet on you—for he knaws you cam wi' 'em, he'll cut yer skin i' such small ribbins 'at they'll be ower narrer for th' fairy lasses to tie their shoes wi'.''

Brotherton was fully aware of the object for which Lord Carlton had that morning sought Mr. Skirlaugh's society. He knew, too, some little by personal experience, and much more by vague report, of the habits and character of that gentleman. It did not strike him as at all improbable that the Squire would be highly incensed, and if such were the case he was quite sure that no respect for Lord Carlton's position, much less for his own, would restrain him from venting his feelings in any way that might suit his pleasure. The awful tale which the groom told did not, therefore, strike him as improbable. Cowardice takes various forms. Brotherton could not have been considered a timid man in ordinary cases. · He had plenty, a superabundance indeed, of that kind of moral courage which enabled him to carry out his own designs in the teeth of opposition. He was not fearful of danger when it was far away, nor particularly timid when near, if he saw any feasible mode of eluding it; but he was entirely without that moral dignity which enables some persons, even if otherwise bad, to face pain and danger in its most unheroic forms with manlike courage. If the agent had been on trial for his life for felony, or on the scaffold about to suffer the last penalty for that crime, it is probable that he would not have borne himself worse than other villains have done in similar positions. But in the present instance, threatened with what he believed to be a very real, but at the same time vague danger, with no stimulus of vanity, no hope of reward to lure him on, his courage rapidly gave way.

" What is to be done ? Oh, Mr. Drury, good Mr. Drury, do let me out and help me to escape," exclaimed he in a suppliant voice.

" Let ye out ! Why if I was to oppen the door, our Squire would pounce down on ye in a minnit, like a kite scraggin' a whitterick. You'd not hev a whole bone i' yer body as big as a copper ha'penny afore I could say Jack Robison."

" What am I to do, then ?" whined he.

" Do ! why not be bellowin' out there like a bull cauf i' a peat moor dykin', bud lig still an' do'nt speak a wod. If ye yowl out i' that form ye'll be scarein' th' pigeons, an' then out they'll puther, an' if he sees 'em flyin', he's sure to knaw what's up, an' then he'll be efter ye soon, I'll uphowd it."

As Bob was finishing his sentence he poked a long willow rod, which he had provided for the purpose, through one of the holes by which the birds entered their abode. The startled bevy, unused to such disturbance, poured forth, flapping their wings, in no little consternation.

" There, then ! It's just as I tell'd yer. Noo he's sure to see 'em, an' you'll soon see him. I'm strange an' sorry I put a new thong on his whip this vary day. It's a real heavy un. You seed it, may be. Bud I mun be off, or he'll be a catchin' me an' all."

With these words the tormentor departed, but his

schemes of mischief were not over. He retraced his steps into the saddle-room; called to one of the "threepenny lads," and handing him the instrument of torture, bade him crack the dust out of it. "Don't do it here," said he, "or you'll scare the pultry, Ben, but go back o' th' sheds."

The agent had the clearest recollection of the big whip which he had seen in the saddle-house. He dreaded every moment that the door would open and the form of the Squire armed with that frightful weapon present itself. Sunk on the floor, for there was no seat, he felt that whatever torture the future life might have in store for him, nothing in this world could exceed the agony of the present. An additional pang was yet added by the boy on whom devolved the congenial duty of whip-cracking. He perhaps had never handled a real riding-whip before. Play no doubt he had with vulgar articles called whips of home manufacture, where a thatch peg does duty for a stock and some platted "tarmarl" stolen from the roof of a neighbouring corn stack, furnishes the lash, but a real whip with a stock of polished Indian cane, a steel hammer inlaid with silver for a hook, and a thong of the whitest of white leather tricked out at the end with a lash of green and red silk cord, was a treasure not to be handled lightly. It were almost a metaphor to call the low, dull sound that the boy's toy whip produced, a crack; but this was an instrument whose report resounded far and near, and raised echoes in every part of the home domain. As the groom had hoped, he devoted himself thoroughly to this new employment. Every time the sound, so congenial to the urchin, struck on the ears of the prisoner, he thought that the enraged Squire, who he believed to be hunting for him, was venting his baffled rage. "It can only be a work of time," groaned he ; "in a few minutes he must find me."

How long the cracking would have gone on, if uninterrupted, our juvenile readers, should we chance to have any, can probably conjecture. Old John Dent, the gardener, happening to come into the yard for a tool which he required, was much scandalised by finding Ben, one of his own particular retainers, doing what he was pleased to call the groom's "idle wark." He at once sent the truant off to his weeding, glad to have escaped a cuffing by the loss of the remainder of the pleasure he had promised himself.

When the cracking ceased, Brotherton had faint hopes that the Squire was in some degree pacified, and begun once more fervently to desire the presence of his jailer. Hour after hour glided silently away, and no Bob appeared. It was too dark for him to see the face of his watch ; the cawing of the rooks saying their evening prayers, informed him that the hour of sunset was past, but his liberator came not. Could he have forgotten him? His mind had been too painfully occupied to think of food ; but now, in the dead stillness of evening, he became aware that he had partaken of none since breakfast. Another hour passed ; the hunger increased. He began to turn his thoughts

to the possibility of some way of escape. Could one
of the doors be forced from its hinges ? Was it possible
for him to climb to the next storey, and break a way
through the roof ? He tried the door, and found that
the strength of no one man could burst it open. He
remembered observing when he entered that the little
trap-door by which access was obtained to the pigeon-
chamber was, as is usual in such places, in the middle
of the floor, and that it was therefore quite impossible
to reach it without a ladder.

Hope, then, there was none. In a state but little
removed from despair, he was preparing himself to meet
the worst, when he heard footsteps. The key turned
in the lock, and the groom stood before him. He began to pour out most heartfelt thanks to his liberator.

"Stop, stop ! Let's have no slaverin' talk like that,
but be off wi' yer like shot, or some o' th' chaps will
be seein' yer, and then it's all up, I can tell yer.
Squire's gen orders that if ony on us sees yer (for he's
sure you're about somewhere), we're to collar yer
straight off, and tak' yer to him. You knaw what that
means."

"No, I don't; surely he wouldn't kill me !" groaned
the captive.

"No, I don't think he would do that ; for, ye see,
ther'd be yer carcass then a lumberin' about, and the
crowner would be gettin' to hear on it, and then ther'd
be an inquest like, and he'd hev to give th' jurymen
a dinner i' th' kitchen, and ax the crowner into th'
room. But, ye know, there's the vaults."

"The vaults! and what are they?" said Brotherton, a thrill of horror darting through his mind.

"What! ha' ye lived so long, and never heard o' them? Why, yer knaw when old Sir Ingram, our Squire's grandfather, pulled down the castle, he left the big prisons and dungeons, and built th' new house up o' th' top on 'em. We use some on 'em now as cellars, but they're mostlins locked up, and no one else but Squire ever goes into 'em, or if anybody does, he niver comes out agean to tell us nowt about it. Some on 'em runs just under this very place where we are a stannin' now. If you was once putten in there, you'd never be heard on no more till there cam a week wi' three Thursdays in it."

The agent took in every word of this audacious lie. He had been accustomed in his youth to hear of the wild deeds of the lawless Scottish nobles "lang syne," and had seen with his own eyes some of the subterranean dungeons of their strongholds. Had it been broad daylight, or had he been in his usual unexcited frame of mind, it is not likely that such an improbable story would have had more effect on him than it now has upon the reader. The conviction that he was the object of fierce, if not murderous, hatred, the certainty that he deserved to be so, and that if Mr. Skirlaugh could know the plans he was projecting, he would be justified in dealing with him as severely, if not quite as summarily, as Bob had described, predisposed him to believe anything.

"Do but get me out of this, Mr. Drury, and I'll

give you all I have in the world!" exclaimed the terrified wretch, who already felt himself, in imagination, in the dungeon, which the mischievous fancy of the groom had created. As he spoke he thrust his purse into Drury's hand.

"Tak' that rammil back; I don't want none on it, man; nobbut be still, and I'll get ye off this time; but just listen to me : there's a little bod been a tellin' me what yer after, and if I tell'd our Squire ye'd not get off, if ye was at Brackenthwaite, or i' Lunnon itself—mind that," exclaimed Bob, striking his right hand violently on his thigh to give emphasis to his words.

The agent began a confused reply. He was cut short at once.

"Be still. Yer more frangy than a blood-foal fost time it's a helter putten on it hëad. Here's Nob, ould Isaac the shepherd's pony; you may ride home on her, if ye like ; but you mun send her back agean afore six i' th' mornin', or you'll get wrong, I can tell yer."

· With many protestations that the pony should be returned at the time specified, the agent mounted, and the groom opening the gate, let him out of the yard into the woodland road.

It was a moonless night, the few stars that were shining gave a faint light sufficient to guide the traveller on his way. The road was a rough cart-track, on which the thoughts of the roadmasters had never expended themselves in the form of gravel. Here and there miniature lakes, which we Lincolnshire men call

flodges, stretched across the whole path. There had
been no rain for some time, but the stiff clay held the
water as in a basin. No sound broke the death-like
stillness, except the splashing of the pony's feet, or
the occasional cry of some night-flying bird. The
intense relief that he experienced in being delivered
from captivity and the dread of the Squire's ferocity,
made Brotherton, notwithstanding hunger, for the
moment somewhat light of heart. Reaction, however,
soon set in. His not unnatural feelings of resentment
against his tormentor were mingled with anxious
curiosity as to the meaning of certain hints that he
had thrown out. " What if the fellow really should
know that which his words seem to suggest ? " thought
he, as the irritating fancy struck him. His reason told
him that it could not be, or that if some part of his
plans were vaguely guessed at, he could certainly out-
manœuvre such a person by a very immaterial change
of tactics. Conscience hinted that the miserable
schemes of self-aggrandisement which led him to plan
evil deeds for the gratification of his worthless patron
must end in misery. Conscience had frequently said
the same before, but the only effect of the voice was to
draw forth the reply, "I must go on and help Lord
Carlton in this. There is no way else. I have sold
myself to the devil, and must make the best I can of
the bargain." Thus he muttered, almost aloud, as the
pony turned a slight curve, where the road seemed, in
the dim light, to narrow to a mere footpath, completely
overhung by bushes. The words were hardly uttered

ere an unearthly yell rung through the wood, and the
foul fiend himself sprung on his pony behind him, and
clasped his arms around his neck. The scream the
victim gave was almost as loud as that of his grim
tormentor. Nob, whose pace had been thus far that of
a peaceable, well-disposed nag, was as much alarmed
as Brotherton himself. Putting her nose between her
legs, she galloped off in a perfect frenzy of terror,
not in the direction of Brackenthwaite, but down the
western slope of the hill. The agent was, by no means,
a bad rider. Scotch peasants in former days were
used to tumble about on the backs of ponies almost as
soon as they could walk. Fear deprived him of all
power of guiding the terrified animal; but he stuck
on firmly, though the pace with which they swept down
the decline was frightful. When he tried for a moment
to give his attention to the pony, the fascination of
the spiritual presence was too strong for him, and he
turned round, in an agony of fear, to gaze on the
incubus on the crupper. There could be no doubt
about it. There sate behind him, distinctly visible,
in the dim light, the form which he had so often heard
described by the cottage fireside, which he had seen a
hundred times in picture-books, and certainly not less
frequently in his dreams. The dark, thin body, the
long, skinny arms, the horrible face,—every trait was
there by which the Scottish peasant distinguished that
being whom one of their writers has called the Pope of
Pandemonium. Each time he attempted to gaze the
sight became one of more unearthly horror. Reason

did not, however, entirely forsake the victim. When he reached the bottom of the hill, although the pace was not less rapid, his seat was, in some degree, less perilous, and he turned deliberately round, determined to speak to his unearthly companion. The frightful visage was within six inches of his own; the horrible eyes, he averred, shone with the very light of the pit itself; and curses, deep and long, rung in his ears— such curses as, to use his own words in after days, when, converted from a life of sin he settled down as a ruling elder and whisky distiller in his native village, " it is not fit for human lips to report."

" Avoid thee, Sathanas, in the name of— "

The exorcism was cut short by Satan grasping him fiercely by the nose. At the same instant of time the pony swerved round a corner, and the horrified Brotherton saw before him what seemed to be the wall of a castle, all on a red glow with intense heat. It had not the appearance of a building which had taken fire, but of one to which fire was the natural element. Tongues of flame—long blue flame—shot through every door and loophole, glimmered in every crevice; and each individual brick shone and " lowed " with the intense heat. " As I am a Christian man," thought he, " this is verily the mouth of the pit; and I am lost—lost for ever, for—" His exhausted frame could bear no more. He fell fainting from his pony.

Some hours after, the man, whose duty it was to see to the fires of the Squire's brick-kiln, went out to make all right for the night, and found the agent senseless on the ground, bleeding from the effects of his fall. In the morning the pony, saddled and bridled, was discovered rubbing herself against the wood-lane gate. It was also observed that Jenny, the monkey, had that night broken her chain, although the good dame, if she had wandered abroad, had returned to her residence with punctual regularity.

Brotherton, to the day of his death, believed that he had had a personal interview with Satan, and dated the sowing of the first seeds of his conversion therefrom; seeds which, as our readers will see, like haws and American walnuts, took a considerable time to germinate. Those who know the wild tales of diablerie with which the Scottish fireside was formerly illumined, as it were, by the very flames of Gehenna, who have read the monstrous legends in the Analecta of Wodrow, the pious covenanting historian, will not be surprised that Mr. Brotherton should have thought he had met the Devil while engaged in plotting to gratify Lord Carlton's unholy pleasure.

CHAPTER XV.

" Believe 't that we'll do anything for gold."

Timon of Athens, act iv. s. 3.

THE night was dark and the wind moaned fitfully in the chimneys in harmony with the sad soft rain that was falling without unheard, save when a gust of more than usual strength drove it against the leaded window panes. At other times no sound whatever broke the deep silence except the dripping of the water from the eaves, as it fell with a pleasant monotony upon the flags of the court below. A solitary man was sitting in a small old-fashioned room. On the table lay a leather travelling desk, a few papers, and one or two books. He might perhaps have been writing letters, but was not doing so now. His chair was turned away from the table, and he sat, his feet upon the fender, with his body bent down and his head resting on his hands. His eyes were fixed upon the logs in the grate as if watching the angular forms into which the heat clove the burning wood. The modern invention of a fireplace in which to burn coal had not yet been introduced into the apartment which he occupied. The expression of his face was unhappy—sad would not be the fit term to use. It was sternly, bitterly unhappy, but had none of the mellow autumnal hue which sorrow if borne manfully gives to the features; neither were there signs of the weak irritability often seen on the countenances of those who do not bear it manfully. If, however, dignity were wanting, there was in its room a dogged frowning earnestness which supplied its place not inaptly. If the man whom we now see before us ruminating on painful subjects were of fairly virtuous life, we might safely predicate that the share of the imaginative faculty with which he had been endowed by nature was very small, that the shadows of his life had had very few rays of light from within to produce beauty by the contrast. If his character were vicious, it would not be unsafe to conjecture that he had wandered far in the paths of sin, and had picked his way among the pitfalls not unwarily; that the thoughts of repentance which had crossed his mind had been kept sternly in check by a strength of will that might have gone far towards making a noble Christian character had it been exercised in curbing evil thoughts and wandering desires. As he raises himself up from his crouching attitude and leans back in his arm-chair, we get a full view of his features as they are lighted up by the dusky blaze.

The faculty of keen, quick imagination is certainly not wanting; there is that about the expression of his dark eyes and the humorous curve of his well-formed full lips which at once precludes any one who can read the soul in the features from coming to such a conclusion. The heavy protruding under-jaw indicates a strength of purpose which the general character of the features would lead us to think had been often exercised in planning schemes of evil. He was thinking earnestly, but no murmur escaped his lips. Such characters are not sufficiently child-like to think aloud. The only bodily action by which the most acute observer could have guessed at what was going on within was the movement of his fingers, which now went gently to and fro like those of one playing on a keyed instrument, and then suddenly, as some bitter memory or anticipation struck him, clenched themselves tightly together. Whatever the thoughts were that troubled him, they evidently occupied all his faculties, for a low tap on the door failed to attract his notice. It was repeated. As he arose his features assumed their ordinarily gay, somewhat *roué* air. He opened the door and received Mr. Brotherton with a hearty shake of the hand.

" I thought I shouldn't see you to-night," said he, " and was just debating whether to go to bed, or waste an hour over a book."

" I was sure to come, Mr. Mackenzie, but I have had a hard day. Lord Burworth finds me plenty of employment without our other cares," answered the new comer.

" Have you accomplished anything satisfactory in our line," asked Mackenzie, setting the other arm-chair for his friend comfortably near to the fire.

"Well, yes, I think I have. I've seen the men, and they're all right, though I'd more to pay than I thought of. There's one thing troubles me. I'm not clear of the way—the road I mean; we must know that," answered the agent.

"Certainly; but there's time enough yet. Come, have something to drink. I can't get any hot water, but there's plenty of cold, and the spirits are on the side-table."

"It's a cold, wet night; we Scots should be untrue to our country if we made a dry bargain," replied Brotherton; and, stepping to the sideboard, he helped himself to a strong glass of hollands and water.

"I won't take any to-night, I've to drink so much when Lord Carlton's here, that I'm as abstemious as a hermit when he's in bed. His lordship's been there all day," added Mackenzie, in a tone that showed some of the contempt that he felt for that distinguished member of the Upper House.

"As I expected," replied Brotherton. "How the ass could think that a man like old Skirlaugh—as proud an old patrician as ever talked treason or spurned his betters for some silly conceit of pedigree —would accept him as a suitor for his daughter, passes my understanding."

"It was a fool's errand; but what you have mentioned was not the most foolish part of it. It might have been possible by some accident that the old man could have been talked round; but what chance would he ever have had with the girl herself? She's one of the handsomest lasses I ever saw; and I hear from those who know her that she has a strong will of her own, and that her father never contradicts her in anything. You may tell her character by the way she manages her horse. She sits him like a queen."

"Where have you seen her?" inquired the agent, surprised that Mackenzie should be able to speak in any part from personal knowledge.

"I've not been idle while you've been across the Humber. I picked up the acquaintance of the son of a certain Jacobite squire—Morley they call him—who lives at Scalhoe, about two miles over there. He thinks it rather a grand thing, I fancy, to know a friend of Lord Carlton's, and has shown me no end of courtesy. This very day he took me to see a duck decoy at—I forget the name of the place, it was his father's, and they've just sold it to old Skirlaugh. While we were on the bank of the pond, and he was explaining to me the uses of the nets and pipes, we heard horses, and up rode the old man, his daughter, and some more people. Like Moses, I was hidden quietly among the reeds, but had a good view of the whole party."

These remarks were probably made more for the purpose of introducing the name of Morley than to explain how Mackenzie had had the opportunity of beholding the lady. After a pause he added,

"Morley of Scalhoe is brother to the plotter, but he's a mere hard-drinking, sporting squire."

"Could you make out anything from his son of the man we want?"

"No, not a word. I touched on the subject once, but my companion, who is able to talk of nothing but dogs, horses, and such like, took fright. Thought for the moment I might be a spy, perhaps. But I've heard something important from another source. A despatch from London informs me that a letter, certainly from Marmaduke Morley, although in a clerk's hand, has been seized. It is to his daughter, the girl that's to marry young Skirlaugh. It says, if we can understand the old fox, that he's coming to Skirlaugh very shortly," said Mackenzie.

"Indeed! pray God we may trap him," ejaculated the agent, in a tone which was either the echo of his pious Scottish education, or one of the first fruits of that conversion which was slowly setting in. "What are your plans, Mr. Mackenzie?"

"To catch him myself, and get all the reward, or to bargain with you to help me, and go shares according to circumstances."

Brotherton gazed on his companion attentively, as if he did not understand him, but remained absolutely silent.

"I think I can catch him by myself, but I'm not anxious. I suppose you'd like it to be a co-partnery job?" continued the former speaker.

"Certainly," answered the agent.

"Well, then, let it be so ; but, mind, I mustn't be seen in it. Not directly, I mean. It may be my vigilance, and all that, which has brought it about, if you like, but not my hand that tightens the cord. I can't afford that, if I'm to share the prize with you."

Brotherton hesitated. He was willing to give any substantial aid he could in capturing the outcast, but shrunk with a natural horror from doing the deed himself. He had hoped that the fouler part of the work would fall to the lot of one so well accustomed to it, and that his share would be of a kind that could be kept in the background, hidden, except from his own conscience, and, perhaps, even glossed over there.

"Oh, you hold back, I see ; well, never-mind, we'll think no more of it then ; I'll do it all. You'll then be clear of all blame, and only lose five hundred pound. It's best, as we say across Tweed, for every old wife to wash her own foul clothes by her own midden," said Mackenzie, with an air of carelessness very well affected.

"I don't like it, I really don't, Mr. Mackenzie. I've no hesitation about the other job, though there's far more danger in it, but to get a man hanged like a dog just for so much money, makes me think I shouldn't be happy again. You know what the feeling is like. Don't you wish sometimes when you're in bed at nights, and the wind is moaning and sighing round about the house as it does just now, that you were clear of the hangings of forty-six."

"What a question to ask a man. Why, no, to be sure. Do you think I would go out of still water if I was afraid of being sea-sick? Come, come, you're tired and unsettled to-night, and hav'n't forgot the fright t'other night at the brick-yard. I shall begin soon to think you're as great a coward as most people are who think they see old Nick," said Mackenzie, gaily.

"As sure as I live, I did see him; and I would not have such another sight for all the blood-money in the secretary of state's keeping. Let's not talk of it to-night. I'll arrange with you by daylight. I don't like it now, I can tell you," answered Brotherton, in a tone which showed fear was contending with avarice.

"Well, well, you'll be all right in the morning, old fellow, I see; take another glass, and I'll join you just for old Scotch friendship and brotherly love, though my head would be the clearer without it."

The Highlander arose, and mixed the spirits for himself and his friend, continuing the conversation all the while.

"This is our plan, you see. The letter that has been stopped, had it reached its destination, would have given the Skirlaugh folks time to prepare for the fugitive, and then they would have baffled us. He would have been smuggled off into Yorkshire, Lancashire, or the devil knows where."

"Pray, don't talk about the devil now, Mr. Mackenzie," broke in the agent in a beseeching tone.

"Upon my word, Brotherton, who would have thought that you who always take upon yourself to lecture me for weakness when to please the peer I get drunk, could be so unnerved by a mere dream. Cheer up, man, or you'll be unfit for any action in this life more serious than robbing a hen-roost, or lagging a vagrant. As I was saying, if they knew he was coming, they would baffle us, and they might except him, even if the letter didn't reach them, so I've written a note in his style, as near as I can imitate it, and I don't think I've done it badly, to be given to his daughter. Can you get it conveyed to her by some safe and unknown hand? They're accustomed to get letters of this sort by all sorts of roundabout ways; here it is," and saying this, Mackenzie took the note from his desk, and handed it to Brotherton. The agent read it.

"I will take care she gets it. It will do exactly. Poor girl! I can't but feel sorry for her, poor thing;" and an expression that showed the man really meant what he said clouded for a moment the weaker schemer's face.

"Pshaw! who would have thought you were so weak. Why you never saw the lass in your life. Now I knew her well when she was a child, have played with her at ball and blind-man's buff, many a time when I've been staying in Cheshire with her uncle, Corbet, who was hanged. She used to call me, Uncle Kenneth, though I was no relation of theirs, and liked me, I fancy, better than any one has done since, or will do

again. But what's all that now but a thing to forget
or remember, just as it gives one the most pleasure.
When we were school lads at Auld Reekie, we used to
kill butterflies. You've played at Scotch and English.
We killed 'em for no fault of theirs, but just because
they were of the wrong colour. This is nothing more,
unless, indeed, there be, as I sometimes think there is,
a slight additional pleasure, just a touch of romantic
pathos, such as Shakespere writes now and then. I
really don't know that I shall not enjoy this hunt a
little more when I think of her grief, she'll do it so
beautifully. There's no acting like nature, man. Gad,
I think I can hear her speak. Shall I tell you what
she'll say ? "

"No, no !" ejaculated the horrified Brotherton,
appalled by his companion's utter heartlessness.

It would have given the Highlander real pleasure to
have enacted the scene, but he felt that if he went too
far in outspoken villany, he might lose a useful ally ; so
checking himself, he replied to the agent's thoughts
which had not yet clothed themselves in words.

"My good fellow, you have one fault, a very grave
fault it is. You are so tender hearted that you take
all these things as seriously as a felon does the condemned sermon. You don't know how very easily
they're borne by women. They haven't the tender
feelings we men have. To them it's almost nothing.
I've had much experience, have watched them carefully, and know all about it. Why, man, in this very
case, of which we're talking, there'll be a few tears;

the old man will hang like a dog, then a few more tears; she'll put on mourning, and put the wedding off a twelvemonth, then she'll marry this young Skirlaugh, who'll tell her he loves her the better for her suffering; they'll settle down hereabouts, and when the children can understand her, she'll talk to them of her martyred father just as coolly as we are now."

"Mr. Mackenzie, it's bed time; we'll talk of these things to-morrow," said the agent, rising and lighting his candle. The demon ride of a former night had made him peculiarly susceptible to spiritual impressions. He felt that the conversation of his companion was little short of fiendish. He closed the door, but re-opened it, only to put in his head and say, "I must have one word with you, on a matter which other business has put out of my head. We must hasten our work here. Lord Burworth told me to-day, that he was very anxious for his nephew's departure. If he learns who you are, you'll have to go at once."

"I suppose he'll be as bad as old Skirlaugh," said Mackenzie, jauntily.

"Pretty nearly. Good night," and so saying he closed the door. "There sits the deepest, cruelest ruffian living," thought he; "a hardened atheist, who has no more hesitation in murder than I have in the ordinary little rogueries of business. I have a very good mind not to help him to capture Morley, for his poor daughter's sake. The reward is a thousand pounds; I shall only get five hundred, but that, with the other eight hundred I have, and the sixty, and the forty, and—and—and—." He had spun a long line of figures ere he got to his bed-room ; and the spirit distillery, to which he looked forward as a haven of rest, stood in imagination before him. "I suppose I must do it," he said, as he began to undress, and yet I have half a mind not. I wonder if I went over to Skirlaugh to-morrow morning and told the Squire everything, whether it would not pay as well." The vision of that terrific potentate arose before him, obscuring the phantom distillery. He felt that come what might he dare not face a being so terrible in his ire, especially with a confession of the manifold wrongs which he was helping to plot.

Brotherton had called Mackenzie an atheist. How little we know of human nature. This hardened criminal, who was prepared for any outrage that could furnish him with money to spend in the gratification of his vicious passions, had a far fuller and deeper realisation of religion, that is, of the spirit world around us, and the future life beyond, than the wicked, but still in a sense conscientious Presbyterian. To Mackenzie the holiest and purest human feelings were nothing, or worse than nothing, a subject for jests of a nature that we cannot reproduce. He laid his plans of death for some, of life-long misery for others, with the deep deliberation of one to whom the atmosphere of sin was so habitual that he had got to take pleasure, such as hagiologists tell us the devils have in outraging the purest and noblest feelings of his victims. So long had he pursued this course, so carefully, almost tenderly, had he watched and schooled the emotions of his own mind, to fit it for his unholy work, that it is probable the pleasure he anticipated in handing over Marmaduke Morley to the gallows was in no slight degree heightened by dwelling on the agony which he knew would be thus caused to the pure-minded girl whom he hated for the very reason that she was pure, innocent, and beautiful. Such he was; we could add darker traits even than these if it were fitting to soil our pages with such morbid anatomy, and yet ere he retired to rest he knelt and said the old Catholic prayers he had learned in infancy at his mother's knee, seemingly without any consciousness of the foul blasphemy he was adding to his other crimes.

It is a strange thing this hatred of beauty and goodness, merely because they are good and beautiful. So strange is it that there are people who have lived long in the world and are not ignorant of some of its evil ways, who are unable to bring themselves to believe in its existence. The testimony of many a broken heart and many an early grave might be invoked to refute such benevolent scepticism.

CHAPTER XVI.

"Come, let's to dinner."
Henry the Fourth, Pt. II., act iii., s. 2.

"On painted ceilings you devoutly stare,
Where sprawl the saints of Verrio or Laguerre,
Or gilded clouds, in fair expansion lie,
And bring all Paradise before your eye."
Pope, Epist. IV. 143.

A DINNER-PARTY was a rare event at Skirlaugh
Manor. When, however, the Squire did make up his
mind to endure such an infliction, it was his habit to
do it in a very handsome manner. He was on this
occasion the more anxious that everything should go
off well, as he had a particular desire to show courtesy
to old Mr. Morley, a gentleman of, as Tom Hearne
would have said, thoroughly "honest principles," and
one who represented a decayed gentilitial family, for
which he had a great respect. Mr. Skirlaugh's reverence was confined entirely to the political principles
and pedigree of Mr. Morley, and by no means extended to that gentleman in his personal capacity.
Both the owner of Scalhoe himself and his sons, he re-

garded as bearish persons, who disgraced, by low pursuits and vulgar habits, the gentle name they bore. The fact, however, that Morley the elder was the brother of that Marmaduke Morley, of whom we have so often heard, and the uncle of Mary, the dear girl he loved almost as much as his own children, and who was soon to be his daughter-in-law, would alone have induced him to perform any act of politeness to him that did not entail much sacrifice of patience. There were other strong reasons why on the present occasion he should be as hospitable as possible.

One of his forefathers upwards of two centuries ago had sold off from the Skirlaugh domain a certain small estate which, after a variety of fortunes, had at last become vested in the Morley family. It was a cherished whim of the Squire to repurchase this fragment, and for twenty years he had been using all his eloquence with Mr. Morley to induce him to part with it. The old man, perhaps, feeling that as it was the only portion of his property not settled in strict entail, it was wise to keep it for some great emergency, had always rejected these offers. Now at length the emergency had come. His own careless husbandry of his resources and the extravagance of his sons had reduced him to the necessity of parting with the land He therefore naturally offered it to one to whom he was under many obligations, and whom he knew moreover to be so desirous of possessing it, that he was prepared to give more than its real worth. The object of or excuse for William Skirlaugh's visit had been to

bring over the title-deeds, which had long reposed in
the London office, and to see the conveyance executed.
Money there was not much to pay, for the Squire
had already advanced a considerable sum by way of
mortgage.

We need not detain our readers with an account of
the manner in which the conveyance was " sealed,
signed, and delivered." Nothing occurred to render
that formidable operation any way worthy of record,
except old Morley's discovery that he had left his
armorial seal at home, and that there was considerable
danger of the deed going down to posterity with the
office seal of the London firm impressed on the wax
instead of the rampant lion of his own ancient house.
The difficulty was a grave one, as he would certainly
have insisted in putting off the execution of the docu-
ment until a special messenger could have been despatched to and returned from Scalhoe, had not his
son Jim remembered that a similar seal was appended
to his own watch. As no other troubles impeded the
flow of business, we will at once adjourn to the apartment where the servants were engaged in setting out
the table and covering the sideboard with the contents
of the well-filled plate cupboard.

The dining-room occupied a considerable portion of
the eastern side of the house, the windows looking
into the Morning Pleasaunce. The furniture was
costly, and seemed to have been little used. The
high-backed walnut chairs, covered with green leather,
on which was stamped a rich gold pattern, might but

yesterday have come from the hands of their maker,
had not the change of fashion already given to them a
somewhat antique appearance. Over the chimney-
piece hung a fine picture of King Charles's general,
the gallant Earl of Lindsey, who fell at Edgehill,
said to be from the hand of Vandyck. All the rest of
the walls and the ceiling itself were covered by the
works of a far more prolific artist. Verrio, King
Charles II.'s favourite limner, had been employed to
decorate Burleigh House, in the south of the county,
and when that work was done had found time to come
somewhat further north for the purpose of painting
the new dining-room which Sir Ingram, the Squire's
grandfather, had just finished. If the knight were not
delighted, he was surely hard to please. Nothing in
unassisted nature, and but few things in applied art,
save the raw contents of a colour-shop, could excel in
brilliancy the works of the distinguished Neapolitan.
Sea-gods, sea-nymphs, cupids, satyrs, fauns, and demi-
gods sported among waves of the bluest ultra-marine,
wandered over endless marble staircases, or lolled on
banks whose vivid green surpassed nature's verdure,
as far as the sums of money that this tawdry craftsman
received for his works did the modest pay for which
Michael Angelo had been content to labour.

The room was seldom opened, except on occasions
like the present. Mrs. Skirlaugh thought its decora-
tions very lovely, and the Squire himself was by no
means ashamed of them, although he had a vague
sense that they were somewhat overdone; still, they

both preferred a smaller and less sumptuous apartment for the ordinary purposes of domestic life. Our
readers would, we are sure, pronounce the work abomi-
nable. The fashion, which is nicknamed taste, has
wandered far away from the showy and theatrical
mythologies of former times, and now disports itself
in doing honour to that kind of painting which its
admirers call photographs of real life, such as " Grandmother's Wedding-Day," or the " Footman in Repose."
If we are to be troubled by bad art, we are by no
means sure that the fleshy Venuses and thundering
Joves of Verrio are not more tolerable than the vulgar
imbecility which now insults us. He, poor fellow, did
his best to copy Raphael ; can their admirers tell who
certain painters of domestic scenes try to imitate ?
His gods and goddesses do bring to our minds, though
in no very pleasing manner, the beautiful mythology
which preceded the dawn of Greek civilisation. What
do the others suggest that any rational man or woman
would care to remember ?

Imagine that the dinner-hour has come, and behold
Mrs. Skirlaugh seated at the top of the table in a rich
brocaded white silk dress, ornamented with silver and
pink anemones, the train tucked up, and the petticoat
short enough to make her small feet, of which the good
lady was sufficiently proud, distinctly visible. On her
head arose an erection of hair, which, were we to
describe it, our lady readers, even those who rejoice in
chignons of the largest volume, would pronounce pre-
posterous. We will abstain, not from any dread lest

their feelings should be hurt by the satire which they
might think to be implied, but for fear that if we treated
the costume of the mother of Isabell irreverently, our
heroine should lose some of the regard that is her due.
On Madame Skirlaugh's right behold the elder Morley
—Squire Morley as he was called when Mr. Skirlaugh
was not present. A little man in plum-coloured coat
and green waistcoat, whose well-powdered, new-looking
wig made his very red face appear more fiery than on
ordinary occasions, when he wore his old one, which
was never powdered, except at the rare times when he
anticipated a visit from one of the neighbouring gentry,
or when he and his sons took a long ride, say to Doncaster, York, or Pontefract, for the sake of enjoying
the sports of the racecourse. His dialect, when he
spoke, showed that in early days he had had the training
of a gentleman, but that constant association with in-
feriors—mixing, indeed, on terms of familiar equality
with the small farmers and yeomen around—had so
confused his ideas of language that, despite his endeavours to talk gentle English, especially after the
punch-bowl had circulated, he constantly slipped into
the vernacular of North Lincolnshire. His wife sat
at the opposite corner to her husband, on the Squire's
right. She was a large, thin woman, with some
remains of personal beauty of the more homely sort.
Theirs had been a love match. Like many of the
lesser Roman Catholic gentry of that time, Mr. Morley,
when young, had found himself almost entirely cut off
from the society of his equals by those violent religious

prejudices which made a Protestant almost afraid to receive a Papist as a guest into his household. He had, therefore, not unnaturally sought for a wife in a rank beneath his own, and found one, if report said truly, in the person of a dairymaid. If that had been Mrs. Morley's original occupation, she was so far raised by marriage that now there was little difference in manner between the pair. Perhaps her more southern· dialect—she was a Warwickshire woman— might render it a little easier for her to avoid slips of the tongue. Her dress, though not so rich, was quite as fashionable as that of her hostess. The mass of hair with which she adorned her head was, perhaps, a little bigger, and the ears of wheat, poppies, and other ornaments which decorated it were several degrees more incongruous.

Jim and Dick, their two sons, who sat opposite to each other near the centre, were considerably rougher than their father. In personal appearance their mother's pattern seemed to have been followed ; that lady's taste was also probably to be seen in their bright blue coats, and large, deeply pocketed scarlet waistcoats. Dr. Chubb we have seen before ; he need not detain us further than to say that his dress was the usual professional light drab. His bright riding boots, a cross between the true jack-boots of the seventeenth century and the ugly top-boot of our fathers' days, showed that he felt he must not unbend so far as to be unprepared for a sudden exit, if needful. Mr. Tempest, the Catholic priest, a rather

fine-looking, somewhat florid man of about fifty, wore
a costume of dark brown, perhaps a little more sombre
than that usually worn by laymen, having about it no
mark of the clerical office, unless the absence of a
sword could be held in those days to indicate that he
belonged to a peaceful caste.

At a time like that of which we are speaking, when
the penal laws were in force, though their rigour had
been mitigated by the decay of the persecuting spirit,
it was not safe for a priest of the fallen Church to
indicate his profession by his dress.

Mr. and Mrs. Jordan alone require notice. They
were the only Whigs present, for the worthy Doctor,
though reputed to be lax in his religious notions, had
far too much regard for the health of his patients to
profess any opinions which might have a tendency to
shock delicate nerves. The parson certainly did
honour to his opinions as far as his own person was
concerned. He was by far the heaviest man in the
room; and if his large, inexpressive, grey eyes, broad
low brow, and full, wide nostrils could be taken as
adumbrations of the light within, was certainly not
deficient in that form of good taste which would make
him appreciate Mrs. Skirlaugh's culinary merits. His
wife was little, simpering, dark-skinned, and possessed
of a sharp, declamatory voice, which had been largely
cultivated by exercise; for her husband, as well as
discharging the light duties incumbent on him as Vicar
of Skirlaugh, Rector of Scalhoe, and Curate of East
Culverness and Gunnulby, kept a school for little boys,

and on his spouse fell many of the minor duties of
that irksome task. It is true she did not teach them
to spell, write, extract cube root, say *musa*, or hammer
out Cæsar. (Why should the very name of the greatest
of the Romans, we would ask in a parenthesis, have
been made hateful to the children of upwards of ten
generations, by associations with the birch and the
cane ? Brutus was content with murder; he would
have shrunk from mutilating the harmless trunk.
Schoolmasters and emperors might surely find in
Latin literature some less illustrious person — one
more nearly on a level with themselves—under whose
shadow to commit their barbarities.) It fell, however,
to Mrs. Jordan's lot to inculcate the equally difficult
lessons of face-washing, hair-brushing, shoe-scraping,
and the thousand other virtues which the three I have
selected so beautifully typify.

Let us suppose the party seated, and the dinner
begun. Would that we had the art of setting before
our readers, in language sufficiently exalted for the
occasion, an account of the good things of which it
consisted. Alas ! the power to call up so savoury a
vision from the forgotten past has been denied to us.
The talk flowed on in a dull ripple during the first
course. Soup and fish, though the latter were carp
from the Squire's own stew pond, were not found
strong provocatives of conversation. The roast beef
came at length, and when he saw it, the Squire's face
evidently brightened. Roast beef was not a particularly national dish in the old days, but in the last

century it had begun to be thought so. The faculty we all have of looking back with reverence to a past that never was a present, on this occasion gave Mr. Skirlaugh no little degree of pleasure. He was not a gourmand, but a man of his nature felt considerable delight in doing a peculiarly English act. He raised the silver-handled carving implements, and cut the meat with a sense of the awful importance of his office, little inferior to that felt by the Druid priests when they severed with their golden knives the sacred misletoe from its parent oak.

" Thank God, Morley, we've our old English roast beef left yet, whatever else we've lost. What with you Papists trying to force your fasts upon us, and the cursed Hanoverians with their turnips, beet, sour craut, and I know not what other abominations, a good, old-fashioned Englishman is like to go without eating altogether."

" The Whigs don't fast, at all events. The Vicar will testify to that," replied Mr. Morley, gazing at Mr. Jordan, who was consuming, at a very rapid rate, very large slices of the sacred food.

" Certainly not," said the gentleman appealed to after a rather long pause, which was quite needed to adapt himself for conversation. " Certainly not ; it was allowed at the Reformation as a condescension to Popery on the one hand, and fanaticism on the other, but was always opposed to the principles of the Es-tablishment. It went out of practice among genteel people—genteel Protestants, I mean, of course ; no

offence, I assure you, is meant, Miss Morley—after
the restoration. I myself always make a point of
preaching against it once a year—usually on Good
Friday."

"I shouldn't have thought your flock much addicted
to that form of sin. Do you preach from the text of
Dives and Lazarus?" asked Isabell.

The Vicar had no time for reply. He was, when
eating, slow of speech. Long before he was able to
begin his response the Squire broke in,—

"It's all very well, Bella, for our friend Jordan and
his brethren to preach against fasting, but their lords
and masters at Westminster make our poor folk fast
far harder than ever the Papists did. Trust a Whig
for going without his own dinner, when there's aught
in either his own or his neighbour's larder. Dives let
the poor beggar pick up the crumbs that fell from his
table: a modern Whig justice of peace would have
sent him in the custody of the parish constable for a
month's imprisonment in Wivilby Gaol. Eating is a
cardinal point of the Whig religion. If Billy the
Third had altered the Prayer-Book as he once threatened, there was to have been another article put in
about the virtue of it, to make up the round two score.
For a Whig to go without eating when he's able is as
unnatural as for a Papist to stint himself in the matter
of drink."

"Even your Church has never imposed a fast upon
drink, I believe?" said Mr. Jordan, inquiringly to the
Catholic priest.

"Certainly not," replied the ecclesiastic.

"And don't you know why?" continued the Squire. "I see you don't, so I'll tell you. I learnt all about it when I was in France. You see, when the Reformation began in that country, about half the nobility and country squires were on one side, and half on the other. They fought and tussled, burnt and hanged one another with the most Christian perseverance, but they didn't for all that seem much nearer getting matters settled. At length the news came that the Council then sitting at Trent was about to forbid the use of wine on fast days. 'Gad,' said the Papists to a man, 'if this is the game, we'll be shot if we'll burn another Protestant. Sooner than be docked of our wine, we'll swear by John Calvin and final perseverance.' The bishops and clergy were alarmed, took fright, like a blood-horse at a bonfire, and fled to the Pope and cardinals at Trent. They were only just in time; the decree had passed the Council, and only wanted the Pope's signature to make it perfect law. He was sitting in the vestry of the big church there with a pen in his hand, all ready dipped in the ink-horn. His name would have been scrawled at the bottom in another minute, when in rushed the French bishops and clergy. They didn't pull off their hats, or so much as say, 'It's a fine day, your Holiness,' but they swore great round oaths that if their wine bins were tampered with they'd have a bran new church and somebody else for Pope. Who it was to be they weren't agreed. Some were for our good Queen Bess,

others for Geneva Jack, and a few said that they
didn't want a Pope at all, but that every man should
do the infallibility for himself. Well, to cut a long
story short, the Pope got frightened. 'I begin to
see,' says he, 'there's a mistake somewhere. I was
only just thinking of what St. Paul said about it as
you came in. Although never Pope, he was a cardinal, high in the confidence of the Holy See. He was
dead for wine on fast days. It will never do for us
to set the example of going against authority. I'll
make it all right, but you know there should be some
slight acknowledgment, some little honorarium in
return. What do you say to a couple of pipes of the
best claret and a hogshead of champagne every Christ-
mas during our Pontificate ?' The bargain was struck.
The Pope got his wine as long as he lived, and so
pleased were the Papists with the result of their
mission, that on their return they burnt at the stake
five Calvinist preachers and seventeen women and
children as some small testimony of the devotion they
bore to the Holy See. You know this is true history,
Mr. Callis. Just give the authorities for it to show
my learning."

Mr. Callis replied that he did not remember having
met with any mention of the circumstances either in
Father Paul or Pallavicino.

"Then they've missed setting it down through some
confounded Jesuitry. Father Paul was general of the
Jesuits, you know. Mr. Tempest will back me in
that."

The priest seemed reluctant to support even so well known a truth by the weight of his authority.

"Ah, well," continued Mr. Skirlaugh, "the fault isn't all on the side of our natural enemies, the Papists; I wish it was. In the countries where they rule a man may eat as much as he likes, off a fast day, at a small cost, but here, thanks to the Vicar's friends, there's not a thing one wants to swallow that is not taxed. Come now, Jordan, you're fond of a dinner, man; what do you say to these new taxes? Why, there's not a thing on this table, unless it be the water, that's not made twice as dear as it should be by their confounded excise laws. Even the water doesn't escape, for, though it's free, yet they tax the things of which our pumps are composed."

Mr. Jordan was understood to say that the fault was not in his friends, who were necessitated to raise money to pay a standing army for the protection of the land against a foreign power. He carefully avoided mentioning by name either the Pope or the Pretender.

"Ah! so you kick the rightful master out of his house, and starve the old servants that you may find victuals for a lot of lazy, lubberly——" The Squire was continuing with singular eloquence in the same strain, when he was interrupted by his wife, who drew the attention of all by knocking with the butt-end of her fork on the table.

"Mr. Skirlaugh," said she, "we have laws here which you as sovereign have no right to break. What-

ever England may be, Skirlaugh Manor is a consti-
tutional monarchy; and one of the chief limitations of
the King's power is the ancient statute which enacts
that no one shall talk theology or politics at meal-
times."

" I stand corrected, madam," replied her lord in a
submissive tone. "I profess I won't so much as
mention God or the King any more to-day in the
presence of my faithful Commons, but will confine
myself entirely to the most opposite subjects—the Devil
and old Noll, for instance."

Mrs. Skirlaugh had gained her point. She had
broken a thread, which, though amusing enough to
some of the gentlemen, was not likely to tend to harmony. She had also succeeded in gaining some
share of attention for the ladies, whose voices had
hitherto been almost unheard. They had not been
quite idle, however. Miss Skirlaugh, with feminine
modesty, had almost entirely confined herself to a
pleasant *tête-à-tête* with her cousin, and Mrs. Jordan
had availed herself of the very good opportunity that
presented itself of getting some medical advice gratis
from the Doctor, who sat next her, by asking several
questions as to the new and very successful cure for
the ringworm which that eminent man had recently
introduced into the neighbourhood.

Near Jim Morley the wild ducks happened to be
placed, and upon him devolved the no easy labour of
dividing them into parts. Jim was not a good carver,
therefore Mr. Jordan, whose habits as a schoolmaster

made him particularly fond of giving advice, threw out
to him sundry hints and suggestions which the young
man did not take in such good part as he would have
done had he studied the manners of polite society with
the unremitting devotion which he bestowed on the
arts of the chase. He was heard to say he could cut
them up very well.

"I am glad to hear it, Mr. James," interposed Mrs.
Skirlaugh, addressing the carver with tender firmness
—"very glad to hear it, indeed; but pray don't say you
can 'cut up' a duck for the future. Such a process
cannot be performed. There are, as you should know,
separate words to distinguish what you call the cutting
up of each kind of game or bird. You say unbrace a
duck, unlace a rabbit, dismember a heron, thigh a
woodcock, rear a goose, allay a pheasant, and wing a
partridge."

Mr. James was profuse in his thanks, but expressed
a desire to know why one word would not do for all
kinds of carving. His teacher was prepared with a
judicious reply,—

"Suppose," said she, "you were invited to dinner,
and had but one dish set before you, you would think
your host a niggard, or the knowledge of the hostess
very imperfect. You will readily understand from your
own delight in the pursuits you follow that one-half of
the pleasure of anything we do consists in talking
about it. Now, if we havn't proper words to express
ourselves, much of that pleasure is lost. But do, Mr.
Jordan, let me give you a little of this hunter's

pudding. I am talking of the names of things, and forgetting the realities before me."

She helped the divine to a large portion, and then fell into a lively discourse with him as to puddings in general. Mrs. Jordan observed it, and felt that a time like the present might be improved in another direction.

"Perhaps, my dear, Mrs. Skirlaugh could tell us how cowslip puddings are made," said she in a loud voice from the other end of the table.

The whole room was attention, for none of the persons present, save the Jordans and Mrs. Skirlaugh, had ever heard of that delicacy.

"I can't tell you now, but I have a recipe for making them which answers admirably. My daughter, I think, will copy it out for you."

"Thank you a thousand times," said the divine, something very like emotion shining in his big grey eyes. "If I were to tell you of our many failures, of the domestic jars that have ensued thereon, I am sure you would sympathise with me. It was only last summer that several pecks of them were gathered by my boys and made into puddings—rowly-powlys, with very rich crust; but when they came to table no one could eat them. I don't know when I have been so much disappointed. I had quite looked forward to it as a little treat. I had eaten them years ago at the Earl of Hembleton's, and have longed to taste them again ever since I lived in the country."

CHAPTER XVII.

"How does the fowler seek to catch his game
By divers means ?   All which one cannot name :
His gun, his nets, his lime twigs, lights and bell :   .
He creeps, he goes, he stands ; yea who can tell
Of all his postures ? "

John Bunyan.

THE advent of a large silver punch bowl was the signal for the ladies to retire, and the gentlemen to draw round the hearth.

" The embargo's off now, and we can talk politics. I've a host of questions to ask anybody who has got news to tell about the forthcoming election. Who knows whether we are really to have a contest, or whether the Whig Squire means to draw in, and save the expense of a fight ?" asked Mr. Skirlaugh.

" I'm sure it will come to a poll. I have had a communication, only this morning, from one of the most influential Whigs in the county, who, after urging me to bring up every voter over whom I have any influence, says it was positively arranged last Tuesday, at a meeting at the White Hart at Lincoln, that our side should fight to the last.   You, Mr.

Skirlaugh, know what the Tories are prepared for
better than I can profess to do," said the clergyman,
with the air of one who had exclusive information.

"Not a bit, my dear sir; I take no interest in the
silly child's play we call politics now. If our quarrels
could be fought out with pike and gun, as we used to
do, and shall, I hope, do again, then I should know
what to make of it; but I'm quite out of place in
your electioneering intrigues. Besides, it doesn't
matter to men like me the value of a sixpence whether
the Whig Squire goes to London avowedly to support
the existing power, or the Tory goes not avowedly for
that end, when we all know that Whigs and Tories
alike will sell their country for a tag of ribbon to hang
in their waistcoat button-holes, or a fine new handle
to stick before their names. For old friendship's sake,
I shall tell such of my people as are freeholders to go
for the Tory; but, for any other reason, I don't care
the crack of a pistol which has it. I doubt if I shall
be at the trouble of going myself to see the fun. I've
seen men with flags in their hands, and heard trumpets
blow, when the silk and the noise meant something,"
said the Squire.

The whole party, except William and the clergyman, expressed sorrow and surprise at Mr. Skirlaugh's
implied decision.

" You must show yourself there, Squire," ejaculated
the elder Morley, who actually paused in the serious
occupation of helping himself to a second tumbler of

punch for the purpose; "you must, indeed. The Kesteven people will think you've deserted the cause, if you stay away."

"And suppose they do—what then? They know that I am ready enough to support it if there's any-thing to be done; but I can't vote if I do go. They'll tender me the oath," answered Mr. Skir-laugh.

"Yes; but your presence will be worth fifty votes. It will bring over a host of shilly-shally people, who'll go the other way if you don't show. Half the poor creatures our parson here takes with him, when they see the Squire there a lookin' at 'em, and may be axing after their wives and daughters, darn't, for very shame, vote agen the land. Why, half their fathers have been bred and born under you, and the rest have pouched hares and rabbits, let alone deer, wild-ducks, and salmon many a time," said Morley, in a tone which showed how anxious he was that the Squire should honour the Lincoln saturnalia with his presence.

"Besides," said Jim, following, as in duty bound, his senior's lead. "Besides, half your folks won't go if they don't think you care about it. And then we want you to talk to some of our own people about getting the penal laws off, and to know if we can't persuade you to subscribe to the Lincoln races. If there was a Skirlaugh Cup there, Mr. Tafferton says, they'd be as good as Doncaster, and better."

"Oh, I see! Then it isn't that you care for the cause, as you call it, or for the penal laws; but that you want to get a quiet, homely man, who has no spite against anybody's life—no, not even a German elector's—to give his money to encourage the gentle art of neck-breaking. No, Jim; if old friendship won't drag me there, you'll not draw me by such silly gear. If gentlemen thought as seriously for six months of the condition of the country, as they do about racing and birding, we should be soon all of a mind again."

"Lord Burworth has given fifty guineas," said Dick, with some hesitation.

"Has he? Now, you see how it is; those folks who want to keep us in slavery know the weak side of such men as you. They know, while your heads are full of horses and dogs, there'll be no room for king and country. I wish, for my part, what you call sport was all at the devil."

"It may be soon," ejaculated Jim. "He was seen here in the wood not a week since."

"Nonsense! What old woman's tale have you got hold of?" interposed the priest, unwilling to see one of his flock make an ass of himself on so serious a subject.

"It's as true as the gospel, Mr. Tempest; I had it from a man, who had it from the very person to whom he appeared. It's a real true story. He got on his horse behind him, and rode I don't know how far," reiterated the last speaker.

"It's all moonshine, man. Why, I've been in that wood at all hours of day and night, and never seen

anything worse than myself," interposed his father, as
if anxious to stop the conversation.

"Well, I don't know what you call nonsense ; but
Mr. Tafferton, Lord Burworth's great friend, who is
down with him shooting at Brakenthwaite, told me
that Mr. Brotherton, his lordship's agent, was here
five or six days since, that he left just when it was
dark, and that he'd no sooner gotten into the wood
than all the boughs began to sigh and sough, just as they
do before a thunder-shower ; and that the devil himself jumped on behind the fellow, and hugged him fast
in his arms ; the horse galloped away, and he would
sure enough have been carried straight to hell if the
girths had not broke. He was found next morning,
with a strange smell of brimstone on his clothes, as
dazed as though he'd been drunk."

Mr. Skirlaugh listened attentively. He believed
the whole story to be mere fiction, as he had no idea
that Mr. Brotherton had been a visitor at his mansion.
The interest of the anecdote to him consisted entirely
in the fact that he thought he discovered, under the
name of Tafferton, the person whom the world knew
as Mackenzie.

"You know who this Mr. Tafferton, your informant,
is, I suppose, Jim ?" said he.

"Oh yes, sir. A very great friend of Lord Burworth's. He's to be made a lord soon. He's a Protestant himself, but is a great friend of the Catholics ;
and is here now partly to consult Lord Burworth about
taking off the penal laws."

"Indeed! Now, I may be wrong, but I have a very strong suspicion, not far removed from certainty, that this fellow's name is not Tafferton. He's a tall, powerful man, rather spare and pale—is he not?"

Jim admitted that the description was exact.

"I believe he is no other than the person who called here with Lord Carlton, a few days back. I am well acquainted with that man's history. His reasons for being here are not what you suppose; and I don't for a moment believe that Lord Burworth would have him in his house for an hour if he knew who he was. I have good reasons for keeping what I know of him secret for the present, for if I told you what I know you would be more likely to commit some foolish act of violence, than to listen to such a man's gossip, which, I doubt not, has been manufactured with some knavish intention."

Jim sank into abashed silence. He was in the habit of deferential obedience to the Squire; but was not by any means satisfied that his new friend was such as that gentleman had suggested.

The break was satisfactory to the giver of the entertainment.

"Gad! the punch is all done," said he; "and we've no time for more, if we're to see any sport to-night. Now then, hats and great coats for the lay-men, and the drawing-room for the parsons. Hillo! are you lay or cleric, Chubb?"

The doctor expressed his desire to join the ladies.

"Then tell them that when we are coming to White

Cross Garth I'll send a boy to let them know, so that they may come into the Pleasaunce to see the end of the fun. Now then, off we go."

And off the whole party set, in the direction of the kitchen court, where a large body of servants, with nets and the other necessaries for the sport, were already arranged, employing the time they had to wait in consuming cans of beer and hunches of bread and cheese.

The "generall manner of taking of land-fowle by night, in champayne countryes, is with the lowbell," saith Gervaise Markham, a man once of great authority in field sports. The custom of netting partridges has become so entirely a practice confined to poachers, that we fear we shall experience considerable difficulty in making our readers believe that, little more than a century ago, it was not only a recognised way of capturing game for the use of the table, but also a very popular amusement, in which not only the sportsmen themselves joined, but almost all the little boys and idle men of the neighbourhood. It may be briefly described as sweeping the stubble fields with a long and very broad net, during the progress of which a deep-toned bell was rung at intervals, for the sake of creating a noise terrible to the birds. The flames of cressets, burning tow attached to long sticks, torches, and all other means of making a blaze that could be thought of, were freely resorted to as an additional means to terrifying the game into repose.

The Squire led the way, down the very lane where

Brotherton had had his fearful ride ; but no evil spirit
molested him or his friends. The stubble fields in
which the sport was to be carried on were near the
wood. For a short time a death-like silence reigned.
It was a necessary precaution that no noise should be
made until the " engines " were ready for action.
When the net-pullers were arranged in proper order,
and the net itself spread out, the low bell, in the
hands of Mr. Robert Drury, began to toll deeply—at
the rate of about six strokes in a minute. This was
the sign for the netters to move on. At the same time
all the cressets and flambeaux blazed out with a flood
of dusky flame. William had, we much regret to say,
little of the sportsman in his nature ; but the novelty
of the scene, and the lurid beauty of the small portion
of the landscape that was visible to him, was very
charming. He did not regard the poor birds either
from the point of view of the sportsman or the
epicure ; but there was something strangely attractive
to him in this picturesque way of taking them.

    Jim and Dick were in ecstacies ; but they had work
to do which prevented them from giving way fully to
their delight. The rabble gathered together on such
occasions was great. They were, it is true, most of
them the children of the Squire's people ; but it by no
means followed that their ideas of the feudal homage
due to that person would have prevented them from
running over the net when in motion, or gratifying their
uriosity to " hev' a look at th' bods," by opening the
hampers and thus letting the captured fowl escape.

When not engaged in withstanding the impetuosity of
the mob, they both at once poured into William's ears
their extreme delight at the sport that had been provided for their edification. Jim "would bet anybody
anything that nobody this side Lunnun had so many
partridges as Squire Skirlaugh." Dick was quite sure,
if they had, nobody except himself understood how to
capture them half so well. It was a strange thing to
him that the Squire, who knew more about such things
than anybody in the whole country side, should care
for them so little. They had hardly satisfied themselves with shouting out their pæans on the capture of
one covey, ere the net paused again, and they had the
delight of seeing another family of birds consigned to
one of the wicker cages that had been prepared for
their reception. William gave attentive ear to their
talk, partly because he took a lively interest in
varieties of character, and partly because he thought
it right to be as agreeable as he could to Mr. Skirlaugh's guests. This little courtesy, almost unthought
of on his part, raised the listener much in the young
men's estimation. The vulgar follower of field sports,
however stupid he may be, has generally some conception that his tastes are lower than those of cultivated people, and is, therefore, usually not a little
pleased when such persons seem to enjoy his conversation. There is a sort of ignorance which puffeth
up; but, happily, among such persons this is com-
paratively rare. They usually fall into the other
extreme, and are but too apt to give to gentle manners

and out of the way knowledge greater honour than is their due.

Several fields were netted in this way. The cages were rapidly filling, the torches becoming fewer, and the time running on. The master of the game ordered his people to their last field, the White Cross Garth. It was at the eastern end of the Pleasaunce, and communicated with that place by a gate. A sunk fence, and a low yew hedge, cut off one from the other. To reach this garth the road had to be traversed for perhaps a couple of hundred yards, when the stile of a footpath presented itself. Squire's Bob led the posse, with one solitary beacon boy trotting by his side to show a light. On the stile sat a little, old man, with a pair of bagpipes under his arm. Seeing the procession come near he begun to play a low, melancholy tune, then well known, which was a great favourite of the common people.

"Houd yer noise, Charlie, ye fool; we're bod-catchin'—you'll scare 'em," shouted Drury, ere he reached him.

The music ceased, and the little man crouched into a corner, evidently afraid he had offended that important personage.

"It's all right, Charlie, I'm not mad wi' yer; but ye mon't skirl now, or ye'll scare the partridges up. We've just done, then we'll hear yer, and gi' ye a bit o' supper maybe," said the groom, patronisingly.

The musician slunk into the procession, immediately behind Bob. Though White Cross Garth was but a small inclosure, several coveys of birds were found therein; but the Londoner, attracted either by the charms of the music in prospect, or by some other lower motive, deserted his companions, and, entering the gate, joined the ladies and clerics in the garden.

The old man, whose singular figure he could now see more clearly, stood immediately outside the fence, with his instrument of music ready for immediate action when called upon.

"Who is that odd-looking man?" he asked of Isabell. "A Scotchman, I suppose, by his bag-pipes?"

"No; he's a Lincolnshire man. Did his pipe make you think him a Scot?" inquired she.

"Yes; I never heard of bagpipes out of the land of cakes. All the pipers we have in London say they're Scotchmen."

"That is because Londoners don't think anything worth having unless it comes from some place a long way off. The bagpipe is our native music, the only one our people play, and the only kind they much care to listen to. When my father was a child, every village had its piper; there are now few of them left. The religion of the common people makes them dislike music."

"I should imagine, by his readiness to perform his part in the amusements of the evening, that the old man is well known here," continued William.

"As well as I am myself. He lives, if he can be said to have a home at all, in a hut on the moors, between this place and Scalhoe; but really principally in the kitchens and stables of Skirlaugh, Brackenthwaite, and a few other such places. Charlie is a necessity of the neighbourhood. We could no more do without him than without our chaplain," replied she.

" Our functions are different, Mr. William ; but you will find that wherever the clerical order is respected, the art of music has been held in honour. The churchwardens of former times, ere Puritanism had trampled on the hearts of the people, were wont to charge regularly in their accounts for the payments they made to pipers for amusing the villagers," said the Nonjuror.

" Bagpipes are instruments of ecclesiastical music at this moment in Italy," added Mr. Tempest.

" One of the great angels in the choir at Lincoln is playing on a bagpipe, and on a stall on the north side of the chancel in Boston church there is a jesting sculpture of a bear playing on an organ, a pig on the bagpipes, and a dog accompanying them on a drum," continued Mr. Callis, glad to give the conversation an antiquarian turn.*

" As we have such good authority for it, I will ask the old man to play," said Isabell. "I should have liked to give him that pleasure at first, but dreaded that I might be charged with frivolity by my superiors."

Mrs. Skirlaugh, the only superior who was likely to thwart Isabell's wishes, made no sign of objection;

---

* The Reverend gentleman might have directed his friend's attention to the angel playing on this instrument sculptured on the corbel over the last column at the west end of the north aisle of Holy Trinity Church, Hull.

so Charlie was invited into the garden, and began to pour forth his sad, monotonous ditties, to an audience far more refined than those before whom he usually practised his art.

"Do you like it?" asked Isabell, in an under tone.

William hesitated. He did like it very much, but "feared the people." He hesitated to say that he was pleased with that which he thought she, like most other so-called cultivated people, would consider barbarous.

"Oh, I see, you, like the rest of the world now, have an ear for music, and despise these uncultivated strains. Now I, who am happy enough to-have none, really enjoy this far more than most of the music I have heard in London; and, really, almost as much as the organ at Lincoln Minster," continued the lady.

William hastened to assure his cousin that it was only fear of uttering an unpopular opinion, that made him hesitate to avow similar feelings.

"I am exceedingly delighted that you are on my side here, for the Morley people—not Mary, of course—persecute the old man, as they do Bessie, the tanner's daughter. If they see you like his music, I should not wonder if it made them more humane to him. You are a great favourite with Jim already: he took the trouble to come into the garden before the sport begun in the field, to whisper your praises in my ear."

The sport was now over. Mr. Skirlaugh and his party came to the gate. The hampers were opened; a sufficient number of the finer birds retained for home use and to be given away to the guests, and the rest turned out among the long stubble. Two men were told off to watch the field during the night, for fear some of the lookers-on should be tempted to return and pick up the frightened birds, who would not regain the wonted use of their faculties till daylight came.

"Stop that din, Charlie," said the Squire, in the middle of a tune. "The gentlemen are just going, and you'll frighten their horses if you skirl now."

This was a hint intended for the guests, as well as the musician. The latter did not pause at the moment, thinking, we imagine, that his duty to the ladies imperatively required him to finish the tune. Mr. Skirlaugh was a man who was used to his commands being instantly obeyed.

"Silence, man!" shouted he; "or I'll cut a hole in that confounded bag, and let all the tunes out at once; or take it from you altogether, and give it to their fine new church at Gainsburgh

> 'to make the great organs roar
> And the little pipes squeak higher
> Than ever they squoke before,'

as the song says."

The terrified old man slunk away out of the Squire's sight, among the bushes; and the party moved onwards to the house.

William had hoped for the pleasure of escorting
Isabell through the mazes of the garden, but was
hindered by Jim, who was again vehement in
his praises of her cousin, whom he averred to be
" one of the pleasantest, freest gentlemen" he had
ever seen in his life, " let alone a Londoner, who are
generally strange high fellows." As a mark of his
extreme approbation of William's good qualities, he
asked Isabell if she thought he would like to see the
Northolme duck-decoy; because, if he would, there
was nobody on earth, as he assured her, who was so
well able to expound its mysteries as himself. Miss
Skirlaugh was of opinion that the said cousin would
be pleased by a sight thereof; so Jim at once hurried
to make arrangements with William for a visit to that
place on the morrow.

During the whole time the party were in the garden
—nay, almost ever since those of the clerical order
had joined the ladies in the drawing-room — Mr.
Jordan and his wife had been in the closest attendance on Mrs. Skirlaugh, hearing her, and asking her
questions on the whole circle of the gastronomic
sciences. That lady, though proud of her attainments
in these high branches of human knowledge, was not
a little fatigued by the catechising she had to undergo,
and heartily wished for some of her husband's political
or religious personalities, in exchange for this vapid
talk. As a judgment, no doubt, for sins of a like kind
on her own part, no relief was afforded her, for the
priest, the nonjuror, and Mary were too courteous to

R 2

interfere; and Isabell enjoyed the retribution too much to think of rendering assistance. As they walked up the garden the two persecutors still stuck to their victim.

"I have really often thought we were very deficient in the uses we make of even the commonest things. Seed cakes and light cakes are the only changes we can have from commonplace household bread. Now, I have heard that in France there are seventeen kinds of hot cakes that are eaten at breakfast," said the Vicar.

"Some are eaten with wine, some with meat, others with eggs, others with fruit," interposed his spouse.

"The Marquis of Luddington told me, that when he was there, it was usual to have for breakfast a delicious, thin, octagonal cake, which was specially made to be eaten with grapes. Neither he nor his valet, unfortunately, could tell me how they were made. I have no doubt you know, Mrs. Skirlaugh?" continued the divine.

"I never heard of them," said the jaded lady; "but here comes my husband, who will, no doubt, know all about it. My dear, our friends are very anxious to know if the French make eight-sided cakes, and eat them with grapes at breakfast?"

"Yes, of course, they do. I've eaten them often enough," replied the gentleman addressed.

"Oh, would you tell us how they are made?" exclaimed husband and wife at once.

"I would if I could, but, you see, I'm not a cook;

all I know is, that they are, as Rabelais says, heavenly eating, *viande céleste ;* but he doesn't tell how to make 'em, he confines himself to their effects ; but, now I remember, Father Tempest is sure to know all about it, for *La vie de Gargantua et de Pantagruel* is a class book in all the theological colleges in France. No man can be ordained priest unless he has shown himself able to explain all the allusions there. You should ask him, by all means."

Mr. Jordan's learning was confined to English and the classics. He therefore rushed off at once to the Catholic priest, confidently hoping to learn from so well drilled an authority all that he wished to know.

Mary walked up the garden alone, behind the rest. The old piper had often been intrusted to bring her letters from her father. These precious documents were in the habit of reaching England by various unsuspected routes. Their first receivers would send them on, as opportunity offered, to the next Jacobite household that was in her father's confidence ; and so, by a roundabout method, they would at last reach the anxious daughter. The last stage of their journey was usually performed about the person of Piping Charlie. The poor old fellow had no politics, little feeling of any kind beyond that which attached him to his gentle art, and to the persons who patronised him ; but he was thoroughly to be trusted. His appearance so late in the evening made her almost certain that he had a missive for her. She was not mistaken. As she passed a tall holly, the old man came from his hiding-place, and, drawing from his inside waistcoat-pocket a dirty-looking billet, put it into her hand, saying, as he did so,—

"I'm not clear sure it's all right, my lady. It was gi'n to me by a man I never seed afore."

CHAPTER XVIII.

" He hereth the melodyous armony of fowles ; he seeth the yonge swannes,
hecrons, duckes, cotcs, and many other fowles weyth theyr brodes."

The Boke of St. Albans.

JIM MORLEY was prompt in fulfilling his engage-
ment. Ere breakfast was over that gentleman appeared at the Manor in full sporting costume, armed
with a very long fowling-piece, and accompanied by
two yellow and white setters. Great was his disappointment at finding that William intended only to
accompany him to see the sights he had to show. He
had vainly hoped that he might have been induced to
join actively in the sport of the season, and was with
difficulty made to understand that his new friend,
having no property qualification—that is, a hundred a
year in real estate, and not being the son of a lord or
lady of a manor, nor a gamekeeper by the appointment of such a dignitary—it was contrary to law for
him to enjoy the sports of the field except as a looker-
on. The Squire endeavoured to help him out of the
dilemma by offering to make him his gamekeeper for
the season, but to this the Londoner objected, not

from any feeling of pride, for such a means of evading
the law was then a commonly recognised practice, but
because the amusement of shooting had few attractions
for him, and he was glad of a dignified excuse for
evading it.

Their route lay across hedge and ditch in a southerly
direction.

Although William had little delight in the sport, the
excursion was a pleasant one. The walk opened out
an entirely new country to his view, and he found his
companion very entertaining. " A little of such people
goes a long way," as an artist once remarked to us
about the conversation of a certain farmer who had
been discoursing to him for a couple of hours on short-
horns, Mr. Swinburne's verse, the price of corn, the
end of the world, and the evils of reform in parliament. But until one tires of it the conversation of a
thorough sportsman, if he be well master of his subject, is a most amusing change to a man from the non-
sporting world.

Jim was a good talker in his own homely fashion,
and although his mind was as blank as that hackneyed
sheet of white paper which John Locke, gent., was the
first person to introduce to the British thinking public,
on all other subjects of human interest, yet on the
questions which the 'Sportsman's Dictionary' and the
'Racing Kalendar' treat of, he was a thorough profi-
cient.

It was interesting to watch such a man, to see the
artistic way in which he handled his fowling-piece as

if *she* were a thing endowed with life, to observe the perfect training of his dogs, and the masterly manner in which, ere entering it, he surveyed each stubble-field, holt, and dingle.

There are not many things more strange than the power of the human mind to resist knowledge on points which are not attractive to it. A man may have been the keeper of a picture gallery for fifty years, and still not know the difference between a Titian and a Teniers; may have lived all his life with a talkative metaphysician, and not learned to distinguish between noumena and phenomena, or accident and substance; may have warmed himself by coal fires ever since he could run, and never perceived any difference between the produce of the Welsh and the Yorkshire coal-fields; or, what is perhaps the strangest of all, may have dwelt for years in a place rich in the grandest associations of the past—Rome, Aachen, or Oxford—and yet know no more of it than some poor wanderer—say a Cooke's excursionist—who has run wild therein for a few hours. Here was a man to whom not only the outer world was a blank, but all that part of his own world which was not immediately connected with slaughter. He knew the habits of every game-bird from the heron to the snipe, with an almost perfect knowledge, just so far as was necessary for him to do, that he might kill them, but not a jot further. The very idea of there being any interest in observing the wild things that God has made for their own sakes, was quite beyond his understanding. So, too, the grass of the fields, the heather, and bracken were familiar to him; he could tell by the tints of the one and the curve of the other where he was most likely to find his prey at morn, noon, or evening; knew that the partridge delighted to sun itself on sandy slopes where the wild thyme and yellow-lady's-bedstraw flourish ; that the heron only frequented the river flats at the fall of the tide, and varied his visits daily with the regularity of the moon itself; that the pheasant is particularly attached to such coverts as possess a tangle of briars among the undergrowth. But this knowledge had not in the slightest degree lighted up his soul, or given him one feeling of sympathy for, or unselfish interest in, the things around him.

Jim's conversation was not only entertaining because it dealt with these things, but because in its way it was so perfect. Most of us spoil our talk by laboured endeavours after variety, or by the natural changeableness that indicates we have no fixed ideas. His never varied. Its text was always slaughter, its objects, or its instruments, except when it diverged to certain amusements that are confined to cruelty, and do not necessarily include death. The local, genealogical, and political gossip of the Squire abounded with anecdote. His tales were often introduced, not as illustrations, but as good things in themselves. With Jim it was very different. He had little more idea of a joke than the deputation of a Missionary Society has. When he told a tale, as he sometimes did, it was as a mere example, which, however tragic or comic, was not repeated for its jocosity or its pathos, but used solely as an exemplar, like the shreds of verse and prose in a Latin Syntax: introduced, not for its own sake, but as an illustration of some truth he was anxious to bring down to the level of his hearers' understanding.

Decoys for taking wild ducks are rare things in England; so we can imagine that some of our readers will be offended when we tell them that, after serious deliberation and after having consulted our wife and daughters, as well as two other persons whose positions give them peculiar advantages for knowing the popular taste of the day—one is a fashionable West End hairdresser, the other a curate in large practice at a well-known inland watering-place—we have come to the conclusion that it is better to leave out of the present chronicle the full and particular description of the same, which Mr. James Morley gave William Skirlaugh. We are sorry that we have been compelled by the advice of our counsellors to make this sacrifice, but the subject, to do it justice, required a long chapter; and those judicious monitors had before their eyes the terrors of the publisher and the reviewers,—awful judges,—whom the poor author, carried away by his microscopical regard for accuracy, is apt to forget until his manuscript suffers from the shears of the one, or his printed pages from the merciless justice of the other.

The Northolme decoy had been formed on a small flat piece of land that lay by the side of a tiny runnel of water. Here had been excavated a pond, much in the shape of that singular object known now as the Three Legs of Man, once the cognizance, if we may use an armorial term so far out of chronological order, of the Isle of Sicily. The centre part was open water, the legs from the feet to the knee, to carry on the simile, were enclosed by network. The side of the hill and the flat around was covered by a dense coppice of alder, birch, hazel, and elder; on the more moist parts grew a dense forest of reeds.

This place, secluded as it was, lay within a few furlongs of Northolme Hall, the purchase which had been conveyed to Mr. Skirlaugh by Mr. Morley the day before. Here our friends lunched. While they are thus engaged we will spend a few lines in the description of a place which we may again be called upon to visit.

Northolme Hall, as it was called from being the only house of any pretension in the parish, for it was not a true Hall, never having had a manorial franchise attached, stood away from the mud cottages, four or five farm-houses, and Norman church, which composed the village, a short quarter of a mile. A little valley lay between, through which a nameless brook found its way to a somewhat bigger streamlet, whose waters in flood time almost reached the dignity of a river. The house seemed to have been built early in the reign of Henry VIII., or perhaps during the rule of his father. It had little of distinctive architectural character about it. Originally, like most houses of

the time, in which people of the upper classes resided,
it had formed three sides of a square. The eastern
wing had disappeared. The centre, consisting of hall
and drawing-room, remained, and on the west a large
range of kitchen offices, two of which had in
more modern days been converted into parlour and
dining-room. As originally constructed, it had been
built of stone up to the floor of the first story; all
above that had been made up of oak rafters, with
pargetting between the open panels. The roof was
covered with large flat tiles, but here as elsewhere
restoration had not been improvement. When repairs
were wanted the place of the old covering had been supplied by the modern hollow tile, which we have so un-
happily imported from Flanders. The result was, that
the roof presented a patched and unsightly appearance.
The windows of the lower rooms were of stone and
strongly barred with iron. It had probably not occurred
to the builders that persons wishing to attack the
house might furnish themselves with ladders, for
those of the chambers above were spacious, though
their size had been increased, in many instances, at
the expense of their gracefulness, by sawing out the
Gothic tracery which once ornamented their heads,
and the oak mullions that had supported it. The
small garden was mostly devoted to culinary vegetables. A large weeping willow grew on a lawn in what
had once been the court in the centre of the building,
and a few gay flowers bloomed beneath the parlour
window. This latter garden was cut off from the

home-field—it was not a park, and had never risen
to the dignity of being called one—by a row of white
pales, and from the kitchen domain by an ivy-clad
wall. The whole place looked cold, damp, and de-
solate. A dignity not its own was lent to it by the
shadow of two enormous ash trees and a few walnuts,
and sycamores of lesser, but still of large, growth.

The refreshment was soon consumed. As they
set out on their journey homewards, William vainly
endeavoured to learn from his companion something
of the history of the place; but he found that he
knew nothing and cared less, and that therefore the
only way of continuing their pleasant chat was to
let Jim take the lead and discourse on some of the
branches of his one subject. Their homeward
course lay mostly through grass fields where there
was little game, so the sportsman was able to give his
whole soul to the theory of his art. He even went so
far as to surrender his birding-piece into the hands of
the game carrier, while he illustrated with bits of stick
and his pocket-knife the proper way of making the
stop-catch of a gun-lock, an improvement which he
had never seen, but which he was certain would
answer. The method then in use he averred to be
not only highly dangerous, but what was of far greater
consequence, singularly awkward. He had not only
known of men who had shot their friends or keepers
by accident through its failing to act, but had seen sad
effects arise from its acting when it should not. He
had twice himself missed beautiful shots with this his

favourite gun "Ben Rayner" during the present season,
and he was, as he assured William, and as might be
readily perceived, a most careful man.

Following his lead, his companion remarked that he
believed most of the bad shooting so prevalent arose
more from carelessness than sheer want of ability.

"Well, I don't know that," replied Jim. Now,
there's my brother Dick, as careful a fellow as I am; a
man that never misses a shot through any hurry or
bustle, that's always up to the mark and never before
his time; yet he can't knock 'em over as I can; and
then there's the Squire, a man who's got some of the
finest shootin' in Lincolnshire, but who doesn't care a
toss about it, perhaps doesn't go out six times in the
season, and when he does go handles his gun like a
hay-fork; yet when he does fire I think he's a deader
shot than I am myself. I like going out with him; it's
a real pleasure to see the birds fall, but I'm always
afraid I shall be fallin' myself, too, some day through
him."

"Do you mean he is careless with his fowling-
piece?" inquired William.

"Careless! I don't know what you call it. It's as
bad as being in a battle to be within forty yards of him,
for a gun in his hands is tied to bring down summut.
Why, I'll tell you a trick of his. I was out with him
only a week or two before you came. We were rabbit-
shooting at Askham Elder Woods, a place full of sand
hoes. Well, there was a smuice through the hedge
just again' where I was stan'in', and I stooped

down to look through it, with my feet wide apart so"—and the sportsman put himself in position for the purpose of illustrating his narrative. "Well, just as I was lookin', a hare came and sat down about twenty yards off, just opposite. I was raising my gun to fire when I seed all the sod between my legs plewed up, and heard the Squire's gun go bang. I thought I' was shot, but it happened all the corns had gone straight between my two feet, but just where they'd have been if I'd been stood as I was a minute before. Od, says I, Squire, you've near done for me this time. If you'd nobut been three foot higher, it would have been a strange good thing for Dick. Well, do you know he laughed as if he'd done a clever trick, and said he always shot straight, but he didn't mean her to go off then, but while he was thinking of sum'ts else, he'd just pressed his finger on the trigger."

"You must find the pleasure of shooting with Mr. Skirlaugh much diminished by the danger, if this be a fair specimen," remarked his interested listener, with singular want of sportsmanlike tact.

"Not a bit. You see he's such a grand fellow to talk to; he's not only a real gentleman, and that's a good deal to a man like me, but he and all his family are the best folks in the country. Why, look at Miss Isabell; she's fit to be a queen; and then there's Mary, my cousin; you couldn't think, to see her and hear her talk, that she was aught akin to us. That's all through livin' wi' them. If she'd been my sister instead of cousin, and lived at Scalhoe instead

of Skirlaugh, she'd ha' been no more fit to marry
Mr. Ralf than I should be for Miss Isabell. I don't
know how it is, for as to family, they do tell me that
we're very nigh, if not all out, as good as they are.
And I'm sure it's not because they are richer than us,
for our Mary hasn't a penny but what the Squire gives
her—no, not for pocket money."

It required great power over the facial muscles on
the part of our hero for him not to laugh outright at
these very true remarks. He did restrain himself, but
not wishing to encounter another equally severe test,
" harked back " to the former part of the discourse.

"I shouldn't have thought," said he, "that any
pleasure you might have in Mr. Skirlaugh's society
would have made up for the risk you profess to run
every time you go out with him."

" Bless ye, when he once gets a talkin', you would
think nothing of it if his gun were pointed at the
middle of your body and you saw his finger playing
wi' the trigger. There's plenty of folks that can
shoot, but there's nobody knows so much or can tell
so many funny tales, or has half so much good in him
as our Squire. I've never been mad at him in my life,
and I never seed my father real cross with him but
once, and then it really was past all bearing."

William expressed a strong desire to know what a
person so beloved could have done that even the nar-
rator thought anger justifiable.

" Well, you see it was this—but now I wouldn't tell
any living soul but you, nor you neither, if you wasn't

like one of the family. You must promise never to mention it."

Our hero gave the necessary pledge, and the chronicler proceeded—

"It was last year, and the Squire had asked my father and me to go and have a day wi' him, as it was the first day of the season. We thought we must mind and be early, so we got there hours afore he was up. He seemed in no hurry when breakfast was over, but at last we were all ready for startin'. You've been in madam's still-room, perhaps,—a little room near the kitchen. Well, the Squire was there, sitting in a chair in the corner between the fire-place and the window, screwing on his gun-lock. My father, who's getting rather dull of sight, was standin' in the door-way, makin' the flint fast in his gun, and I was outside in the yard having a spree wi' one of the servant lasses, when all of a sudden there was a bang enough to awake the twel'month dead. I thought at first the world had certainly come to an end, and should have begun to say the 'De Profundis,' only I couldn't remember how to start. The cannons lettin' off at Hull garrison is nothing to it. Well, in less time than you can think, wop comes a big black thing down atween me and the young woman I was talkin' wi', as big as the stone of a cheese-press. If it had hitten either of us we should have been crushed as flat as a barn floor. To make a long story short, just when the Squire was all ready for startin', he found out his powder was damp and wouldn't go, so as madam wasn't by he slipped into the still-room and put it in the oven

just to take the cold air off, and then fell to thinkin',
first about a tale he was tellin' my father, and then
about his gun-lock. If he'd let it stay in one minute
less it would ha' been all right. It's that last
minute that always does the mischief, Mister
William. The Squire, thank God, wasn't hurt at all,
not a hair of him singed. The oven went clean
through the window and missed him, but a great blast
of flame and soot flew out at the door and singed every
bit of hair off one side of my father's wig, and it was
a bran new 'un, bought at Lincoln not a week before.
You really should have heard him swear. I often
hear him rap out when there isn't a gentleman, a
priest or a parson, by, but to hear him then, when the
Squire wasn't over fower yards off, and the ladies,
maybe, close to, was something fearsome."

"Were not the ladies very much alarmed at the
accident? The report alone was enough to have
frightened them very much."

"I can't say about the young ladies. I never seed
'em. Madam wasn't, but to hear her rate the Squire was
something dreadful. I'd rather hear ten men like my
father swear again' one another for a summer's day
than that. However he bore it I can't think, but he
did, and just saying, 'I'll never do so again, Lucy,'
walked away, got another powder flask in the stables,
and stayed out till it was as dark as pitch."

CHAPTER XIX.

"Rien ne peut l'arrêter
Quand la chasse l'appelle."—*Louis XIV.*

THE conversation, of which we have given but a brief abstract, lasted until the shooters had passed over a considerable stretch of meadow and entered upon a wild region of sand-hill, as perfectly bare as the sea-shore itself, except that here and there grew patches or rather lines of that hard wire-like grass which may be familiar to some of our readers, from their having seen it on the dunes which protect the coast of the Netherlands from the storms of the German Ocean.

Path there was none. The whole region had an appearance of bareness, only relieved from absolute desolation by the purple heather and sweet-scented ling which flourished in the peaty soil of the valleys. As the sand-hills hid the prospect of the neighbouring slopes entirely from the traveller's view, except when he crossed their tops, it was a place where any person not well drilled in local knowledge might have wandered about for hours without finding himself any nearer to the place of his destination. Jem was, however, in no danger of being lost, as he had been in the habit of amusing himself there, ever since he was old enough to stray away from the paternal homestead. Thus, every hillock, however much like its neighbour it might seem to others, had to his practised eye a peculiar form and character of its own. He had therefore not the least hesitation about his way, but plodded on, with William by his side and the setters at his heels, as unhesitatingly as if he were traversing the high road leading to his father's home. The sun had set, but it was by no means dark. They were on the point of emerging from this wilderness, and already the row of tall poplars that marked the northern extremity of John Stutting's property was in sight, when the dogs sprang from behind their master and almost pounced upon a fawn which was couched among the heather. They were a moment too late. The agile creature sprang away, and the dogs dashed in full chase after it, followed by Jem, hallooing and cheering them on at the very top of his loud voice.

William remembered the conversation that had taken place between his relative and the tanner, and he knew, also, that Mr. Skirlaugh had, no longer ago than that very morning, cautioned Jem that he was on no account to injure the deer. But he had, as it seemed, no power to hinder the atrocity he was compelled to witness. To make Jem heed him in his present mood, when under the full influence of the madness of the chase, would have been very difficult, even could his voice have been heard; but to make him hear anything, when he was shouting at the full pitch of his own voice, was a manifest impossibility.

When under strong excitement we usually find inaction the most difficult of all forms of labour. William did not stop to think what good he should do, but set off running at the top of his speed, vainly hoping, perchance, to come up with his companion, and induce him to call off the dogs. If so foolish a thought shot through his brain, a few seconds must have dispelled it; but he still ran on as fast as he could. The dogs gained rapidly on the quarry. Their speed was much less than that of a full-grown deer, but it was more than a match for the young creature they had roused. The frightened animal ran directly for Stutting's homestead; but this, which should of itself have been a hint to the hunter, only gave an additional zest to the chase.

Before reaching that place a highway had to be crossed; the form of the piper sitting on a heap of stones caused the fawn to curve out of its direct course in a northerly direction. This gave William a great advantage, as he kept on in a direct line. The animal quickly doubled again, and running within a few yards of him, its pursuers obviously gaining on it at every bound, leapt from the high bank of the stream into the midst of Bessie's island garden, followed at the same instant by the two dogs and William Skirlaugh.

Jem Morley was but a few paces behind; he was, however, too late. The fawn, in its leap, had entangled itself in the net with which Bessie protected her flowers from such intruders, and would, in an instant, have been in the jaws of its pursuers, had not William, with a presence of mind worthy of one whose life had been devoted to the chase, at the very instant crushed down the net with his foot, while he grasped both dogs firmly by their collars. The hunted animal, with a bound, cleared the stream, and rushed for protection to Bessie, who was seated at the cottage door, in conversation with her father and another person. The dogs lurched violently forward, almost dragging their captor into the beck beneath. At the same moment he felt Jem's hand heavily on his shoulder, whether in the form of a blow or an endeavour to save him from rolling downwards, he was not quite sure. He remained stooping, still grasping the dogs, until he was quite sure the fawn was safe, and then arose, prepared to receive a volley of abuse, if not physical violence. The face of his companion was swollen with passion,, but the chase had, for the present, deprived him of all power of articulate utterance. The young men stood for a second or two, gazing in each other's faces in a manner which indicated that high words might not unlikely be soon succeeded by blows. This dumb show was, however, terminated by the advent of Stutting, accompanied by a companion fewer in years and as muscular as himself. From the seat beside his door, where he had been refreshing himself after the work of the day was over, he had been a witness of the whole proceedings.

"James Morley," said he, " I have seen the course you have taken. I thought Ralf Skirlaugh might per-adventure have kept you from law-breaking, harrying God's creatures, and spoiling my goods. It seems you care no more for Ralf Skirlaugh's will than you do for mine, or for the Lord's. Had your beasts killed that dumb thing, as I live I would have made you so that you should never have hunted deer more. You may thank the young man who is with you that you are able to go home. And now go; and remember that if you, or any of your kin, be they man or woman, come here again, I will use them as I would wild beasts. If the law of God won't hold you in, force shall. I profess I will show no more mercy than do the Christians in America to the Red Savages, whose land the Lord hath given to the saints for a possession."

Jem, who hated the tanner for many bygone affronts, would by no mans have shrunk from doing battle with him, notwithstanding his superior strength, which could at any time have given him the victory. Now, however, such a contest was out of the question. He was blown with running, and John had by his side a companion who was unlikely to have any chivalrous scruples as to the singleness of the combat; but he was loth to beat a retreat without a sufficient excuse for delivering a volley of the notable oaths for which the Morleys of Scalhoe were celebrated. He therefore put himself in a threatening attitude, so as to command the plank that connected the isle with the mainland.

"Go, I tell you, man," cried Stutting. "Go, or the presence of your companion shall not preserve you longer. Go." As he said this he walked forward upon the narrow bridge.

"For heaven's sake leave the place; you are in the wrong," whispered William. Jem knew resistance would be useless, so with a broadside of curses he leapt the stream, regained his father's land, and walked sullenly away.

The companions paced onward in silence for some minutes; at length Jem exclaimed in a tone very much like that of a naughty boy who is trying to be good, "Gad, I'm a fool—a natural fool. You'll not think anything of it, I hope, Mr. William. I can't help it; I can't, upon my soul."

After a proper rejoinder from his companion he continued, "I'm very sorry—more sorry than I can make you believe; but, Gad, if it was to come over again, I must do the same. There are some men who, if you keep 'em away from the sight and smell of liquor, never want it; but once let 'em see it, no power on earth can hinder 'em from getting drunk; and I'm just like that, only it's not drink wi' me, though I do have a randy bout now and then; it's partridges, ducks, pheasants, and 'specially deer, that oversets me. If the squire should get to know, he'd be very mad; but maybe he'll not, Mr. William."

Mr. William took the broad hint, and relieved his companion's fears by promising that he would not perform the part of an informer.

The person whom we saw in company with John Stutting was a farmer from the south of the county, a respectable, upright young man, of the same religious persuasion as himself, who had been for some time engaged to his daughter. When the sportsmen took their departure the others entered the sanded kitchen of the cottage. Bessie busied herself in setting out the table for the evening meal, and the two men fell into grave conversation as to the evil times in which they were living. Such talk has been but too common with persons holding their gloomy views in all ages of Christian history. The events which had just occurred had added an additional shade of sombreness.

"I have half a mind, Isaac, to sell up all I have and go to America again. I would at once if I didn't think that Bessie could ill bear the sea. These fellows make England well nigh unbearable to an honest man. One day I'm fretted by the tax-gatherer, the next our drunken parson wants his tithe; then somebody comes for a church-rate, or the Commissioners of Sewers are down upon one; and worse than all, one is liable at all times, clean against law, to have one's property harried by a pack of graceless Pagans, who call themselves gentlemen. Gentlemen, forsooth; there'll be no more good in Old England till the gentlemen are all turned adrift, as the monks were. Why should there be respect of persons on earth?—there's none in heaven."

The future husband of the tanner's daughter was too much accustomed to Stutting's manner to dream of expressing any doubt as to the truth of this last very questionable statement. The nearest approach that was seemly for him, was a suggestion that Jem Morley's bad conduct arose from propensities not essentially connected with aristocracy.

" They're all alike, Isaac. The only difference is, that they don't all get in my way. There are three sorts of 'em. First, there is Skirlaugh, and men like him—mere heathens; worldlings with no more idea of the Gospel than a flint-stone has of a fire, till you strike it; men who love justice and hate iniquity for this world's sake. Their hearts are eaten up with pride, and their minds full of hard things. If they had their way they would grind us between two heavier millstones than ever the Whig Parliament in London will be able to set rolling a top of one another. And yet I don't deny that if these men had grace, there might be much good in them. There's a worse sort than them. Fellows like Woorme, of Todholme; fellows who call themselves gentlemen, and are as particular that esquire should be put after their names, as you and I are that ours should be written in the book of life; who run after any of the big men when they see them, whether they be Whig or Jacobite, as if their clothes would cure sick men, like the handkerchiefs that had touched the body of Paul of Tarsus;

and if they meet a poor man, snap him off as if they belonged to a different world from his, and had only come down here on a visit of pleasure, as you might go down into a Yorkshire coal-pit. These are mostly sons of linendrapers, ironmongers, publicans, and such like, who've had lands left to them by miserly relations, and have bought their gentility ready made, as sailors do their clothes,—that's why neither of 'em fit. But neither of these sorts hurt me. It's the Papist kind, who spend all their time in hunting, racing, drinking, and what's worse, who take a real devilish delight in persecuting me, because I am a God-fearing Christian man."

"If it wasn't for Mr. Skirlaugh, father, Jem Morley, and them that go with him, would be ten times worse than they are. I know he tells them every time he sees them, that they're to let our things alone," interposed Bessie, who had a strong regard for Miss Isabell, which reflected itself upon her father.

"Very likely, lass—very likely; and much good it does. Why do you think old Skirlaugh has any more power over them than I have? I tell you they're mad; drunk with their superstition, which shuts their eyes to everything in this world that's cleanly and of good report, and opens them wide to all foulness and evil doing. A Papist can no more be a good man, as the world counts goodness, even, than a wild beast that delights in blood can be gentle as a lamb. It is against nature. They are idolators, members of the foul synagogue of Satan, and heirs of the retribution prepared for the devil and his angels."

"But, father, Miss Mary Morley, who is, as they say, to marry the young squire, is a Papist, and I am sure she is a kind-hearted lady."

"Tiger-pups are sweet, soft things to play with, till their claws are grown. It's a shame that Ralf Skirlaugh should marry his son to a heathen; a crying sin and shame. Are there not plenty of worldly women hereabouts, to pick from, without seeking one who worships stocks and stones? Don't you know, child, what the Scriptures of the old covenant say of idolators, and remember that there was an excuse for the old heathen who worshipped Moloch, which there is not, now that the light has come for those who pray to Mary, Peter, and other dead men and women, and deny the Lord who bought them? I would rather take into my house a lion or a mad dog, than a Papist."

Bessie was too well aware of her father's peculiar views—opinions she, as was natural, in a great measure shared—to seem to contradict him; as, however, many little circumstances had led her to have a liking for Mary, she recounted several anecdotes which told very much in that lady's favour. The tanner heard her narratives to the end, with the condescension of one who is so sure of his own position that it is a pleasure to hear all his adversary has to say. When she had done, he looked at her gravely, and said—

"Bessie, you have often heard me read to you, and

tell of Hell—of the lake of fire and brimstone which burns for ever and ever, just below the green fields and cool waters. Now, if there be one thing clearer than another, alike from the letter of Scripture and from the faith, that God puts into the hearts of his elect, it is that all idolators shall have their portion there— whatever their works have been. I don't deny that some of them have done what men call good works; but I am sorry, heartily sorry, when I see or hear of them; they profit nothing to save from everlasting burning, and they do take off from the hate one should feel to the enemies of God. 'Do not I hate them that hate thee, oh Lord,' is fitter in the mouth of a Christian woman, like thee, than what thou hast now spoken."

The girl was silenced, perhaps convinced. Her father enlivened the evening meal with other theological discourse, the tone of which is sufficiently indicated by what we have recorded.

CHAPTER XX.

Heel.—Silence, and let us proceed, neighbours, with all the decency and confusion usual on these occasions.

1st Mob.—Ay, ay ; there is no doing without that.

All.—No, no, no.

Heel.—Silence, then, and keep the peace. What ! is there no respect paid to authority ?—FOOTE. *The Mayor of Garratt.*

MR. SKIRLAUGH never had any serious intention of depriving the citizens of Lincoln of the benefits that his presence might afford them at the election of a knight of the shire. He cared nothing whatever for politics, as commonly understood—had not the least interest in the result of the contest, but the Tory candidate was a personal friend of his own, and a man who carried the extreme principles he professed so very far, that there was but a shade of difference between the Toryism of the one and the open rebelliousness of the other. The hair that divided them was the oath to the ruling dynasty. This Mr. Skirlaugh firmly refused to take, while his weaker brother swallowed it, without, as far as could be seen from his conduct, its making any change in his devotion to the exiled family. Devotion is of different sorts. The

Squire's was of a kind that would not have shrunk
for an instant from translating itself into action; that
of the candidate consisted principally in talking treason and drinking disloyal toasts, when among his own
friends. The Squire, though lax of tongue, was
habitually sober, the candidate was more in harmony
with the times in which he lived; and when he had
consumed more punch than he could control, he was
sometimes in the habit of giving public vent to opinions which even the free-spoken Mr. Skirlaugh
thought it unwise, if not dangerous, to utter.

William had, during the last few days, more than
once suggested that the time was arriving for his departure. He felt that to stay much longer in such
congenial society would unfit him for the life of retired
drudgery to which he seemed destined. He knew,
too, that his affections were becoming rapidly fixed on
one who he was certain could, if she thought of him
at all when out of her sight, only regard him as a mere
pleasant casual acquaintance, and to whose hand,
raised as she was by the accident of social position so
much above himself, it would be impossible for him to
aspire.

Notwithstanding all that men, wise with the wisdom
of this world, have endeavoured to prove to us, we are
not always masters of our own actions. Fate, accident,
providence, use which word you will, is stronger than
our resolutions for good or evil. In spite of the firmest
resolves to the contrary, the young lawyer was seldom
alone without his thoughts turning to Isabel. Her

lightest words clung to his memory; the sound of her voice was in his ears, even when the Squire, who to his praise be it told, seldom repeated himself, was narrating his raciest stories. He felt that the time when he ought to have gone, had he valued his own peace of mind, was long past, and that it was now, at all events, little short of a duty to himself, if not to another, whose happiness he valued far more than his own, to hasten his departure. When this deliberation was mentioned to the Squire, he would not entertain the idea for a moment.

"My good fellow," said he, " the election is just at hand; you must stay and see the Skirlaugh people in force. That is a sufficient reason for your lengthening your visit; but I have a better and a really very grave one. My son will be home soon, perhaps in a day or two, and you must see him for two reasons. In the first place, you and he are both good fellows, and will no doubt like each other; and, secondly, because he' will soon marry Mary, and I shall want some legal advice as to settlements. The poor girl hasn't a farthing now, but she must have something in the way of a dowry. It won't do for Marmaduke Morley's heiress to be wedded like a pauper. Her father has lost all his own, and her mother's fortune, also, in the service of the King, who will no doubt make it up handsomely some day; but till the time comes, we must provide what is fitting Now I can't talk on these things properly when Ralf isn't here."

This seemed a sufficient reason for protracting his

visit for a few days, which William did not see how to evade, though he felt that he ought to put it aside manfully, but the desire of indulging a little longer in what, however pleasant, he felt was but a dream—the first, and perhaps the last, of his waking life—was too strong for his better judgment. It was therefore arranged that he should stay till after the election, in the hope of young Skirlaugh's return, but that if the traveller did not come back within a very few days of that event, he should go to his office-desk again, without making his acquaintance. A letter notifying this was written to his uncle in due course, who was already anxious for his nephew's return, not only because there was much business which required his attention, but also because he found his days pass slowly without his companion.

Mr. Skirlaugh's intention of going to the election had been kept a profound secret. Not only were the Whig squires and parsons of the neighbourhood in complete darkness on the subject, but also nearly the whole of his own people. Such of them as had votes, and most of his tenants and other dependents were possessed of small freeholds, had notice to assemble at a certain point of the road, remarkable in their minds as the site of a small public-house, known as the "Crooked Billet." They had all received orders to be at that place at nine o'clock in the morning. Long before that hour, not only the kitchen, parlour, and passages of the said hostelry were crowded with thirsty men, but the court-yard, and even the road adjoining, were occupied by a motley throng of persons, who, if they had not now a vote to give, were very happy to drink the beer the Squire had paid for, as a pledge that if ever they should be raised to the rank of freeholders, their votes and interest would be entirely at his service. The orders were for beer to be given to all comers who wore the proper-coloured ribbons in their hats; but wisely was the precaution taken of only issuing them the day before, so that Mary Moss, the hostess of the establishment, was unable to lay in such a stock as to create any great amount of intoxication in the neighbourhood. The public-house stood, as these old wayside houses of refreshment were wont to do, at the junction of four roads. One of them led from Scalhoe, and riding down this, at a little before nine, might be seen Mr. Morley, accompanied by both his sons. Their presence was not unlooked for, but was by no means a welcome addition to the party.

"Did our Squire tell 'em to come to tak' care on us, I wonder?" asked a red-vested farmer of his neighbour, as they sat on a bench beside the door.

"No, man," replied the person questioned, who was happy in possessing exclusive information, his daughter being one of the housemaids at the Manor. "It's not a likely thing, and I wonder you should ax such an a question. He none tell'd 'em to come, but they know he's aboone this sort o' thing hiself, and so they think they'll look big by makin' theirselves look like our maisters."

"The road's as free to them as it is to us; but I'm not a goin' to hev it said that I arn't fit to tak' care o' my sen at 'lection time wi'out them drinkin', pot-huntin', swearin' fellers puttin' their sens for'ad to look a'ter me," rejoined the first speaker, who, after so long an address thought it necessary to refresh him-self with a deep draught of beer, and then went on: "I wonder our Squire stan's it; he's ower good-natur'd by half. Why, there isn' a thing in the place that they don't powch or make away wi'. It's not the deer, only; it's hares, pheasants, rabbits, every thing in the world. They're as fell as a otter for fish, an' all. I wouldn't so much as look at 'em if I was him."

"You don't know everything, Robert. You see Miss Mary, who's niece to old Morley, is to marry the young Squire this back end, and it wouldn't do to fall out wi' th' girl's relations, though they are a low lot. And then they do say, neighbour, how far it may be true, I don't know, but they do say that young Lon-don chap is to hev' Miss Isabell, and he's strange, an' thick with Jem and Dick, and 's out spreein' about wi' em every day, be owt it be Sundays."

It was, as the malcontents had anticipated; no sooner had the Morley party arrived than they began to assume the post of leaders. Their first act of sove-reignty was to declare that Mr. Skirlaugh had in-formed them of his determination to stay at home; their second was to intimate, if not broadly affirm, that he had requested them to guide his people through the perils of the election. Advice they scattered freely on all hands. One man was told at what inn he had best put up his horse ; to a second the mysterious process of recording the votes was explained in elaborate detail, and a third was cautioned in a whisper, loud enough to be heard by many of the bystanders, that he wasn't to let Justice Woorme see him, for if he did he'd make him vote "yallow," because of that mortgage he had on his place.

All this was very offensive. The Morleys were not popular. Their religion, their manners, the vulgar admixture of coarse familiarity and bustling dignity which they assumed, and their entire want of tact in dealing with their fellow-creatures, tended to make a body of men who were quite independent of them resent an assumption of authority which their own landlord would never have thought of exercising. They were, however, all three, quite deficient in that sense of the incongruous which makes some of us know when we are doing. an unpopular act, without a plain statement of our delinquencies being growled into our ears.' It is not improbable that something very like a quarrel would have arisen, had not the noise of wheels startled the throng, and the green and yellow chariot of Mr. Skirlaugh appeared in the distance.

Carriages were rarities in those days. The one that was now before the eyes of the people, and that of the Whig Lord at Brackenthwaite, were the only vehicles of the kind that most of the crowd had seen, and this particular chariot was but seldom visible. The Squire

treated it with the same care that Sir Hudibras did his
learning—seldom used it, for fear of wearing it out.
Horseback was his favourite mode of travel. It was
only on great occasions, when he felt that display
was a duty, or when the ladies had to go a long
distance, that this stately machine was unswathed
from its many coverings, and dragged into the light of
common day.

When he halted at the door of the Crooked Billet,
it was observed to contain not only the Squire himself, in his own proper person, but also his daughter,
his guest, and his chaplain. A loud cheer greeted Mr.
Skirlaugh, as he alighted, and shook the nearest of the
bystanders kindly by the hand. A few sensible words
of direction, and one or two good-humoured jests removed the ill feeling that the intrusion of the Morleys
had caused, and the great man drove off—not, however, without a hint to his coachman, to keep on the
grass at the side of the road as much as he could, for
fear of scratching the paint on the carriage-wheels—
leaving behind him the impression that the Lord of
Skirlaugh Manor was certainly one of the greatest
people on earth.

The carriage, with its inmates and outriders, had
not been the only addition to the party. Close in its
rear came Squire's Bob, with a body of followers whom
he called his voters. Bob was himself a freeholder.
He had inherited a small bag of guineas from his
grandmother, and had saved several more in the service of his master. These he had judiciously invested

in one of the villages of the Isle of Axholme, in what is called a *land end*—a local term, which it may be needful to explain, as the phrase does not convey a distinct meaning to the uninitiated.

The Trent, as people know who look at maps, is a winding river. One of the main roads on the Isle of Axholme, skirts the west bank of the Trent, but for obvious reasons of convenience, does not follow every twist of the stream. The fields in those days were all open, many of them are still so, and the numerous freeholders, among whom the arable land was divided, held it in long, narrow slips, called *lands*. Each of these lands was raised by continual ploughing one way into a high ridge for the purpose of drainage, and the furrow between them was a sufficient boundary. The highway cut across these strips, leaving a small bit of land belonging to each allotment between the river and the road. These were, and are still, usually called *land ends*, and from their nearness to the river, and the extreme richness of their soil, were very valuable. Their size fitted them exactly for spade labour. Mr. Robert Drury had bought one of these land ends, dreaming, perhaps, if things prospered with him, that it would form the nucleus of a larger property, and in the meantime be a safe investment for his capital. Bob was, however, not only in the proud position of being a voter himself, but in the still more exalted one of being able to influence several other people. His sister had married a person, half fisherman, half smuggler, who lived at Barton-upon-Humber ; and not

only he, but several of his kin and allies, were delighted to oblige Bob, by going to Lincoln at the
Squire's expense. It is not probable that they had
any views whatever on the political questions involved
in the contest, but they had strong reasons for wishing
that the Squire and his retainer should continue to
think well of them.

As Bob had the care of his own convoy, he was relieved from attendance on his master, who, for the
sake of being able to descant upon the interesting objects
on the way, took, after leaving the Crooked Billet, the
longer but much more picturesque road which runs on
the brow of the hill above the villages. Drury did not
think that his friends would appreciate the scenery of
the villages so much as the fleshly cheer which he had
orders to provide for them at Merespital, he therefore
went by the shorter route. When he and his party
arrived at the St. George and Dragon, the old inn was
full to overflowing. Mr. Sargisson, its master, was
sober at the early hour when our friends arrived, and
he and every one of his people were busy serving out
food and drink to the gay crowd of travellers whose
yellow, white, and blue ribbons indicated that they
were journeying to the local capital with their souls
bent on politics. Bob was fond of good cheer, and
still fonder of good company. He knew, however,
that he should have enough of both when he arrived at
Lincoln, and therefore preferred, on the present occasion, to sacrifice these lower desires to the shrine of
his love.

Our readers are, we think, aware that he had a tender regard for Nell, the servant in whose company he was first introduced to their notice. That maiden was still absent from the inn, engaged in attendance upon the poor woman at the almshouse. To that cottage Bob directed his steps as soon as he had seen his companions comfortably seated, and had, as he expressed it, "just weshed the dust out of his mouth." He found the place scrupulously neat, the cripple sitting upright in her bed, supported by pillows, employing her hands in knitting, while at long, distant intervals, she let drop a few words to Nell, who was sewing by her side. Conversation it could not be called. What she said to her companion seldom extended to more than a few words of remark, or a brief question. She was not, however, quite silent. Her lips constantly moved, often in inaudible whispers, sometimes snatches of songs, the prayers she had learned in infancy, and words that had, in after life, made a deep impression upon her, mingled in discordant and often painful confusion. Her mind was evidently failing through weakness of body, but, like many others in her condition, she had, at times, a strong craving to hear news which she forgot the next moment, or only remembered in such a fragmentary fashion, that if any portions of it were produced again, the teller was startled by the variations they had undergone.

Drury had, on several occasions, been sent over from the Manor with presents of food, and was well

known to Anne Mason. Although he spoke to her on
entering, she seemed hardly to notice him. The
animated conversation which passed between the
lovers seemed quite lost upon her. Bob had told his
companions that they were to be ready to start on
their journey in a quarter of an hour, but double that
time passed away in Nell's society, without the groom
discovering that it was time for him to depart. Yet
neither he nor she were quite at their ease. The
swain had sufficient effrontery for most of the occasions of life, but the dull, scarred features, and
cold grey eyes of the sufferer, unlit by any sentiment
that he could understand, acted on him with a
strongly depressing effect. The occasional mutterings
of prayers and verses, which were certainly not of a
religious nature, added to his discomfort.

"Nell, my lass," said he, in an undertone, "I
mun be goin'; she's strange and dour. I wonder
you're not scared to be wi' her by your sen at
darklins."

Anne noticed something in his manner which
indicated that she was the subject of remark.
"What's that ye say about me?" said she, in a
shrill voice.

Bob was silent. Nell, to help him out of the difficulty, said, "He thinks you're not so well to-day, you
don't talk much."

"No! and wherefore should I talk, there's nobody cares to hear me now. Tell Madam Skirlaugh I'm much obliged to her; and Miss Mary

that I wants strange and bad to see him we was talkin' on."

Bob promised to deliver the messages, and arose to depart. As he was moving towards the door, Anne called him back.

" Thou mo'nt go yet," said she. " Thy lass has got summut to tell thee she's forgetten. Sit thee down here," and she pointed to a seat near herself. " Tell him what that man frae Barton said, Nell."

" Bless me, mother, I'd forgotten all about it, and I didn't know you even heard what he said."

" I was like to hear when he tell'd a thing like that. If ye'd lived among trouble as I hev, ye'd not forget things as ye do," rejoined Anne.

" It's may be as well that she's named it. It's just this, Bob. A few days sin Brother Dick frae Barton was here, and he came in to sit half an hour wi' us, and he tell'd me as how there had been somebody, he called him a gentleman, but didn't say who he was, had been axin' him ower and ower agean which was the straight way frae Skirlaugh to Barton across the closes. He said he knew the public road, but he wanted to learn about th' pad they call th' smugglers' trod. This is a thing chaps like him keeps to their sens, and so he wouldn't tell him nowt about it."

" Umph! And he didn't say who this gentleman, as he called him, was? " asked Bob, musingly.

" No, not a word."

" Then I mun try and find out, for I'm sure there's summut up that shouldn't owt to be. I'll tell ye a trick I played on a gentleman o' that sort 'at com' to our house pychin' about, when I come back, but I mun be off now."

And giving his lady love a hearty smack on the lips, the groom departed to put himself at the head of his convoy.

END OF VOL I.

BRADBURY, EVANS, AND CO., PRINTERS, WHITEFRIARS.